A
FATAL
WALTZ

A
FATAL
WALTZ

An Ella Shane Mystery

KATHLEEN MARPLE KALB

First published by Level Best Books/Historia 2025

This novel is entirely a work of fiction. The names, characters and incidents portrayed in it are the work of the author's imagination. Any resemblance to actual persons, living or dead, events or localities is entirely coincidental.

Kathleen Marple Kalb asserts the moral right to be identified as the author of this work.

First edition

ISBN: 978-1-68512-966-8

Cover art by Level Best Designs

This book was professionally typeset on Reedsy.
Find out more at reedsy.com

For my former agent Eric Myers, without whom Ella Shane would never have made it into the spotlight, with deepest respect and appreciation.

Praise for A Fatal Waltz and the Ella Shane Series

"I am in awe of Kathleen Marple Kalb's masterpiece, *A Fatal Waltz*! 'What sacrifice would you be willing to make to discover the truth...or suppress it?' Ella Shane, the duelling Duchess of Leith, and her husband are newlyweds who find themselves in the midst of two desperate situations. One is close to home, affecting the sister of a dear friend because of a quandary of identity that could result in a career-ending and damaging scandal. The other is an investigation given to the Duke regarding a decades-old youthful indiscretion between the British Royalty and the New York high society.

"Both require finesse but show the underbelly of deep-seated prejudices bolstered by diverging views of Christianity and Justice. Once again, the Duke and Ella are caught in the deadly crosshairs of those who would do anything to suppress the truth... even murder. A fantastic read that keeps you on the edge of your seat. Who are the devils, and who are the angels?"—Wendy Bayne, author of the Crimes Against the Crown Series

For *A Fatal Reception*:

A 2024 top-10 pick from Aunt Agatha's Reviewer Vicky Kondelik: "*A Fatal Reception* by Kathleen Marple Kalb is the fourth book in a wrongly-neglected series, which I am very glad has found a home with a new publisher."

"A delight! Opera diva Ella Shane is about to wed her very own wicked duke. But the nuptial plans go awry when a society matron brains a fellow patron of the arts. Written with great charm and wit, this lively, entertaining romp through Gilded Age New York will have you eagerly awaiting Ella Shane's next adventure."—Mariah Fredericks, author of *The Wharton Plot*

"Marple Kalb has a knack for combining humour, mystery, angst and romance in just the right proportions to keep you on the edge of your seat." — Wendy Bayne, author of the Crimes Against the Crown series

Praise for the series:

"Kalb writes with vivid assurance. Her stories are well paced and well layered. Ella's matrix – the characters who surround her—are as interesting and flawed yet human as she is herself., as is the theatrical setting…This book is by a woman who knows how to tell a story."—Aunt Agatha's Mysteries on *A Fatal First Night*

"This series is truly one of my favorite cozy-mystery series! I love the mix of opera, history, romance, and mystery…and I find each book impossible to put down!"—Goodreads reviewer Ashley

Chapter One: Marital Privileges

My first production at the Met would have been enough. Or perhaps my first autumn in New York as a wife. Certainly, it would have been quite sufficient to find oneself entangled in blackmail, murder, and the succession to the British Throne.

Instead, we had all these—and more—in that September of 1900.

The opening night of *Xerxes*, a marvelous old Handel piece the Metropolitan Opera had revived for me, was a sensation. In the trouser, or male soprano, leading role as an ancient emperor, I carried the show, which the Met staff had carefully designed to display their latest acquisition to best advantage. The Diamond Horseshoe showered me and my castmates with applause and flowers, then congratulated me further at a reception at the home of one of the 400.

A far cry from my upbringing as an Irish-Jewish starveling on the Lower East Side. But, of course, now, I am not only Miss Ella Shane, leading light of the opera, but also Her Grace Ellen, Duchess of Leith, wife to a senior Peer.

At the end of the night, though, in the bedroom of my Washington Square townhouse, after I'd traded my reception gown for my favorite peignoir, lavender with violet ribbons, removed my stage makeup and loosed my hair, nothing mattered but being alone with my husband.

It's still rather amazing that I have one.

Though we had an immediate attraction when we met, Gilbert St. Aubyn and I spent close to a year trying to find a way to be together, and working out the terms of our marriage, which was by no means a certainty for a couple from such vastly different parts of the social spectrum. In the end, though, we were both willing to bend just enough to get down the aisle…and had been quite ridiculously happy since.

That night, despite the late hour, we had fallen into our usual evening routine in our, formerly my, bedroom. Unlike many aristocratic couples, we consider sharing a bed one of the principal pleasures of marriage, and not merely for the obvious reason. While Gil maintains what he calls a dressing room, where he retires to hide and read when he wants to be alone, we both enjoy the proximity of the marital chamber.

I sat down at the vanity and started brushing out my hair, watching Gil undo his white tie, snap out his collar studs, and unbutton his stiff white piqué waistcoat. Unlike most men of his class, he neither needs nor desires a valet, since he grew up well-off, but not rich, with no expectation of, or desire for, a title.

He had spent the evening standing a step or two behind me, beaming with pride at his wife's success, but now we were alone, I could see he was troubled, from the furrow at his brow, and the carefully precise way he moved. It meant he was distracted.

Since I knew he was as happy for my success as I and loved standing behind me and observing the scene, I did not take it as the insult one might fear from a lesser man. Something else was going on here.

With the insight of several months of marriage, not to mention a lifetime of dealing with the prickly moods of my cousin Tommy and other close male friends and relatives, I knew it was best to wait and let him talk when he was ready. When a man's troubled, pushing only annoys him.

Gil put the waistcoat and tie down on a chair and walked over to me, holding out his hand for the brush. "May I?"

"Of course, *mes epinards.*"

He smiled a bit at the nickname. French for "my spinach," it was a joke between us. *Mon chou,* translated as "my cabbage," is the usual French endearment between husband and wife. But as I told Gil, he's far too elegant to be cabbage.

He held the silver-backed brush and gently took a lock of my hair, twining it in his long fingers for a moment, clearly enjoying the feel and the closeness.

Before my marriage, I had heard some men are very drawn to their women's hair, taking great pleasure in seeing it down, which is, after all, something only allowed to a husband. Gil did indeed find my strawberry blonde locks quite appealing, and sometimes helped me brush at night, gently running the bristles and his fingers through the waves, watching the way they caught the low light of our oil lamp.

After a few strokes, he met my gaze in the mirror. "So, I am going to take advantage of marital privilege."

"I rather thought we had," I teased. Legal terms often creep into his informal conversation because he trained as a barrister before a number of relatives died in an assortment of outbreaks and battles, leaving him, quite unexpectedly, with the coronet.

"Not that marital privilege." Gil smiled faintly. "The marital privilege of confidentiality."

"Of course. That's always been understood."

"Yes, but I generally prefer not to give you information that might cause you concern—or even endanger you."

"You can tell me anything, you know."

"I do." He ran the brush through again, this time lightly wrapping the hair around his fingers at the end. "Your hair looks like honey."

"It benefits from a good brushing." For a moment, we enjoyed a warm glance in the mirror, contemplating some of the other privileges of matrimony. A momentary distraction, no more.

"You know I had some business in London before I came over to meet you."

"Yes. You said family affairs."

"It was, though not all our family." He took another stroke. Watched me. "And I've kept busy while you were rehearsing."

"Yes. You've seemed to be out and about a great deal. I assumed you were enjoying the city."

"Sadly, no." He toyed with the brush. "How much do you know about the Prince of Wales?"

"*That* Prince of Wales?"

"There is only one. It's rather the point." Another careful stroke, perhaps to dilute the edge from his tone.

"Of course. A somewhat naughty fellow by all accounts, but also apparently quite kind in his way."

"Which rates a great deal with you."

"Yes. And I've read that he has little or no class or religious prejudice, which rates even more."

Gil's eyes held mine in the mirror, and he stopped brushing for a measure or so. "With me as well, *mo chridhe*."

The Scots Gaelic endearment literally means "my heart," and while it can be simply translated as a way of saying "sweetheart," from Gil, it carries a deeper resonance. At some level, he means it as a statement of fact: he's calling me the center of his world.

Quite a thing to live up to.

He started brushing again. "So, the Prince is the second of Her Majesty's nine children and had the considerable misfortune to follow the brilliant and charming Princess Royal, now Empress Frederick, who was undoubtedly her late father's favorite."

"Fathers and daughters often have a special bond," I observed, with a faint twinge at the thought. My father had died of typhoid when I was a babe in arms.

"They do. I hope to find out one day."

"God willing," I agreed. I, too, was hoping we would soon be blessed, but I had thought Gil shared the aristocratic male preference for sons, even though he already had two adult heirs with his late first wife. A discussion for another moment, since I did not wish to be reminded how long we'd been wed with no sign of a baby. "But he was still the heir."

"He was indeed. And her Majesty and the late Prince Consort had impossibly high ideals for him."

"No doubt."

"And he, perhaps equally understandably, wished for some sort of freedom and life of his own."

4

"Don't all boys?" I asked. "I can think of a certain young gentleman of our acquaintance…"

Gil smiled at the thought of his younger son and made another careful stroke. "They do. But the stakes were rather higher for His Highness."

"Of course." I met his gaze in the mirror. "This is fascinating insight into the Royal Family, but what has it to do with us?"

"Well, you will know that I occasionally do a favor for a friend."

"Yes." At least one of those favors had resulted in an unexpected and entirely welcome visit to me just over a year ago. Not to mention the apprehension of a killer who was now settling into a well-earned life sentence.

"A friend of a friend, who is close to the court, asked me to look into a very delicate matter."

"How delicate?" The Prince of Wales, after all, was known to have been just about everywhere and done just about everything. Including many liaisons with women, respectable duchesses were not supposed to know about…unless HRH happened to decide he wanted a respectable duchess on the given night.

Not on your bloody tintype.

"More delicate than anything I ever imagined." He took a breath. Contemplated again. "You will know that the Prince visited New York many years ago as a boy."

"Before I was born, I believe."

"Correct. 1860, to be exact. He was eighteen."

"Ah." The light was starting to dawn. "Eighteen and away from his family for the first time. And free to enjoy himself."

"Precisely."

"I'm sure he did." I smiled. "Cabot's Great-Aunt Cecily danced with him at the Academy of Music Ball. She will still tell the story on occasion."

"No doubt one would." Gil nodded and began another careful, gentle stroke with the brush, watching my hair catch the light. "He was unmarried and apparently rather innocent at the time."

"I believe he married the Danish princess a few years later."

5

"Exactly. At the time, he was a rather rakish fellow, but there was no real hint of scandal attached to his name...until the next year."

"The incident with the lady of ill repute at the Irish army camp that some still claim killed Prince Albert?" I asked. My knowledge was not from research, but from a society grandmamma on my first London stand.

"Yes." Gil shook his head. "If every man dropped dead on finding out that his son had—er—there would be no men left."

We shared wry smiles. Marriage does give one a bit of sophistication, after all.

His smile faded as he continued. "In all fairness and honesty, I must tell you though, a connection of the friend who asked me to look into the matter has in fact dropped dead, and likely not from the shock."

"Really."

"That's part of the reason my friend asked me to investigate. He was a distant relative...some sort of cousin, but please don't ask for specifics."

"No cause for concern in this house," I assured him. "One advantage to marrying into an Irish family. We assume we're all related to one another."

"One of the many advantages, sweetheart."

Another smile, easier and more genuine. Watching him, I realized he'd been a bit tense and quiet in recent days. I'd given it scant attention, and no acknowledgement because I'd been preparing for my debut at the premier opera company.

"I'm sorry," I said.

His eyes widened. "For what?"

"For not knowing you were troubled." I met his gaze. "I was so absorbed in my Met debut that I didn't pay attention-"

"I hid it well, *mo chridhe*." Gil shrugged. "And I would never expect-"

"But you should. That's part of being a good wife. I can do better by you."

"I cannot expect you to read my mind."

"No, but you can expect me to at least notice when you are concerned." I sighed. "I'm still learning..."

"You're doing brilliantly." He leaned down and kissed the top of my head. "I have no complaints. If anything, I'm relieved I didn't have to answer to

6

you."

"All right." I vowed to myself to be more observant, but realized the best I could do for him right now was let him tell the story. "So, the Prince?"

"So the Prince," he said, returning to brushing. "He was an ocean away from his rather doctrinaire papa, and a resourceful and energetic young man, no matter how well supervised. It seems he enjoyed some female companionship during his visit to New York."

"Great-Aunt Cecily says he was a flirt." At the time, she would have been an important Knickerbocker matron, past her first youth but probably still beautiful, certainly with the same gleam in her eye as she had now. I suspected she gave as good as she got from Princey.

"More than a flirt, unfortunately." Gil toyed with the ends of my hair. "There was apparently a young lady or two. And a liaison or two."

"A *young* lady?" I gave him a puzzled look. "Don't these things generally involve somewhat older, married ladies?"

"Generally, that's the way—for any number of good reasons." He nodded, his face a little tight. "Young princes have needs and wants, of course, and it's better to take care of them in some safe circumstance."

"If their families are enlightened enough to allow them to." I did not envision Prince Albert looking the other way while his prized heir frolicked with some appealing matron.

"And that was rather the rub with the Prince." Gil nodded, starting another stroke. "It's fair to say the late Prince Consort was far less than enlightened in this area. And, because of the long tradition of young princes being, er, initiated by older ladies, his watchers kept a very close eye on such females."

"When they would have done better to look out for a girl?"

"It appears so. The story goes that there was some kind of very quiet romance, with the help of at least one of the gentlemen traveling with him."

"Well, perhaps it was just an innocent flirtation." I leaned back as he took a new stroke. Whatever pleasure the brushing was for him, it was equally lovely for me. We have become quite good at sharing various pleasures. "Back then young ladies were quite closely watched, and it was a very grave matter indeed for a girl to surrender herself."

"It still is. Even if a prince were involved."

"Of course. The world is not especially tolerant of young women having adventures." Not that I'd had any, of course. Heaven help me, I'd married the first man I'd kissed. Good thing I chose a good one.

"And yet, the story goes, a young lady did indeed have one with the Prince." Gil stopped brushing for a moment and twined his fingers through the end of my hair. "Though history has always accorded the honor to the—woman—in the army camp, it seems at least one New York miss helped His Highness dispose of his innocence."

"Probably a much riskier proposition for her, you know."

"True. But more consequential for him."

"Really? It's the Prince of Wales. Wouldn't you be rather disappointed if he hadn't been up to a bit of naughty?"

"More than naughty if with an innocent young girl." Gil's face took on a stern cast.

"True. But if she plotted, and actually managed to slip past his chaperones, she was willing, and at least somewhat aware of the risk involved. And, anyhow, it was forty years ago."

"Yes."

I met his troubled gaze in the mirror. "By now, surely, it's just a wicked little story she tells to shock her grandchildren. What's the harm?"

"There may have been—issue."

My eyes widened. Gil put down the brush.

"And there is at least a tiny chance that the child, if child there was, could have been legitimate."

"Legitimate? You mean…"

"His Highness was very young, very infatuated, and more than a little drunk on at least one occasion. My friend says he has a vague memory of something that might have been marriage vows…though that, of course, might also have been the drink."

"But if it was not the drink…"

"Somewhere in this city of yours, there may be an heir to the throne. Not to mention a woman who would be the true Princess of Wales."

8

"Good God," I breathed. The mind reeled...or at least mine did. "But why now? It was forty years ago."

"Because he will soon be King."

"The Queen..."

"Is fading. No one is entirely certain how quickly, but by all accounts, she is definitely in decline." He took a breath. "You know, Shane, it's not just the Prince. If this was a true marriage, and the woman is still alive, or even remained alive for a period of time..."

"The entire line of succession could be illegitimate."

"Two generations' worth."

"What a mess."

"So you can see why my friend needs a clear answer in this matter as quickly and quietly as possible."

I nodded. "And it just happens that you are in the city for your wife's first Met season."

"My wife, who has more than a few connections in the society and opera worlds. Do you think you could arrange a tea with Great-Aunt Cecily?"

"It would be a pleasure."

"Excellent." He put down the brush.

I met his eyes in the mirror. "Does it ease your mind to share all of this?"

"Greatly." He let out a breath and rested his hands on my shoulders. "Marital privilege is a good thing."

"I agree, *mes epinards.*"

His fingers moved to the ribbon tie on my peignoir. "I'm fond of other marital privileges as well."

Chapter Two: A New Day Brings New Troubles

The next morning, I slept deeply into midday, as has been my habit since the beginning of my performing career. When I was on the road with the Ella Shane Opera Company, sleeping late was essential, the best way to stave off the exhaustion from eight performances a week and grinding train travel. The Met's schedule, though, is far lighter; in a repertory company, one's production is part of a rotation rather than a single long stand. Nonetheless, after the late opening night, with the full run of *Xerxes* ahead, it was still wise to get as much rest as possible.

Not to mention a bit of quiet time with my husband.

When we are staying at the Washington Square townhouse, my cousin and manager, Tommy Hurley, sleeps a floor down from us in his own little private space. An excellent arrangement, and one that still leaves plenty of sleeping space for visiting friends, relatives, and guests.

Our visitors are not a problem once they're safely tucked in. They can be a bit much, however, when they're awake and running about. We seem to have a constant stream of people coming through the house, especially during a production, which adds a whole new layer of visitors to the usual. On any given day, we're surrounded by any number of the friends we've accumulated from years of hard work and good works. And Tommy and I would not have it any other way. We've enjoyed sharing the house and filling it with our dear ones, ever since we bought it with our first serious earnings from my singing and his boxing victories.

The happy chaos does make life a bit wearing for newlyweds, though.

Only behind the locked door of our bedroom, formerly my maiden-lady redoubt, can Gil and I be guaranteed any privacy. Which simple fact provided additional motivation for me to linger.

Or would have, if my spouse were so inclined.

Unlike me, Gil, the son of a resolute Highland Scotswoman, was not in the habit of lying abed. From earliest childhood, his days began with a long walk and a cold bath. Even now, he generally wakes with the sun, filled with energy and enthusiasm for the new day.

It can be rather annoying for those of us who awaken slowly, cautiously, and generally less than cheerfully.

Nonetheless, he's usually happy to seize a chance for time alone in the midst of the whirlwind that is our lives, so I was not surprised to see him when I woke.

He was mostly dressed, in trousers and shirt, waistcoat open, no tie yet, sitting on his side of the bed with a book, apparently quite absorbed in his new edition of Abraham Lincoln's letters. Several months of marriage had done nothing to diminish my appreciation for my man, either in looks or demeanor. At the moment, with his collar loose, dark hair a bit mussed, and the midday light picking up his sharp features and giving his ice-blue eyes a bit of glitter, he was looking rather astonishing.

And I had good cause to know he was rather astonishing in other ways, as well.

"Gil." I stretched, and ran a hand down his arm. "Good morning."

"Ah, Sleeping Beauty wakes." He put down his book.

"You could have awakened me."

"That would not have been fair."

"Still…" I pretended a pout.

He laughed and reached for me. "I'll wake you properly now, *mo chridhe*."

"Best way to start the day."

Even though we had been married for months, I was still amazed at how the crackling attraction of our courtship had transformed into an intense and loving bond. We had always shared a deep connection of mind and spirit, but the way that had evolved into a companionate marriage was surprising. I would never have expected it from the careful, reserved way he behaved toward me in the weeks before the wedding, but once we were duly married, we discovered that neither of us was troubled by the alleged lack of passion said to plague the respectable classes.

Some very pleasant time later, Gil was slowly buttoning the back of my lilac-wool day dress, pausing occasionally to kiss my neck or earlobe, and we began to discuss the day ahead.

"Are you resting about the house today?"

"Mostly. We have a few friends for dinner, I believe."

"Father Michael?"

"Always. The new cook at the rectory is someone's sister and perfectly awful."

"Poor priest." He finished the last button, and his hands moved to my waist. "Food is practically the only pleasure he has, after all."

I leaned back into his arms and gave him a quick kiss. "I am powerfully fond of cake, but it does not compensate."

Gil laughed. "Too true. I have a few errands today, but I will be back for dinner."

"Good." I did not ask about the nature of the errands, because if it were something he could tell me about, he would have.

As we pulled back from the embrace, he held me for a moment and gave me an assessing glance. "You know, a bit of womanly insight might be just the thing."

"Oh?"

"Yes. Would you be able to join me for a late-afternoon tea at the Consulate?"

"The Consulate? Are you quite sure?"

"Absolutely. You are an excellent judge of character, not to mention a delightful distraction."

"But isn't this a discussion about delicate matters, among men?"

"You can always ask to admire the Consulate's famous sundial garden if necessary." He grinned. "I like the idea of a shared effort, if you're not too tired."

I grinned back. "I am never too tired to work with my husband."

"Just what I like to hear. I shall come back to collect you in time for tea."

"Lovely. In the meantime, I think I shall spend a few hours relaxing on my chaise lounge with a good book."

Little did I know how much I had just tempted the fates.

"About time, sleepyheads!" Tommy called as we reached the landing. He walked in from the parlor, looking maddeningly neat and well-rested, even in a russet tweed jacket that perfectly picked up the dark auburn of his hair. His blue-green eyes are a match for mine—but his smile is all his own. "Decently rested, Heller?"

"Yes, thank you." I narrowed my eyes.

"And I've almost finished that new book of Lincoln's legal correspondence, if you'd like to read it next," Gil added.

"I would, now that you mention it. Cabot is trying to get me to read Roman history, and it's slow going."

Gil shook his head. "I've never been too enamored of ancient history."

"Well, except, of course, for Xerxes, King of Persia…" Tommy shot him a wink. "Come along, you two. There's coffee and—"

We never did find out what our excellent cook, Miss O'Hanlon, had made to go with the coffee, because just then, the telephone in the foyer rang.

We all turned to see Sophia, the young housemaid, racing to the receiver like a baseball player barreling for home plate.

"HurleyresidencemayIaskwho'scalling?"

She just might need a wee reminder on telephone demeanor.

"Miss Ella!" she called, turning to me, eyes wild. "It's Madame Marie!"

Marie de l'Artois, the Met's resident Queen of the Night, is my favorite singing partner and a good friend besides. As a fellow performer, never mind a caring friend, she would never call so early unless the situation was dire.

I took the device. "Marie! Is everything all right?"

"Nothing's all right!" If I hadn't known it was her, I would not have recognized the frantic shriek. "It's Paul!"

Her husband, recently named a civil court judge. Something terrible must have happened. I waited.

"He was taken in a police raid at a sporting house!"

The honeymoon, one had to assume, was well and truly over.

Chapter Three: Even the Best Men...

This disaster, naturally, completely changed the plan for the day.
I assured Marie I was on the way and grabbed my hat and a light
jacket. Gil gave me a quick kiss, offered to do what he could, and
reminded me to be home in time to prepare for tea at the Consulate before
heading off in his own direction.

I suspected the Consulate would be a fine distraction now.

Tommy tucked me into a cab with condolences and a similar offer of
help. I told him to wait until I knew more. What I didn't say, but he surely
understood, was the two of us would soon be heading out on an investigation
of our own.

First, though, a conversation with the injured party. A conversation that
must be among women. No woman would want to discuss such matters
with a man in the room, no matter how kind, perceptive, and helpful the
man.

Quite bad enough this had happened. No need to add to the indignity.

At Marie's Brooklyn brownstone, a suspicious quiet reigned.

By then, it was about one, and the two older children were likely still in
school, while baby Joseph was no doubt napping. Still, though, it was very
unusual to walk into a silent hall at that home.

Marie's housemaid nodded to the parlor, where I found the lady of the
house on the settee, with a pot of coffee and a plate of little sandwiches
on the table. As a fellow singer, she completely understood my exhaustion
today, though she didn't share it.

Xerxes did have a good role for her, but she had not taken it, since she'd spent the late summer singing "Queen of the Night" at a Boston festival and spending time with her husband's parents. The Winslows were not overly enamored of her career but did appreciate the prestige of a diva in the family. Marie, now, was between productions and was supposed to be enjoying a few quiet weeks as a prosperous Brooklyn matron.

Perhaps not.

On the settee, in a lovely sky-blue wool crepe day dress with soft white crochet lace collar and cuffs, all setting off her delicate silver-blonde beauty, she looked as serene as ever. The only sign of trouble—and only to those who know her well—was a tiny crinkle between her brows, and a twist to her rosy mouth. This, in another person, would have been screaming and rending of hair.

"Ells, thank you so much for coming over." She held out her hands, and we embraced.

"Of course. What on earth happened?"

"Well," she sighed as I sat. "It's not quite what I thought it was, but it's still bad."

"What kind of bad?"

She started pouring coffee, and the rich scent stopped me cold. I realized just how tired I was from the performance the night before.

Marie caught my expression. "Poor you. I dragged you out of bed, didn't I?"

"Not quite. I was on my way down to breakfast, well…something."

"I thought as much." She handed me the cup, and I wrapped my hands around it. "When you're ready, Coralie made nice plain jam sammies."

"Oh, thank heaven."

A grin. "Nothing better after a late night than a simple, nourishing meal. And the least I can do, since I've dragged you into this mess."

"Nonsense. You've been in the midst of any number of my dramas."

"And delightful dramas they are." A light, rueful chuckle. "This may be a bit less so."

"Not all of mine have been delightful," I reminded her. I waited. Whatever this was, she would have to work her way to it in her own time.

"Well, first, the good news is, Paul was not there as a client."

"I had no doubt."

"Neither did I." She ran a finger around the rim of her cup. "I've never even seen him glance at a chorus girl. It didn't seem possible."

"Not a bit of it."

"But I almost wish it were. This is much more of an issue. After all, just about every man has slipped at some point."

"Too true. Even the best men-"

"Are still men." She nodded. "Exactly."

"So this is something else? Is Paul trying to help someone who's in danger?"

"Close." A little smile. Then a breath, as she forced herself to say the next words: "Paul's sister owns the house.

"What?" It was a shock, but not for the obvious reason. "I thought Paul only had a brother."

"He did."

I stared at Marie, who blushed and looked a bit uncomfortable. "I don't-"

"He had a brother, but now he has a sister." She was trying very hard to be matter-of-fact.

"All right. None of my business..." I tried to be matter-of-fact, as well, and not nosy.

"Do you remember that story Hetty did a few weeks ago of the Civil War veteran

who died in Yonkers? Everybody thought he was a man, but when they went to bury him, they found out he was a woman?"

Now, I begin to understand. "So, he's now living as...she?"

"Yes." She took a breath. Thought for a moment. "I didn't know until last fall's run of the *Princes in the Tower*. A woman came backstage...she was rather tall, and her clothes were a little fussy. But she had Paul's eyes and a kind smile. I thought, perhaps a cousin, because she asked after Paul and the children. And then Paul walked in, and just stared at her."

I'd completely missed this; our production last autumn had threatened to devolve into chaos with a dressing-room murder, the wrongful arrest of an important player, and Gil's involvement in a second, entirely different, case.

Marie, as far as I knew, had simply come in, sung her role, and returned to her family. Obviously, there had been a great deal more happening in Marie's life than I'd suspected.

Yet another important issue I'd missed. I needed to do better by my beloveds.

"He didn't know?" I asked.

"I don't think so." She took a sip of coffee, reflected. "He said 'Allen!' and stood there staring for a moment."

"And then?" I asked. I knew what many men would do at the discovery that their brother was living as a woman.

"It's 'Alice,' now, she said. And she told him she'd never trouble him again, she just wanted to see how he and our family were doing—and figured it was safe to come to the theatre after a show."

"What did he do?"

Marie smiled. "He shook her hand. Said she's still family."

"That'll do."

"Yes. Though it's not like we can have her over for tea, of course." She sighed. "They agreed to exchange letters, and she sent us a lovely porcelain figurine for the mantel. A Dresden woman playing piano—apparently their mother has one."

"A sweet gesture."

"Yes. What little I know of her is she's sweet and kind." A shrug. "I didn't know what she'd been doing until Paul was arrested. Apparently, she owns the sporting house since it's one of the few ways for people like her to make a living. But Paul says she really tries to run it fairly and decently."

"As much as such places can be." My turn to sigh. "I can't find it in my heart to judge any woman who's desperate enough to work there."

"Neither can I. My sisters worked in shirtwaist factories."

"I cleaned houses with my aunt—and my mother and I did piecework. I have no trouble understanding how a girl might consider another way."

"Virtue's not worth much when your belly's empty and your sight's failing."

"Not at all." I took a long draft of the coffee, feeling the warmth all the way down, letting it push away the memory of the tiny, freezing tenement room of my mother's last days. "So, she's found a safe and relatively decent way to live her life."

"At least as we see it." Marie nodded. "She had, until the police raid last night."

"But police raids are part of the cost of doing business for a sporting house, aren't they?" I knew a bit of the underworld from reading Tommy's *Police Gazette.* Well, and other things.

"Yes. But a raid when a civil court judge just happens to be visiting his sister who is the proprietress? With other secrets of her own?"

"Has there been a blackmail demand?"

"Not yet."

Thinking, I reached for one of the jam sammies, took a bite. Delicious. Fine, rich white bread, a thin layer of fresh creamy butter, and the heady sweet-tart, slightly floral, taste of good ripe strawberries. Probably marvelous even if one hadn't eaten since just after last night's show. "Well, Tommy and I have a few old friends on either side of the law in the shadier parts of town. Perhaps we can ask around."

"You don't need to—"

"Oh, please." I took another bite of my sandwich. "It will be fun. A nice change of pace from receptions and drawing-rooms."

Just a little over-optimistic on my part.

Chapter Four: Their Graces to the Consulate

Back at the house, my lady's maid, Rosa, had taken time from her reading to lay out my very best afternoon dress, soft gray satin with a beaded net overlay, and a matching broad-brimmed hat trimmed with plumes and a swirl of point d'esprit veiling, secured with a flower pin in the same iridescent beads. Harmonizing gloves and an adorable pair of black suede shoes with sparkly steel buckles finished the outfit, and Rosa, with her backstage experience, was able to get me into it in record time.

"Quite elegant, Miss," she said with the final tweak to the hat's angle. "Every inch the Duchess."

"For the British Consulate, I'd best be."

She held out the gloves, and I slipped the lavender fancy diamond off my left hand. "Someday, I'll find a way to fit this under gloves."

"But today is not that day." Rosa chuckled at our almost-daily joke as she took the ring and locked it in my jewel box. "You really should have it fitted on a necklace finding so you can wear it on days like this."

I shook my head. "Much too sparkly. Pearls are quite enough."

"Well, when they're these pearls, for certain." She clasped the radiant single strand of old Scottish pearls around my neck. "...and the bracelet?"

I held out my wrist, allowed myself a moment to admire it. The Tallach pearls had an exotic pale, creamy gray tint and unique shimmery glow. Nothing else looked like these rare freshwater jewels, at once so simple and so astonishing. The pearls had been in my mother-in-law's Highland Scots family for generations, and she'd brought them to her marriage.

Gil's sister had worn them from her debut until her Foreign Office husband was posted in far away, and more to the point, tropical Australia, and his mother had presented them to me on my birthday a few months ago. The thought of the Countess made me smile. She was in Edinburgh with her sisters at the moment, celebrating their aunt's centenary, and planned to join Gil and me for our December trip to San Francisco.

"Do you want a little rose-petal salve, miss?"

I looked at myself. I was a bit pale from tiredness, but if anyone at the Consulate were the narrow-minded sort who considered me a bare step up from a streetwalker, even a hint of the cosmetic arts would only play into their biases. Better to present an innocent, if wan, face.

"Best not," I said, rising from my vanity.

Gil was in the foyer, laughing with Tommy and Father Michael, undoubtedly about the amount of time it took me to change. I suspected it, but I was absolutely certain when all three looked up at me with the sheepish faces of boys caught at something naughty.

"Lovely, Shane," Gil said, holding out a hand for me at the landing.

"Thank you kindly." I smiled at him and cocked an eyebrow at the other two. "Hiding out from a temporary cook again?"

Father Michael blushed, as even a cleric will do when cursed with the fishbelly-pale complexion of the Irish. "Yes. I'm collecting Tom for a visit to the boys' school, and then we'll be back here for dinner, likely about when you return."

"I suspect you'll do more good for the world at large," Gil said. "Tea at the Consulate can be rather…"

I held Gil's gaze. Surely, he knew he could trust Tommy and Father Michael with this. He blinked slowly. *For later discussion.* Fair enough.

"Well, at least you've got Heller to keep you company," Tommy said, a gleam in his eye.

"Is Cabot coming to dinner, too?" I asked rather pointedly. While I did, after all, need to arrange a tea with Aunt Cecily, Cabot Bridgewater's aunt and the matriarch of his Knickerbocker clan, I also wanted to push Toms back just a bit on his happy cupid act.

Cabot is Tommy's dear friend, a description everyone in the family circle understands, since we are aware of, and untroubled by, the fact that Tommy is not the marrying kind. Equally importantly, no one outside dares question them, considering Tommy's past as a boxing champion and Cabot's unassailable social cachet. Well, at least not question publicly.

What nasty things people think in private is not our concern.

"As a matter of fact, he is joining us." Tommy's glare made it clear he knew exactly what I was about.

"Well, then," I said with a radiant smile, "we shall look forward to seeing him in a few hours."

"Bet you will."

Gil and Father Michael exchanged glances, both clearly holding back chuckles. Despite the many changes in our lives, Tommy and I were still as close as sibs—and still sparred like them.

"Come along." Gil held out his arm to me. "We do not wish to be late."

I took his arm. "I doubt anyone is watching the clock for a Peer."

"Punctuality is politeness, as well you know, Shane."

Clearly, His Grace was putting on his best Peer of the Realm face for the Consulate.

I held back a smile and composed myself into elegant calm during the cab ride.

As I'd learned over the months of my marriage, being a Duchess was simply playing a role like any other. Just as I had to dress, stand, speak, and generally behave like an ancient king or a boy swain on the stage, so I played a part when I appeared as Her Grace, Ellen, Duchess of Leith. Of course, this role was a non-singing one, and often barely a speaking one. It was mostly a matter of demeanor.

When we arrived at the Consulate, though, demeanor was the least of our problems.

The cab stopped and generously paid off, Gil handed me down and offered his arm once more. We proceeded inside, the door magically opening before us. Inside, a blank-faced footman closed it, carefully not making eye contact with either of us, as expected of a British servant.

Outside may have been Manhattan in the new 20th century. In here was clearly the empire on which the sun never sets...and the corresponding behaviors. I was suddenly and sharply aware of myself as the child of Irish and Jewish immigrants.

Particularly all the Irish the English left to starve, including my own people. The Great Hunger is in our blood and bones. Even today, many of these British aristocrats would not even see me as human were it not for the protection of Gil's title and name.

"Aldrick is Scots." Gil's whisper, accompanied by a squeeze of my hand, told me he knew what I was feeling. "His people died on Bonnie Prince Charlie's side."

I nodded.

"Ah, Your Graces." A balding ginger-blond man about Gil's age strode into the foyer. His green eyes twinkled as he used the formal address. "What a pleasure to meet your Duchess at last."

"My lady wife, may I present Sir Aldrick MacKinroy?" One of Gil's brows flicked in amusement as he walked through the formalities.

I held out my hand, and Sir Aldrick bowed over it. "Delighted to meet you."

After I pulled my hand back, he turned to Gil for a far less formal handshake.

"Well, Leith, I hope you're prepared for the conversation to revolve around opera. I had the privilege of seeing Her Grace sing in London and Boston, and I should love to hear a few backstage stories if she's willing to tell them."

The direct, and admiring, reference to my work was unexpected—and welcome. In most of the drawing rooms I'd visited since my marriage, people either carefully ignored my profession, or spoke of it as if it were embarrassing.

"I expect I can find a tale or two," I said. "And perhaps you can tell me a bit about reading law with my Barrister."

He shot Gil a grin. "Oh, it would be my pleasure."

In the magnificent Consulate drawing room, with French doors giving on a garden, the tea and shortbread were as fine as one might expect, and the conversation sparkling, indeed centered on opera and performance matters. While it was clear to me Sir Aldrick understood the nature of our partnership, it was equally clear he did not intend to bring up the most sensitive matter between him and Gil in my presence.

Finally, I sent Gil a significant glance and nodded to the French doors. "I have heard the consulate garden is magnificent this time of year."

Gil smiled. "I have seen it recently, but perhaps Sir Aldrick would not mind if you stepped out for a look?"

"I would be honored to hear your impressions." He rose and opened the doors. Outside, it was still a lovely early-autumn afternoon, the light barely starting to fade, and the air beginning to become cool as it does in the hour or so before sunset this time of year. The garden was, of course, an English one, a small, jewel-like courtyard, with bright blue asters, bronzy-red chrysanthemums, and greenery beginning to darken and turn from the cool nights. Lovely indeed. As I studied the black-eyed susans around a weathered bronze sundial, I had the distinct impression someone was watching me.

I looked up. An older gentleman, portly, with a heavy but well-trimmed gray beard, was staring down from a second-floor window, holding up a curtain to get a better look. Even from this distance, I could see the unfortunately common lustful glare I'd seen on any number of stage-door johnnies. Inside, I cringed. But I straightened my spine and tilted my head up to meet his gaze squarely.

Taken aback, he let the curtain drop.

I took a breath, watched the flower heads nod in the breeze. Despite the title, despite the protection of Gil's name, despite my own prestige, property, and not-inconsiderable bank account, when some random man wanted to look at me as if I were an object, still I was no better than any tenement skivvy.

A new century had not changed that fact. I wondered if anything ever would.

Not a thought I wanted to share with Gil, who would likely have marched up the stairs and taught the fellow a lesson in manners. When he came to the French doors, I smiled and followed him inside, to finish the tea with a few admiring words about the asters.

They were a far safer topic.

Chapter Five: Family Dinner

By the time we got home, it was full dark. As Gil and I walked up the stairs, I remembered him squiring me home a year ago, and was again amazed we'd found a way to be together. Not easily, and not without each of us being willing to give a great deal.

But worth it.

"I'm reminded of last autumn," Gil said, his voice soft and low, the Northern burr noticeable as it often was when we were alone. He had kept hold of my hand after helping me down from the cab, and his fingers tightened on mine.

"I prefer this year." I squeezed back. "Wedded bliss is not underrated."

"No," he said, opening the door, "it is not."

"And neither is a family dinner."

It was not a casual remark. Even from the foyer, I could hear a cacophony of masculine voices. We appeared to have walked in on a dispute over some sort of four-hands card game. Tommy and Father Michael were arguing with Cabot and his playing partner, who seemed to be unfamiliar with the way the game was played in New York.

Understandable, since he was still settling into city life, and our house.

Adding to the din, the squawking of Montezuma, our Amazon parrot, who clearly did not approve of the disruption to his territory.

In short, pandemonium in the parlor.

"We are going to have to calm the waters yet again," I said.

"Perhaps we can convince them to discuss something uncontroversial like women's suffrage."

"Well, that's very nearly uncontroversial in this house."

"Not quite." Gil gave me a pointed scowl, as I knew he would. "I still think the vote will harm women more than their votes will improve the world."

"And I am still amazed that you hold this one entirely antiquated view." I shook my head. "One would think that after everything you've seen from any number of women, including ones in your own family…"

"One would be wrong." Gil nodded to the parlor. "We'd best step in."

"Gentlemen!" I called as I walked through the pocket doors.

The scene we confronted was, unfortunately, not at all unusual for us. Tommy and Father Michael were at the card table, laying out a hand, apparently in the process of explaining why it was the winner.

Cabot Bridgewater was lounging back in his impeccable, gray glen plaid suit, his deep-blue eyes gleaming with amusement. He is the classic blond Knickerbocker type, from a family and money so old they make the Pilgrims seem nouveau riche.

His card partner was known to be a bit of a hothead, living up to the reputation of gingers everywhere. At the moment, he was at the mantel, arguing with Montezuma.

"James, never pick an argument you can't win." Gil's tone was dry, but his eyes gleamed with joy as they often did when regarding his younger son.

"Pater! Belle Star!" Jamie turned from Montezuma to us, immediately looking like the naughty little boy he so often was. "I'm surprised you were at the Consulate. I thought you were planning a rest day after the performance."

"*Alba Gu Brath!*" crowed Montezuma. Scotland Forever, in Gaelic, his greeting for Gil because my half-Highlander had taught it to him.

I held out a hand, and Montezuma swooped over to me. Cabot met my gaze with a trace of a grin as Gil continued:

"An old friend wanted to meet your stepmother, and she was kind enough to give up a few hours of her recovery time." The phrasing was formal enough to tip off everyone in the room—probably including the parrot— that more was in play, but no one was really in the mood to pursue it just now.

"Well, that's kind indeed." Jamie and his father exchanged their usual handshake and half-embrace greeting, and then he turned to me and ducked around the bird to plant an enthusiastic kiss on my cheek.

"Very elegant, Belle Starr." Jamie nodded to my outfit as he pulled back. Upper-class Britons often use the French name for a stepmother, *belle-mère*, but he'd changed it to the famous outlaw's handle as a teasing endearment. Fine by me.

"How are classes?" I asked, as Montezuma swooped back to his favored perch on a high bookshelf.

Though Jamie had completed his initial studies at Oxford, he was starting a graduate program in science at nearby New York University, with a professor who was breaking ground in the new field of criminology. Not surprising for the son of a barrister, I supposed, but definitely not an expected path in his social circles.

Gil, being Gil, was proud as punch. Well, after the initial token grumbling, he was.

"Fascinating." Jamie's face glowed. "Right now, we're studying poisons. Did you know there are still no reliable tests for many of the most common ones?"

"Most intriguing. But not at the moment," I said, walking over to the whatnot and pulling out two small pewter candleholders and a pair of creamy beeswax candles. "Let's leave the poisons for now. It's sunset and time for candle-lighting."

"Oh, that's right." Jamie beamed. "I love this."

"So do we all," Gil agreed. "It is a wonderful tradition."

As the daughter of a Jewish mother and Irish Catholic father, I observe both of my parents' faiths. As far as I'm concerned, the Lord knows who I am, and He'll sort it out when the time comes. In the meantime, I take joy and consolation in honoring each of my parents in their own way. Which means Shabbat candles on Friday nights, and Sunday morning Mass. And, when I need to feel closer to them, a *yahrzeit* candle for my mother on a Friday, or a Sunday candle at the feet of the Virgin at Holy Innocents for my father.

Our observance is by no means an Orthodox Shabbat. We do not keep kosher or follow any traditional restrictions on work or activities—as a performer, I simply cannot—but we take the time to bring God into the room and feel the warmth and Spirit together. Faith and family are universal.

The only problem for me is reciting the blessings over the candles. My Hebrew is uneven at best because I did not have a conventional religious education. For most of my life, I've lit candles in private, whether in a corner of my Aunt Ellen's home, or my own parlor. After Tommy and I moved into the townhouse, he took to joining me. While we do light candles on Fridays in my dressing room, my costumer Anna Abramovitz used to recite the blessings because her Hebrew was so much better.

Now, though, as the ranking woman in a good-sized household, I could not hide.

Nothing for it but to do it.

Everyone, including Montezuma on his shelf, was quiet, waiting.

I picked up the box of matches and took a breath.

Even though I had my usual worries about the Hebrew, as I lit the candles, the warmth and joy of faith and family took hold, as it always did. Once I finished the blessings, we stood together watching the candles for a moment of quiet.

And then Jamie—of course it was Jamie!—broke the serene silence:

"So, what's for dinner?"

Chapter Six: A Fine Morning in Washington Square

The next morning, I fully intended to sleep late.

But when the sun filtered through the blinds, I opened one eye and reached for Gil, hoping for the marital pleasure of a lazy morning snuggle, only to discover myself alone. Quite enough to ruin any possibility of lying abed, considering Gil might be anywhere and up to anything if he'd felt the need to slip away. And, under our agreement, I could not ask him, assuming I found him.

Normally, this would not trouble me overly much. But I knew large, dark, and deep forces were at work here. My beloved, even though he is a border lord and not a Londoner, might be unable or unwilling to acknowledge that he was dealing with some very dangerous people. But I, as someone whose family had seen the back of the British Empire's hand, had no such qualms.

And no doubt what awful things the Court might do if Gil brought an answer they didn't like. Perhaps he needed some protection out there, wherever "there" was.

I resolved to bring up the idea with Tommy, as I pulled on a simple violet merino morning dress and quickly pinned up my hair, since there was no telling who might be about the house, even at this hour.

And so it was.

"Belle Starr!" Jamie called as I walked down to the landing. "New experiments today! See you for dinner—thank Miss O'Hanlon for lunch!"

He waved a pail with one hand and grabbed his hat with the other, then blew out the door in a whirlwind. I made a mental note to offer Miss O'Hanlon an extra half-day at some point. Keeping a nineteen-year-old man fed, especially a big, tall one like Jamie, was a full-time job of its own.

"Don't slam the door!" I called pointlessly.

Watching him stride off, jacket and coat flying, I reflected that I probably owed Sophia some extra consideration, too. Since none of our staff lives in, Jamie had taken over the old housekeeper's quarters on the top floor, tucked off the studio, and he'd likely turned it into a treehouse retreat right out of those penny dreadful boys' books.

"Heller!" Tommy called from the parlor. He was happily ensconced in his chair with the morning papers and coffee. Just coffee. In addition to the coffee pot, the tray held two empty plates. The scattering of pastry shards suggested Jamie had been through. "Did I eat everything in sight like that?"

"More. You were fighting and training, and we'd just started making money, so you could afford everything you wanted."

"Probably so." He laughed. "Jamie polished off the bacon and eggs Miss O'Hanlon brought out for him, then came in here and looted my tray for dessert."

"She should be feeding him porridge," I said, reaching for the bell. "Easy to make and very filling."

"Not to mention nutritious for a growing boy." Tommy gave me a sharp glance. "He's done growing, isn't he?"

"I don't know…but it's Gil's problem if he needs new togs."

"Miss?" Mary O'Hanlon, our very skilled and quite adorable young cook, appeared in the doorway with a new tray. "I thought you and Mr. Tom might need more refreshment after Mr. Jamie came through."

"Indeed, we do. Thank you for seeing to him. I believe we owe you an extra half day for your trouble soon."

Her green-gray eyes gleamed. "Well, now that you mention it, Mr. Coyne was talking about a matinee one of these weeks."

"Was he now?" Tommy grinned.

Mr. Coyne, also known as our cousin Rafe, a handsome handyman finishing his accounting course, was courting her in a manner so careful and courteous as to be glacial. A matinee would be a major escalation from their Saturday afternoon walks with her dear friend Rosa and a rotating cast of Rafe's male acquaintances and relatives to meet the proprieties. Since Rosa was far more interested in writing than courting, the expeditions always ended with Rosa dashing upstairs to record her observations about the squire of the day, leaving Rafe and Mary awkwardly alone in the foyer, until Rafe took his leave with a handshake that suggested he feared breaking Mary's fingers...or being burned by them.

"He was indeed talking about a matinee—or at least I got him to talk about it. And more than time, too." Mary grinned right back at Tommy. "I'll let him know I have a half-day and see what he says."

"Take the smelling-salts," I advised. Rafe's absolute adoration was a matter of fun in the house, because it was so obvious and sincere.

Mary laughed, a sweet flush coloring her cheeks. Rafe was not the only one who was smitten—which made it all the more darling. "I'll likely need them. I will let you know, if I may."

"Of course. Good luck." Tommy grinned. "Though I suspect Rafe is the lucky one."

"Indeed, he is." She winked. "Do you need anything else?"

I surveyed the fresh coffee and scones. "Oh, I think we're quite nicely provided for. Thank you."

"Of course, Miss. Mr. Tom." She was still smiling and flushed as she took the old tray and headed back to the kitchen.

I topped off Tommy's cup and poured my own, pausing to take a good deep breath of the rich steam. "Ah. It's entirely possible I will survive."

"Good." Tommy glared a little. "Eat something. You spent yesterday running from pillar to post, and you never eat enough during a run."

I reached for a scone. They were the delicious raisin ones with cinnamon, nutmeg, and a lovely light sugar-and-spice glaze. A working artist does need to keep her strength up. "Important to eat a proper breakfast."

Tommy took one, too. "Always."

"Do you know where Gil went?"

"Grabbed a slice of toast, mumbled something about corroborating a story, and blew out of here. Looked very much like you saw with Jamie just now—only about an hour earlier and without a lunch pail."

I laughed. "They are a pair."

"They are. And thoroughly off the board for the day. So what's on for you?"

"Well, you're aware of the whole mess involving Marie's husband," I said, breaking off a corner of my scone.

"Caught at a sporting house. Not charged, though, right?"

"No. We suspect there will be a blackmail demand."

"A very reasonable expectation. Was he at the sporting house for the usual reasons?"

"Not quite."

Tommy's eyes widened. "What other reasons are there?"

"Well, the proprietress is his sister."

"I thought Paul had a brother."

"He used to."

Tommy gazed at me for a moment, puzzled, as I'd done to Marie the day before. "How..."

"As I understand it, Alice's soul was born into Allen's body," I said. "I don't pretend to know..."

"But it would be a terrible way to live." He nodded. "With no good solution."

"Exactly. Apparently, she's decided to live as she is, not as people feel she should. And running a sporting house is likely one of the only ways to do so."

"No doubt." He shook his head. "So she's found a way to survive. And, also to make herself and her brother a nice juicy target for blackmail."

"Quite possibly."

"Perhaps I should go down to Five Points and have a look around."

"Not alone," I said.

"No tagging along."

"Well," I replied irritably, "I can't just sit here waiting for something to happen."

"You'd best. The Met's headliner—or more to the point, the Duchess of Leith—can't go running about the rough part of town asking about a house of ill repute." He glared.

"No," I agreed, draining the last of my cup. "But Eddie Hurley can."

The glare sharpened. "Absolutely not, Heller. You-"

"You know I'll just follow you." I put the cup in the saucer. "Meet you down here in ten minutes."

"I don't like this," he called after me.

"Your opposition is duly noted."

And ignored.

Chapter Seven: The Hurley Boys Ride Again

Ten minutes later, I bounded down the stairs in my roughest boots, a pair of gray wool pants Tommy had outgrown more than a decade ago, an old fencing practice shirt, and a heavy black-and-gray tweed jacket. I'd skinned my hair back into a tight knot, easy enough to cover with a worn gray cap, and the cap bill provided some useful shadow for my face. A pair of fraying fingerless gloves hid my wedding and engagement rings, and smooth, ladylike palms.

I hadn't worn the outfit in probably ten years. When Tommy was fighting, I used to pose as his younger brother at his matches. My mentor, Madame Lentini, disapproved of boxing and banned me from attending them… as myself. Knowing Tommy's and my deep bond, not to mention my determination, as she did, she'd also allowed as how she had no control over what a younger Hurley brother might do with his time.

She'd meant it, and I understood it, as tacit permission to go and support Tommy, as long as I did so in disguise. Eddie Hurley had proudly cheered his big brother on to the title and enjoyed a night on the town afterward—though he'd been quietly sent home before the celebration got too rowdy, so Toms didn't have to worry about me.

Soon after, I began to see real success in my opera career, and Tommy decided he would be much happier, and safer, managing my affairs. Of course, with a bit of encouragement from his mother and me. And Eddie Hurley disappeared into the box at the bottom of my closet with his clothes.

35

Until today.

"Big Brother!" I called, jumping down the last two steps and landing in a pugilistic pose.

"Stop it," Tommy growled. "I hate this."

"Oh, you do not. We're doing something important." I stopped at the foyer mirror and settled the cap properly on my head. I make a perfectly convincing boy on stage, if a rather pretty one, and I do just fine in the real world, too. "And it might be fun."

"Five Points is not fun."

He appeared behind me in the mirror, meeting my gaze with a dubious and concerned expression.

"You're right. But it's an excellent change of scene from tea at the Consulate."

"Now that, I'll believe." He slapped my back. "Let's go."

Far downtown, long past the genteel precincts of the Ladies' Mile and Washington Square, Five Points is crowded, loud, and dirty. Unlike the Lower East Side, which is where you go when you arrive in the city with hope for a better life, Five Points is where you end up when hope is gone. Many people get out of the Lower East Side with nothing but bad memories and grim determination. If they get out of Five Points at all, almost nobody leaves without scars.

Often from blades or bullets.

Of course, I already had a scar from a blade, the slash wound I'd sustained when I stepped in front of Gil when a madman came at him. I'd learned my lesson in that knife fight. Well, two lessons: I don't ever want to be in a knife fight again—and if I am, I can't lose track of the knife, even for an instant.

The attempt on Gil had left me wounded, but it had done plenty of damage to him, as well as Tommy, because they'd seen it happen, making both more protective of me. Sometimes quite irrationally so.

Today, though, Tommy's protectiveness was not irrational. Danger did in fact lurk at every corner in Five Points, where a casual jostle in the street could—and did—spark a fatal fight on any given day. As we walked deeper into the area, we decided our best strategy today would be to simply observe.

Especially in a place like this, you can't move until you know the lay of the land.

Even in the toughest part of town, one of the best places to start is the newsstand. Everyone buys newspapers, and the paper man knows all of them, and often their habits. We bought a couple of the most salacious tabloid papers and chatted for a few moments about the various ways two young men with an afternoon off might amuse themselves.

The paper man mentioned Alice LaJoy's house, with the comment that "she's good people for what she does."

We nodded to keep him going, not that he really needed the encouragement, as he warmed to the theme, happily spooling out tales of trouble from a more problematic house on the next street over, known for fights and the occasional throat-slashing.

And then, quite unexpectedly, he pointed. "Well, look there. That's Miss LaJoy now."

"How about that," Tommy said, and I nodded, turning our gaze in the direction of a trim figure stepping out of the apothecary, a bag over her arm.

"See? You'd never know she ran a place like that if you didn't know."

It was not the only thing you would not know, at least from this distance.

Alice LaJoy was taller than most women, but quite slim. I couldn't tell much about her face because of the broad-brimmed black hat with veil, but her black coat was neatly fitted over a well-corseted feminine form. She moved with a graceful light step, glancing about the street before turning in the direction of the fruit seller.

Whilst she examined the produce, Tommy and I finished our conversation with the paper man and started walking down the other side of the street, carefully cultivating an unobtrusive attitude. Once Alice had her bag of apples—a very good choice this time of year—we followed. It was easier than it sounds; the streets of Five Points are always thick with people, and Toms and I were dressed perfectly to blend in. Alice was also easy to follow: she was tall enough to stand out a bit, and the shaded gray plume on her hat added more height, so we had no trouble keeping sight of her.

After a few blocks, Alice turned down a side street and up the walk of a brownstone. It was notable only for the immaculate whiteness of the stoop, clearly freshly chalked by a diligent staff.

For a moment, Tommy and I stared after her.

"All right," he said finally, "you know what we really need to do."

"Gather some information." I nodded. "Only one place to do that."

"Think you can nurse a pint and stay out of trouble?"

"Eddie Hurley never met a pint he didn't like."

"That's what I'm afraid of."

"Well, Da Morrissey pours a good one. Let's go."

Morrissey's is the safe place in Five Points. Everyone comes through Morrissey's, and Da Morrissey knows everything happening in the neighborhood. If we want to know about Alice LaJoy and who might want to blackmail Paul, Da Morrissey would be able to give us some direction.

"Champ!" Da Morrissey, a small gray-haired man who looked like a half-size copy of his four large sons—a policeman, a fireman, a priest, and a gangster—cheered as we walked in. Morrissey's had been there as long as anyone could remember, with sawdust on the floor and smoke in the air. "And Eddie—how long has it been?"

"Long enough," I growled in my lower register. Da Morrissey had never acknowledged it, but he likely knew there was something unusual about Eddie Hurley.

"He's been away upstate," Tommy said quickly. "Got sent up for an assault."

"Wasn't my fault the fool up and died," I added, throwing myself down on a stool.

Da Morrissey's blue eyes sharpened on mine. "We're not having any trouble here, my friend."

"No, sir." I mumbled like the misbehaving boy I was.

"The first thing Eddie wanted when he got off the train from upstate was a pint at Morrissey's." Tommy smiled at the barkeep.

"Well," Da Morrissey said, allowing himself a grin, "we can certainly arrange that. Just one, though. I don't remember this young fella having much tolerance for the drink. And certainly not after working the farm for a few years."

"Fair enough," I said.

Da Morrissey drew two perfect pints and set them down in front of us.

Tommy paid, put some coins in the tip glass, and took his first sip, nodding to me.

The stout was bitter but not bad. I'd never admit it to anyone who isn't Irish—especially not Gil—but I do enjoy the taste. I smiled at Da. "Ah."

"Been waiting for that, eh, son?"

"Sure have."

Tommy shot me a glance. "Thinking maybe I take my little brother here out for a good time this evening."

"What kind of good time?"

"Oh, you know, a manly good time." Tommy shrugged. "I'm not fond of the sporting house, but the boy has to learn for himself."

"Not from you. You're always at church. They're going to make a priest of you yet, Champ." Da Morrissey laughed at the neighborhood explanation for Tommy's extended single state, given more credence by his friendship with Father Michael, and good works with Cabot. If Da suspected anything else, he'd never suggest it of the Champ. And considering one of his sons—not the priest—was also conspicuously unwed, he saw no reason to ask.

"The Lord works in mysterious ways." Tommy chuckled as he took another sip.

"Well, if the boy's looking for that sort of fun, he couldn't be safer than Alice's. The girls are clean, and she treats them right. But not cheap."

Tommy chuckled. "My cousin pays me well."

"Though she'd probably faint if she knew what you were doing with the money," Da Morrissey said.

"Heller's all proper," I said, scowling.

Tommy slugged my arm. "Don't run her down. She's offered you a place to stay till you get on your feet."

"She's good people," Da Morrissey said, nodding. "Doing us Irish proud in her own way. Just like you, Champ."

"Thanks." Tommy raised his glass to the barkeep. "We do what we can."

"That you do." Da Morrissey smiled, looked to me and reflected. "Suppose this one needs to let off a little steam after being upstate."

I tried to look like a steaming boy instead of the happy wife I actually am. Tommy was going to have a good laugh at my expense over this later.

"So, Alice LaJoy's?" Tommy asked.

"Best of a bad lot. And they just had a police raid there, so you're probably safe for a while."

"Coppers still doing raids on the routine?" Tommy asked.

"Usually. The other night was an odd one. They'd been to Alice's just two weeks ago, and I know she'd been paying up because the bagman was in for a drink after."

"Strange," Tommy said. "Maybe I'll take Eddie to the fights instead."

"Might be wiser. Just till things cool off. Weird, though."

"Yeah?"

"Alice is a good lady, for what she is. Talks nice—I think she's from some fancy family somewhere. Pretty manners and sounds like she's from someplace else. Maybe a little—different—but nothing bad." Da shrugged because it didn't matter much. "Tries to treat the girls right. Almost never have any fights there, and you know that happens all the time."

"Happens everywhere." Tommy and I exchanged wry shrugs. Appropriate since I'd just been paroled for a brawl that went bad.

"Isn't that the truth." Da Morrissey nodded to me. "Hope you stay out of trouble, kid. You're young enough to do better from here if you work hard."

"Don't worry, Da, we'll keep him on the straight and narrow." Tommy shot me a grin. He was enjoying this.

"Good thing. Might want to make sure he goes to Mass every day. My oldest is pastor over to Saint Joachim's, and he'd be glad to keep an eye."

"He's already signed up to help at Holy Innocents near our house. But if he needs a touch-up, we'll send him your way."

"That'll do." Da gave me a sharp but sympathetic glare. "You watch yourself, now, son."

He was clearly about to impart more wisdom when the door slammed open behind us.

"Ah, well, I've got another customer. Hope to see you two again soon…but not too soon."

Tommy and I returned to our drinks.

"Drink quickly, but not too quickly, Heller," he hissed. "The more people here, the riskier this gets."

"Calm down. I play men for a living, remember?" I took a swig of my beer and savored it. That wasn't acting. Yes, I really do enjoy a proper pint.

"Still. I know you want to help Marie, but—"

I was enjoying the sensation of the stout slowly sliding down my throat when I heard the voice of the new customer.

"Whisky, neat."

I almost spit out my beer.

Toms and I both turned sharply to the sound. Even with an overly pronounced Scots accent, it was unmistakable. If it hadn't been, the tall frame swathed in a rough brown overcoat and the ice-blue eyes under the brim of the rather battered fedora left no doubt.

Oh, dear.

Tommy and I became very interested in our pints.

It didn't work.

I heard Gil exchanging a few indistinct words with Da Morrissey, and then he walked our way, moving between us and motioning for a new round.

"Thanks kindly." Tommy nodded to him, carefully maintaining the pretense that we didn't know each other.

I had a hard time believing this had anything to do with his aristocratic errand...but it *was* Gil.

"Robert Stewart," he said, holding out a hand to Toms.

"Tommy Hurley, and my brother Eddie."

No way to avoid shaking. Or, the eye contact.

I was going to be in so much trouble when we got home.

"Mr. Morrissey tells me you two are some of the best hired muscle around. If I can meet your price."

"Depends on the work," Tommy said.

"I'm also told the skinny one is crazy." Gil's eyes sparkled. He was enjoying this. "I don't want trouble. I just want a job done."

"He's not crazy. He's just a little—"

"Don't take well to being insulted." I held Gil's gaze as I growled out another sentence: "Been known to teach folks a lesson in manners."

"Ah." Gil nodded to me, then turned to Tommy. "Nothing wrong with manners."

I gave him a hard nod.

"Anyhow, I need someone to watch out for a lady who's been putting her nose where it doesn't belong."

"Some ladies will do that," Tommy said.

"This one is a caution." He flicked a glance my way, but kept talking to Toms. "Likes to run out and get into trouble. You'll have to keep up with her."

"We can do that," Tommy said. "Won't be cheap, though."

"Oh, I'm sure I can afford you two." He grinned. "I'll send details."

"Leave it with Da Morrissey."

Gil nodded. "Will do."

He shook both our hands, the grin taking on a particular wickedness as he shook mine, and then walked out.

As he did, I noticed a couple of the other barflies watching him. One of the old codgers, a slumped pile of tweed, at the far corner, narrowed his eyes with a poisonous expression that seemed somehow familiar.

"We have to stay for a few minutes," Tommy said. "Have to be careful of appearance."

"I know." I reached for my new pint, and Tommy took it from me.

"One's enough for you, young man."

As I glared at Tommy, I glanced back at the codger. Of course, I'd never seen him before. Must be distracted. "Oh, fine."

"Drink slowly," Tommy said with a little smile. "Not going to let perfectly good

stout go to waste."

"Indeed not."

Chapter Eight: Back at the Hearth

"The Duchess of Leith should not be wandering about Five Points."

"The Duchess of Leith wasn't wandering about Five Points." I returned my husband's icy glare as I shrugged out of my heavy tweed jacket. He had been waiting for me in our bedroom when Tommy and I returned from Morrissey's. "Eddie Hurley, Tommy Hurley's crazy little brother, was."

Eddie's big brother, in case you were wondering, had headed right to his own room to nap off the stout. It had been a while since he drank like a boxer.

Just as well, since Gil and I had unfinished business.

He was not interested in my explanation. "If something happened to Eddie, it would also happen to the Duchess. And more to the point, to my wife and potential child."

Oh, we were taking that tack, were we? While I wasn't tipsy, I was not in the mood to take any nonsense, either. "Well, if anything happened to Mr. Robert Stewart, it would happen to the father of my potential child."

"That's different."

"Is it, now?" I crossed my arms and glared at him.

"It is, Shane, because you carry that child. Yes, I am responsible for supporting and protecting the child, but you give her—or him—life. It's biological fact."

I would have delivered a withering riposte on biology if not for the stumble on the pronoun. "Her?"

Gil shrugged, unexpectedly sheepish and adorable. "I was rather hoping for a daughter."

"I thought aristocratic men wanted sons."

"What I want is a safe and healthy child." He tried for a pointed glare, failed, and gave up. "And I already have, as the expression goes, an heir and a spare."

"Dreadful way to talk about one's own flesh and blood."

"I agree." Gil took a long breath and let it out slowly. "Some of my so-called peers tend to see their children as chess pieces to move on a board."

"Not you."

"No. My boys are my boys…even the older one." Rueful smile.

"At least you got to see him in London."

"Since you were already rehearsing, there was no need to make a stand about his ignoring you. I will not be so indulgent next time." Gil's jaw was tight. "No one is allowed to disrespect my wife."

I nodded. Part of the reason I'd left early was to give him a chance of a meeting with his older son without the contentious issue of my presence. Charles, who seemed rather more traditional than his father or brother, was doing his best to pretend I didn't exist. It might have been snobbery, or prejudice, or something less offensive but more difficult: the pain of seeing another woman in a place that should have belonged to his late mother. Whatever Charles' motives, I didn't want to be the reason for their estrangement.

"It's not necessarily disrespect," I said. "In any case, you won't be in London until after the San Francisco tour. That discussion can wait."

"It can." His angry expression faded. "And in the meantime, we have Jamie."

"We do. He is a joy."

"That he is." Gil took a breath, and I could practically see his thoughts shift. "But, after sending two sons away for the appropriate education, I believe I'd enjoy having a daughter."

"A son seeks his fortune, but a daughter is yours to keep?" It was Aunt Ellen's maxim—and likely the reason one of my cousins would end up a maiden aunt one day.

"It sounds rather silly, I admit…"

"It sounds adorable."

"Yes?" The awkward expression faded to a grin.

"Yes. You want to be an indulgent papa to a sweet little girl."

"Probably a feisty one if she takes after any of the women in my family, never mind you."

"So she'll lead you a merry dance."

"Like her mother." He reached for me. "I know we have an agreement not to ask about things the other doesn't need to know…"

"And you also know I never go anywhere even moderately interesting without Tommy."

"I do." He took a breath. "And I don't doubt he does an excellent job of protecting you."

"There's not much to protect me from. We're truly only gathering information in the matter of Marie's husband."

"All right." His voice belied the words, and he quickly followed with another thought. "Is Coughlan involved in this?"

"Not so far."

"Involve him."

"What?"

Gil held my gaze. "Coughlan is dangerous in ways you and your cousin are not. If he's watching over you, you might as well be locked in the castle vault."

"Are you serious?" I glared. "You really want me to ask Connor to hold my hand while I do a bit of investigating? That's humiliating for everyone."

"I suppose."

"Please try not to worry."

"I've come close enough to losing you. I won't let it happen again." He reached for me.

I sighed, but let him pull me in. "I'll be careful."

"See that you are."

I did not offer any details as to how I would be careful. I had no intention of bringing Tommy's and my old schoolmate, Connor Coughlan, now a powerful gangster in Five Points, into this. As long as I made no specific promises, I wasn't lying.

Besides, Gil and I were still newlyweds, and we had much better things to discuss...and *not* discuss.

Or we would have—if the calendar had not intruded yet again.

"Miss!" Rosa called. "Aren't you dining with Mr. Bridgewater's aunt today?"

"Oh, dear," I sighed. "Great-Aunt Cecily."

"The one who danced with the Prince?" Gil asked.

"None other." I sighed. "She follows the old Knickerbocker schedule. Dinner is at five."

"Five?" Gil's eyes widened. "We were at tea at the Consulate at five yesterday."

"One does not argue with the matriarchs. You must be well aware of that little fact."

A pointed glance, reminding him of our own beloved matriarchs.

"Well, then, we can't be late. This will be a most useful information-gathering session." He took off my cap, and my hair fell partway down.

For an instant, he stared at my hair, and I stared at him. I don't think I'll ever be bored with that expression.

"Miss?" Rosa asked.

Gil cleared his throat and handed me the cap. "Get moving. I'm not taking Eddie Hurley to see the Knickerbockers."

As I turned to go, I shot him a wink.

Chapter Nine: Dinner with the Matriarchs

Another change into another elegant costume. Knowing I was going to a Knickerbocker home, and the Old New York fondness for restrained luxury, I chose a very simple lilac cashmere and silk jacquard dress with matching floral embroidery at the open, but not salacious, square neck and cuffs. And, of course, the pearls.

Actually, quite to my own personal taste, though I admit to occasionally reveling in an extravagantly frilly blouse or shimmery beadwork. And I do sometimes enjoy going a bit décolleté for Gil, but only when appropriate.

A brief ride further downtown took us to the original Bridgewater manse. Cabot lives in a palazzo built to his specifications on the upper end of Fifth Avenue, but unlike many other wealthy New Yorkers, his sense of history is too strong to allow him to destroy the old family seat.

By the standards of Gil's ancestral home, an ancient, and quite uncomfortable, castle near the border with Scotland, it isn't especially notable, but on this side of the pond, it is breathtaking. The initial brick home was likely built in the early 1700s, and renovated and expanded over the years, always in a comfortable but not showy way.

Inside, all was warm and welcoming, with candles and gas lights lit and a fire burning in the parlor. Perhaps even a bit too warm, considering my cashmere dress and the September evening, but I would never complain about warmth and comfort.

A maid opened the door and motioned us into the foyer. The focal point was a large landscape painting I recognized from an art history book. A famous Colonial painter's rendition of a field near the house. For a moment, I fell into the history, imagining what was here before the busy urban neighborhood.

The world before ours.

"Your Grace."

I glanced behind me to see if Gil was there. Five months into our marriage, I still had not gotten used to the idea, of answering to the honorific. Most of the time, I was able to concentrate very hard and remember that yes, that also meant me. But Great-Aunt Cecily was the living rule of the Knickerbocker matriarch, and Cabot had told me she could be very frightening when she wished.

I had only met her once and had not spent nearly enough time with her to know…and I certainly was not at ease after the day's events.

A musical laugh from probably a foot below my chin told me that she had decided to be merciful, at least for the moment.

Great-Aunt Cecily was impossibly tiny, well below five feet tall, still very upright, but with a frame that had probably been dainty in her youth and was now downright fragile. But her eyes, even now, were extraordinary, deep blue and gleaming with devilment, emphasized by an elegant dark-sapphire velvet dinner dress. Her face was far less wrinkled than one might expect, and her features still held the pleasing aspect that had made her a belle before Victoria was Queen.

"Well, you *are* a Duchess now, dearie. Best stand up to it."

"I do my best," I offered as she took my hands in her little bird claws.

"I've heard that you do. Cabot sings your praises when he's not singing Thomas's. That cousin of yours is very good for him, you know."

"He's very good for Toms."

Great-Aunt Cecily's eyes held mine, canny and careful. "A man needs good friends if he's not wanting a wife."

"Very true."

She nodded. I nodded. All that was necessary.

With a careful smile, she continued: "So you and your Duke have finally returned to our shores."

"It was only right to spend the late summer at Leith and in London since he has kindly agreed to come for the Met production."

"You spend most of your time together, do you not?"

"As much as we can."

Great-Aunt Cecily glanced back at Gil, who was with Cabot and his mastiff Noble, discussing the care and feeding of the magnificent creature. "Better to keep your man close, dearie, especially when he looks like that."

There was nothing I could say. I could feel the start of a blush. Hopefully, it made me look like a blissful bride.

"Not to mention that it already takes longer to get a child at your age, and if he's halfway around the world…"

My faint blush turned truly volcanic. I tried to mumble some appropriate reply and could not even produce a voice.

"Auntie! What are you possibly saying to make poor Ella blush so!" Cabot strode over to us with an apologetic expression. "You *know* people don't think it's nice to ask newlyweds about their expectations anymore!"

Great-Aunt Cecily grinned. Evilly. "What's the point of marrying if not to produce a babe or two? I was merely suggesting to the Duchess that she should stay on the same side of the Atlantic as the Duke if she was hoping to fill her nursery."

I felt Gil's hand on my arm and looked back to see he looked as embarrassed as I, and definitely more annoyed. "Well, Mrs. Bridgewater, my dear wife is a bit shy about such matters, and I should really prefer if you found another topic of conversation."

His tone carried a good bit more steel than the polite words implied, and Great-Aunt Cecily beamed up at him.

"Ah, I like you. Jumping right up and defending your woman. None of that lily-livered London aristocrat here."

"Hopefully, you'll see the Duke's mother the next time she is visiting," Cabot offered. "She's Scots, Highland Scots."

"Delightful. You will bring her here on her next visit."

It was not an invitation. It was an order. I wondered how the Dowager Countess would get along with a matriarch who'd spent a few more decades perfecting the art. And I couldn't wait to find out.

"We would love to," I very carefully did not look at Gil or Cabot.

"Come along, children. We shall talk in the parlor for a few moments until our last guest arrives."

"Oh?"

"An old friend of mine wants to meet you two, and of course, I obliged her."

Gil and I nodded, bemused. Who might this elder consider an old friend?

"Don't worry, she won't be late for dinner. One isn't." Great-Aunt Cecily gave a decided nod. "My cook has prepared a perfectly fine, if not overly elegant, repast. I could wish for a caterer like Cabot's, but…"

"I told you she takes only a few clients, Auntie, so she can spend most of her time with her family."

"As a good woman should."

If it were anyone but Great-Aunt Cecily, I would have risen to that bait, but I did not see any point in arguing the facts of modern female life with her, and just followed her into the parlor.

The furniture was simple cherrywood with dark brocade upholstery, clearly refurbished on a regular schedule. On the mantel and the walls, more old paintings, antique silver and pewter, and a few Chinese vases. None of it fancy or ostentatious, but all fine, old, and likely priceless, left out to be enjoyed and admired in the unpretentious Knickerbocker style.

Unpretentious in tone and living, that is. Not in their view of their place in the world. The old Dutch settler aristocracy, just like their British counterparts, is firmly convinced that they are as good as or better than anybody. They brook no airs from anyone.

Not even the Prince of Wales, as we would discover.

Gil, of course, could not breathe a word of his true errand, so we started amiable small talk with the hope that the matter of Great-Aunt Cecily's dance with the Prince of Wales would come up.

Had she been an Astor or one of the lesser Belmonts, never mind a dollar princess, we would not have had to wait long. As it was, since the Prince's ball was only a small bright moment in a fascinating life, and the rulers of the Sceptered Isle of only modest interest to someone of Great-Aunt Cecily's importance, it took a bit of effort to steer the conversation in the right direction.

After a few futile attempts, with one eye on the foyer and the upcoming visitor, Gil finally resorted to a bit of fiction. He allowed as how the last time he had been in London before our marriage, the Lords had been in an uproar over the latest scandal involving His Royal Highness. It was no doubt an exaggeration, but desperate times, after all.

"Ah, yes. What a very bad boy he is. Always has been, you know." Great-Aunt Cecily grinned. "You know I danced with him at the Academy of Music Ball."

"Did you, now?" Gil asked, carefully cool.

"Not much of a dancer. I bet you're a much more congenial partner, and I know my late husband was. But he was the Prince after all."

"Only a boy, then, right?" I gave her an encouraging smile.

"But no innocent, that one. I know the story about the woman at the Irish camp and how poor stiff Albert dropped dead over it…but he'd have been dead ten times over if he knew what happened here."

Everyone who was not Great-Aunt Cecily blushed.

"Oh, for heaven's sake. We have no dainty maidens here." She shook her head. "Your generation is far too nice about these things. Just because people do not talk about them does not mean they've stopped doing them."

We waited, despite our embarrassment, sure a good story was coming.

"Let me tell you, in my day, we knew how to have an adventure. As long as a girl was smart enough to pass herself off as an innocent at the altar—and not get into trouble on the way there—there was all kinds of fun to be had."

Cabot, poor thing, looked like he might faint.

Gil's flush was positively incandescent.

I was trying not to giggle. My own innocence had been a major concern in the final days of our courtship, and once disposed of, became something of a wry joke between Gil and me. We agreed—*now*—that we really ought to have just taken advantage of our signed marriage contract and started enjoying the privileges.

Neither here nor there.

"What kind of fun?" I asked, since I was the only one with working vocal cords.

Great-Aunt Cecily gave me a sharply assessing glance. "You're the kind who went in like the lamb to the slaughter, aren't you? Silly girl."

"Auntie." Cabot managed some kind of warning tone.

"Well, anyway, I can tell you two have remedied that—and good for you."

Gil looked as if he was hoping the Oriental rug would swallow him.

"Auntie?"

"Well, really, what girl wouldn't want a taste of the Prince if she could?"

I had seen pictures of the young Bertie, and I certainly had no desire for a taste, then or now. But to each her own, I supposed.

"Plenty of girls did, let me tell you. So did many of the matrons. If Alexander hadn't been such an attentive spouse, I'd have considered it."

We all breathed a silent prayer of thanks for the late Mr. Bridgewater's uxoriousness.

"At any rate, you can be sure Princey had a very good time in the States."

"I've heard stories that there were a few particular ladies?" Gil asked, his tone carefully casual.

"In addition to all of the little liaisons?" She nodded. "There was one. Actually, the daughter of my dear friend. I hadn't thought of all this in ages. Poor Lavinia."

"Lavinia was her name?" I asked.

"No, no. Lavinia Ten Broeck is my friend. Her daughter was Bertha. It was a joke, Bertha meets Bertie, you know."

"Of course." Gil nodded.

"But no joke the way it ended." Great-Aunt Cecily sighed and glanced at the parlor doors. "Please don't mention this tonight. Bertha died not long after. She went upstate to help with her sister-in-law's new baby and just died. Lavinia was crushed. Terrible to lose a child."

We were silent for a few measures. Everyone in the room knew Great-

Aunt Cecily had buried her son, Cabot's Uncle George, a few years before, and very nearly died herself.

"At any rate," the matriarch said, calmly shaking off the worst of her sadness, "that Prince of yours was quite a lot of trouble."

"Indeed." Gil nodded. "Well, hopefully, he's learned his lesson in the intervening years."

"I tend to doubt it." The devilish gleam returned to Great-Aunt Cecily's eyes. "And I wouldn't blame him in the least. Have fun while you can, don't you think?"

"Well," Gil replied, cutting his eyes to me, a gesture not lost on our hostess, "there's a great deal to be said for that."

"Mrs. Ten Broeck!" the maid announced.

Great-Aunt Cecily smiled at Cabot. "I was trying to tell you, silly boy. Lavinia is joining us for dinner. She's a great opera fancier and she wanted to meet you two."

Gil and I tried to look blasé instead of thrilled.

We must have succeeded, because Great-Aunt Cecily patted my arm. "I promise, dear, she's really quite delightful, and will be most helpful to you socially if you let her."

"I'm sure it will be a pleasure," I said.

"A pleasure," Gil echoed.

Lavinia Ten Broeck was, if anything, smaller and more delicate than Great-Aunt Cecily. Certainly paler, and without her friend's sparkling demeanor. She was in widow's black, severe and high-necked, draining any color her ashen skin and pale, watery eyes might have had. Unlike Great-Aunt Cecily, she actually seemed old.

"Your Graces," Lavinia said, holding out a hand to Gil, who bowed over it. Where Great-Aunt Cecily had accepted the pleasantry with a wicked little grin, Lavinia merely nodded, studying Gil with a sharp, assessing gaze. When it was my turn, I offered a hand, and she clasped it lightly, the way women did in times long past; in some very old circles, like these, women still do not shake hands because it's considered mannish or immodest.

"Well, you certainly don't look like a boy now," Lavinia said.

"I should hope not," I replied. "Offstage, I'm a woman like any other."

"I've heard you sing, dear. Not like any other."

"Just so." Gil beamed.

"Good to see a man who's proud of his wife," Great-Aunt Cecily said.

Lavinia shot her a little glare.

"We live in a different world, Lavinia. A married woman doesn't have to sit at home and wait until she has expectations."

Clearly, Great-Aunt Cecily's views on how women should order their lives were a bit more nuanced than I'd thought from her earlier comment about Greta Dare's catering business.

Mrs. Ten Broeck's return glance suggested she was not given to nuance.

"I believe I've met one of your relatives," I said, trying for a quick and diplomatic change of topic. "Nicholas Ten Broeck?"

"My nephew." She did not smile.

"Oh," Gil said. "I've also had the privilege."

Lavinia's mouth twisted as if she'd taken a generous bite of a lemon. "Much too

modern, that one. Lets his wife gallivant about to the suffragette rallies when she should be taking care of the children."

"Well, I was quite favorably impressed," Gil said.

"Nicholas is an old schoolmate," Cabot added, pouring oil on the troubled waters. "Good man, and very intelligent."

The maid appeared in the doorway and nodded to Great-Aunt Cecily.

"Ah!" She clapped her hands. "At precisely five o'clock, as it should be, dinner is served."

"You really should ring the dinner gong, Cecily," chided Lavinia. "The forms are to be obeyed."

"And we do, in larger company. This is a small family meal." Great-Aunt Cecily pointed to the dining room and took Cabot's offered arm.

Gil offered an arm to Lavinia with an apologetic glance to me.

"Next time, Cabot, you shall bring Thomas."

"Of course, Auntie." Cabot's small smile gave no hint of how pleased he was by the mark of acceptance, but of course, I knew.

"Well, I am sorry that we are an odd number," our hostess said, as she sat, "but I'm quite sure we'll manage a lovely conversation."

"No doubt," Cabot agreed.

"Perhaps our Duchess will favor us with a backstage story or two, which would no doubt greatly please Lavinia. In the meantime, we have a delightful meal to enjoy."

She motioned to the table, with a beef roast and side dishes set out in the thinnest china I have ever seen, pure white with the deep blue Chinese design that suggested early—and priceless—pieces. The porcelain reminded me where I was, and with whom.

The Knickerbockers are much like Gil's ancient aristocratic family, only with a good chunk of New York instead of holdings in London and northern England. They simply do not notice money and status, and care very little about possessions. This incredible antique china was merely what Great-Aunt Cecily had been using since some female relative gave them to her on her marriage, when they were already a beloved and well-used family set, and she would use them forever.

The china—and the simple meal served on it — exemplified the family's astonishing style, at once breathtakingly privileged and completely unpretentious. As I gently touched the plate at my place, Gil shot me a small, reassuring glance. He knew, just from that tiny gesture, that I was suddenly, sharply aware I was the only person in the house who was not born to this.

"As usual, Cecily, a lovely setting," Lavinia pronounced. "The chrysanthemums are especially pretty this year, I think."

"Not as pretty as the company," Cabot observed, with a twinkly grin to the two matriarchs. He raised his wineglass. "To the ladies."

"The ladies!" Gil raised his, and enthusiastically joined in.

"Boys, boys," Great-Aunt Cecily remonstrated, though her cheeks were pink and her eyes sparkling. "Flattery is entirely unnecessary."

"But welcome." Lavinia raised her glass to Cabot with a smile. "Respectful appreciation is a wonderful thing, even for ladies of years and discretion."

"And entirely appropriate," Gil added. "It's always good to offer tribute."

Lavinia's gaze sharpened on Gil. "You are not a Londoner."

"You've a good ear, Mrs. Ten Broeck. I'm from the North, and my mother is Scots."

She nodded. "The burr is quite nice. Softer than those sharp London consonants, I think."

Gil blushed a bit, probably as much at being caught without his ducal pretensions in company as at the commentary. "Well, it was always a delight to hear it in my mother's voice, so I suppose I have picked up the same."

"Though when he speaks as a Peer, he sounds like the Queen's Court," I assured Lavinia.

"Them." Lavinia scowled.

"Actually," Gil said, sending me a subtle glance, "my lady wife is right that I speak appropriately in the House of Lords. But I do not have the same speech pattern as the Royal Family."

"No?" Cabot asked.

"No. None of them will admit it, but the Queen and most of her children have a noticeable Germanic accent."

"He's right," Great-Aunt Cecily agreed. "When I danced with the Prince of Wales at the Academy of Music Ball, I had a bit of trouble understanding him. Partly because he was rather shy and mumbled...but also because of that accent."

"It must be rather disconcerting to talk to the heir to the British Throne and discover he sounds like a German," Cabot observed.

"But of course, they're more German than English with all that intermarriage," Gil said. "The habit of finding spouses in the *Almanach de Gotha* has taken its toll."

"Probably in many ways. Too much of the same bloodline weakens the stock." Great-Aunt Cecily took a sip of her wine. "One reason we Americans are so healthy is that we have a wider pool of acceptable marriage partners, so we bring in lots of good, strong new blood."

"People are not like your horses, Great-Aunt." Cabot's tone was only mildly scolding.

"It is a dangerous slippery slope," his matriarch continued. "Cousin marriages are all too common...and before you know it, they'll be marrying siblings like the Ancient Egyptians. They don't think the usual rules apply to them."

"You're right there." Lavinia, who'd been quiet through the discussion of Germanic bloodlines, put down her wine glass with a surprisingly loud clink, her hands suddenly shaky and her face tight. "They may not be carried around in sedan chairs anymore, but they still think they're untouchable. Above everyone."

The pain in her voice and fury in her eyes told us there was a great deal more going on there than the usual American disdain for the Crown. Indeed, I'd seen Irish people who didn't radiate that kind of incandescent fury when speaking of the British royals. And we had far more than taxation without representation to hold against them.

I glanced to Gil, who gave me a slow blink in acknowledgement.

He was thinking the same thing I was. The sheer intensity of Lavinia's reaction strongly suggested there was a great deal more to Bertha's connection to the prince than a light flirtation. We might actually be in the presence of a real lead.

At the moment, though, we were in the presence of a Knickerbocker matron who had no intention of allowing her guests' digestion to be disrupted by bad feelings. Great-Aunt Cecily looked at Lavinia, patted her arm, and then turned to me with a carefully light and cheerful expression.

"Well, dear, I shan't ask you to sing for your supper, of course. But I do wonder if I might convince you to tell us how you came to choose this lovely Handel piece for your Met debut."

"I'd be delighted to." I grabbed the opportunity to restore convivial calm. "You see, we were looking for a piece with a good trouser role that hasn't been seen in some time..."

Chapter Ten: More Frank Talk with Dr. Silver

The next day, Sunday, was Dr. Silver's half-day off from her clinic, and I invited her over for tea with Marie, partly for social reasons, but also with the thought of gathering a bit more insight into Miss LaJoy's situation.

If we happened to talk about my own hopes for the immediate future, well, that would just be a happy coincidence. And it was no one's business but mine if I had a particular wish in my heart when I lit a candle at the Virgin's feet after Mass at Holy Innocents that morning.

Or if my eyes lingered a bit too long on the babe in her arms.

In any case, Dr. Silver, in addition to being a fully qualified and extremely competent physician, is a good friend and good company. A visit with her is a treat on the merits.

The day began as a mostly typical Sunday at our house: Tommy and I headed off to church, and Gil and Jamie to a museum. Being from the far more Catholic North of England, neither are bothered by the idea of Mass, but as Gil once told me, aristocratic British men only go to church when their women make them. I had no intention of launching that fight or getting in the way of the Saint Aubyn men's father-and-son expeditions.

Besides, that Sunday, we were all going to end up together at an evening benefit for the settlement house. Normally, of course, I try for a quiet day when I'm performing, but there was simply too much to do. And, honestly, benefits are far less demanding than carrying a full opera, so rest was not as critical as it might otherwise be.

Marie arrived shortly after church at her Brooklyn parish, looking quite lovely in cornflower blue with the sort of blossom-bedecked hat one expects from a judge's wife on Sunday morning. Dr. Silver, who tended to her spiritual needs on Saturday mornings at a rather modern temple on the West Side, was in her usual work clothes of dark suit and plain white shirtwaist, though with a bright carnation on her lapel. After the usual exchange of pleasantries, including inquiries as to the health and activities of Marie's three wee ones and Dr. Silver's high-school-age daughter, Marie brought the physician up to date on the current disaster. She finished by explaining Paul's presence at the sporting house, with the simple and carefully matter-of-fact observation that his brother is now his sister.

Dr. Silver's kind hazel eyes widened, and she took a deep sip of tea, but she didn't appear at all disgusted or upset. Rather, concerned.

"So," I began, pouring more tea, as I took the hostess's job of moving the conversation ahead, "how exactly does this work?"

"Well." The physician inhaled the delicate floral aroma of the orange-blossom tea as she contemplated.

Marie and I waited.

"As I understand it, people believe their soul and body do not match." She took a bit more tea. "They feel they've been born into the wrong body."

"That's what Alice told Paul." Marie nodded. "She said she'd always been Alice but living in Allen's body."

"How sad," I said. "And there's nothing to be done?"

"Nothing known to science at the moment." The doctor's face took on a very melancholy cast. "It's terribly difficult. One can either convince oneself to live as someone they are not…or go somewhere and live as they believe they are, at the risk of being found out."

"They're not always found out," Marie said. "Not in life, anyway. Remember that woman Civil War veteran in Yonkers?"

"That's right." Dr. Silver reached for one of the shortbread petticoat tails and took a delicate bite. "I heard of a case when I was in training. An old lady, somebody's aunt on Orchard Street, died, and when they went to bury her, they found she was—well, an uncle."

"Nobody suspected?"

"Not a one. Apparently, she'd come over from the old country as a woman. What she was back there, who knows?"

"A maiden lady?" I asked.

"She'd been married, but the husband was long dead. So we'll never know."

"The Civil War veteran in Yonkers left a widow," Marie said. "A very stunned widow."

"No doubt." Dr. Silver shook her head. "In any case, it's not unheard-of. But it's a very, very difficult life. I would think Paul is extremely unusual in maintaining any contact—many families would likely consider the unfortunate person an abomination and cut them off."

"As Paul's family did do." Marie ran a finger around the rim of her cup. "But Paul loves his sib. And he shouldn't suffer for it."

"Well, we're doing what we can," I assured her. "Blackmail is a difficult and ugly thing."

"True." Dr. Silver shook her head. "I hope you can find a resolution. Even without the blackmail, Paul's sister is not facing an easy or pleasant life."

"That's part of why he's tried to maintain some kind of contact," Marie said. "He doesn't see her as evil or an abomination, but just as his sib trying to survive however she can."

"Paul is a good and kind man." I reached for a cookie. Since Marie and I were performing that evening, I had to keep my strength up.

Dr. Silver nodded. "I think you're all doing the best you can, considering the way the world is at the moment."

"And isn't that the rub." Marie shook her head.

We all sighed together.

For a moment, we all studied our teacups, unsure where to take the conversation next.

"And speaking of delicate matters," Marie said, an impish gleam in her eyes as she reached for a shortbread, "should we be concerned that our newlywed has no expectations so far?"

Trust Marie to find a way to bring up the topic and spare me the embarrassment of asking. If she had a little fun in the effort, well, that was only fair. And after that awkward and painful discussion of Alice's life, it was almost soothing to return to something so utterly unsurprising.

"Not at all." Dr. Silver shot me a reassuring glance. "Women in their thirties often take a bit longer. And you did yourself no favors leaving him in London for a couple of weeks while you came back to rehearse."

"It was the Met," I remonstrated.

"It was." Marie shook her head. She is the Met's reigning Queen of the Night, a virtuoso in a fiendishly difficult role, enabling her to set her own terms. "And it's also your family."

"True." While I'd heard a honeymoon baby was to be avoided at all costs, I would not have been disappointed if it had gone that way. But since it hadn't, I was continuing my schedule unless and until something changed. Admittedly, while quietly worrying that it hadn't.

The doctor watched me carefully. "Ella, dear, we talked about this before you married. And I gave you strict orders not to worry at least until your first anniversary."

"I know."

"But women do still fret, you know," Marie said.

"Also, entirely normal." The doctor took a sip of her tea. "But it is far too early for any serious concerns. And, the worrying itself can sometimes become a problem. So, try to just enjoy your newlywed days."

"Sooner than you think, you'll be confined to the couch...and then supervising nursery tea." Marie's tone was teasing but gentle and reassuring.

Between Dr. Silver's cool practicality and Marie's warm confidence, I could not help feeling better. It was true, I reflected: some things only happen when they're meant. After all, I hadn't met Gil until I was ready to consider marriage.

Not to mention an odd, very vivid dream I'd had months ago in which I saw my late parents, and they told me I would have two beautiful babies. Dr. Silver would think that was absolute rubbish. Tommy's mother, my very Irish Aunt Ellen, would consider it definitive.

I would take comfort where I could.

I topped off the teacups.

"Thank you both for the encouragement. Now, did you hear that Hetty's editor is trying to get her to write about the fall fashions again? Claims the new fall shirtwaists are 'important and interesting women's stories...'"

Both understood the subject change—but it was simply too good not to discuss, and we happily jumped in. Good thing Hetty's editor doesn't answer to us.

Chapter Eleven: Dueling Developments

After our tea, it was down to business. I'd shamefully neglected vocalizing and fencing practice the last few busy days, squeezing in only a few minutes of scales to keep the instrument supple. Now, though, with a quiet afternoon ahead of a light benefit performance, I was able to work in a fencing lesson. It was a real treat; my instructor, the Comte du Bois, otherwise known as Mr. Mark Woods of the Bronx, had just enough time in his calendar for me.

The Comte and I were in the midst of our final battle, a sharp, intense back-and-forth testing both of us to the edge of our abilities, when I heard the studio door open. Montezuma called *"Alba gu Bragh,"* which told me who it was, but I didn't have time to think about him.

A few measures later, when my instructor and I were at the center of the room, having fought to a draw, we both turned to the new arrival.

"Monsieur le Duc," said the Comte, "perhaps you'd like to join your wife?"

Gil grinned. His eyes had a wicked gleam I knew well. "I believe I would, if she's done with her lesson."

The Comte grinned back. "She is, as always, at the top of her skill."

"Thank you, *Monsieur le Comte,*" I said.

My instructor and I exchanged formal bows to end the lesson, and he put his foil in its case, while Gil took a practice foil from the cabinet.

"Enjoy your match," the Comte said, then bowed and shot us a wicked little grin before walking out and closing the door behind him.

Of course, he knew just how much we liked the play.

Gil doffed his jacket, waistcoat, and tie, and unbuttoned his collar.

I admit I enjoyed a good look at my spouse as he did so. Not that it distracted me from the match to come.

"So," he said as he picked up the foil, "how goes your quiet day at home?"

"Delightful so far," I swept my foil back and forth. "Tea with Marie and Dr. Silver, a bit of light vocalization with Montezuma, and a fine fencing match."

"And another match now."

"Just so." I met his smile with my own. "And you?"

"Well, I am coming to the conclusion that we are going to have to widen our investigation a bit...and we may need a story to explain it."

"Why so?"

"Well, your reporter friend may be able to find us some old records or information."

"That's true. The *Beacon* morgue could have contemporary accounts of the visit. At the very least, it could tell us where he was and when."

"Right. But we can't tell her why." Gil shook his head. "It's not fair to her."

I smiled. Most British aristocrats—and most men, for that matter—would have seen it only from their own point of view in risking exposure. He understood we would be putting Hetty in an untenable position, because of her professional commitments as a journalist.

"I love you," I said.

"I love you. Why, particularly, now?"

"Because you are quite a man. Enough serious talk." I tapped my foil on his. "We'll figure out something to tell Hetty. In the meantime..."

He stepped into fighting stance. *"En garde?"*

"En garde."

We started slowly, but not casually, parrying lightly back and forth. Gil is a decently skilled swordsman, but not a professional like me, and we're both well aware of that fact. When we duel, it's strictly for enjoyment.

At our very first meeting, we had crossed swords, as I made him fence with me after he made an insulting comment about "theatre people," by implication questioning my honor. Of course, we're long since beyond that—but fencing has never stopped being a great pleasure.

"You don't seem to be overly tired by your match with the Comte," Gil said.

"I always have enough steam left for a match with my husband."

Shared smile.

"Was Dr. Silver's visit simply a social call?"

The phrasing and the careful neutrality of his voice suggested he was trying not to ask other questions.

"Not entirely," I admitted. "Marie and I wanted some insight related to Paul's situation."

"Ah." A short, sharp exchange as he backed me up a bit. "And did you gain it?"

"We did. I don't need to trouble you with the details, but essentially, he was at the sporting house because his sister is running it."

"His sister?"

"Well, there's rather more in play," I said. I did not want to explain the entire matter here, or ever, if at all possible. "It's a long story, but she's been cast out of the family, and this is apparently the only way she can make a living."

He shook his head as I took the lead and backed him off a bit. "A matter more for pity than condemnation, I would say."

"Exactly. And she pursues this—profession—as ethically as she can."

"Ethically." He considered for a moment, then launched a new attack, which I fended off neatly. "Did you discuss anything else with your physician?"

"Matters of a womanly nature, perhaps?" I asked, launching my own attack.

"Perhaps."

"I am told there is no cause whatever for concern."

He smiled. "You did ask her."

"Of course I did. She offered reassurance...and a little advice."

"What's that?" He barely parried my next attack.

Distracted, a bit. Myself, as well.

"To enjoy our newlywed days."

"In a particular way, perhaps?"

"Well, of course, if one is playing a lottery, one can increase the odds…" I launched a sharp new attack, and he met it.

For a few moments, there was no need to speak, if we'd even had the breath for it, as we went back and forth across the studio, the match kindling intensity between us as it always did.

We ended, at the center of the floor, swords still crossed, both a bit out of breath.

"Draw?" he asked.

"Draw." I agreed, as he reached for me.

"Increasing the odds, you say?'

"Doctor's orders."

"Why don't I just put away the foils…"

It should surprise no one we were almost late leaving for the settlement house benefit.

Chapter Twelve: Good Works and Good Fun

Since the Met's Grand Sunday concerts do not start until December, I was free to do the occasional benefit, and of course, any time I could sing for the settlement house that had helped my mother and me, I would happily do so. Marie was in this one, too, as were a number of our other friends. Not a surprise, if you know how many performers come from humble beginnings.

With Marie and me as the headliners, our *heldentenor* pal Marc Kane, born Koziekiewicz, pitching in with his best Wagner piece, and an assortment of ballerinas, Broadway stars, and vaudeville folks, it was a great bill, with a very enthusiastic audience.

For the last several months, Marie and I had been doing the death scene from *The Princes in the Tower* as our benefit piece, but we'd decided to do our Romeo and Juliet instead, just for a bit of variety—and fun. And, since we had other good friends in the cast, we had all decided to put together a light sing-and-dance number to "Ta-ra-ra Boom Dee-Ay" for the finale.

Send 'em home with a laugh.

Afterward, the whole cast was laughing too, talking and bubbling, everyone relaxed and a little keyed up from the joy of performing as we worked our way back to the dressing rooms. Gil and I walked back hand in hand after he surprised me in the wings, spinning me around to the last bars of the exit music. A real treat before the duty of the backstage visits. Benefits of course are a bit different, and the donors expect to hobnob with the cast in return for their generosity.

Often, it grates, but for the settlement house, I was more than willing to tolerate it.

Same for most of my castmates.

We adjourned to our respective dressing rooms to await the onslaught, promising to catch up at the end of the evening, and put on our shiny happy faces, while wiping off most of the stage makeup, since it is not particularly good for the skin, as well as looking far less than respectable on the ladies.

Rosa was the only one waiting for us; Tommy and Cabot were dropping by Marc's dressing room for a quick visit — and probably to plan a musical night out. I sat at my vanity, and she handed me a cloth and opened the cold-cream jar.

Before I started cleaning my face, Gil took my other hand and slipped the lilac diamond back in place. It was still warm from its time in his waistcoat pocket, and I leaned back and gave him a light kiss, knowing Rosa would not acknowledge it.

"A delightful show," he said. "You all clearly enjoy working together and brought the audience along."

"Every once in a while, the audience wants good fun instead of wrenching drama, don't you think?"

"I am entirely in favor of good fun." Gil grinned. "Especially when I get to meet my wife in the wings and give here a twirl."

"Well, that was definitely a treat." I returned the grin, as Rosa made herself very busy smoothing out my street clothes. "An excellent change for all the offstage drama we've had lately."

"A bit too much drama."

We turned to see Connor Coughlan standing in the doorway.

Tommy's and my old schoolmate from the Lower East Side was now one of the most important—and dangerous—figures in Five Points. On the strength of our long friendship and the fact that I'd saved his life a year ago, he claimed the right to look to my safety and happiness. Gil tolerated this, partly because he knew he could not stop it, and partly because he found it useful.

In black tie, his black-Irish brown hair slicked back, Connor looked like any other fine gentleman. Except for his eyes, which were shamrock-green and absolutely cold. And probably the last sight of the world for more of his fellow miscreants than I wanted to imagine.

"Good to see you again, Coughlan," Gil said.

"And you, Saint Audrey." They shared a nod, and Connor turned with the warm smile he saved only for me. "Ellen, you're blooming. Marriage agrees with you."

"It does." I held out my hands, and he took them, giving my fingertips a gentle, respectful press. While he may be the toughest of a very tough crew on his own turf, in my world, Connor is never anything less than kind and considerate. We have a longstanding mutual agreement not to spend too much time thinking about why he saves a special place in his heart for me—and why I permit it.

As he let go, he glanced back at Gil, and I understood he was here for more than a generous contribution to the settlement house and visit to old friends.

"Did he call you in?" I asked Connor.

You would not think it was possible for a Peer of the Realm and a murderous gangster to look like sheepish little boys, but you would be wrong.

"I am not standing in your way as you try to help your friend," Gil reminded me. "I'm merely looking to your safety while you do."

I glanced over to Connor, whose embarrassment had given way to wicked amusement when he realized someone else was in bigger trouble than he.

His eyes were twinkling as he moved straight past the question of his involvement to the matter at hand: "Do I understand Madame Marie's husband was pinched in a certain police action recently?"

I knew when I was outplayed. Might as well just go on with their plan, at least for now. "He was. At Miss LaJoy's."

"Ah. As good a lady as might be in such a vile line of work."

"That's what I've heard," I agreed.

I knew, though Gil might not have, what a major concession it was for

Connor to even acknowledge Miss LaJoy's existence. With three sisters and a good Irish boy's adoration of his late mother, he famously had no truck with that particular criminal endeavor. He refused even to handle the usual protection rackets on sporting houses, preferring to leave the whole area to others. Not that he didn't make a more than adequate living with other forms of extortion, intimidation, and leg-breaking.

"Do I further understand that Eddie Hurley is taking an interest?"

"Eddie Hurley," Gil said with an icy note of his own, "is supposed to be staying out of trouble."

"I imagine we can keep a good eye on young Mr. Hurley," Connor said, shooting me a grin. "If Mr. Hurley doesn't stick his nose any further into matters where he doesn't belong."

"Mr. Hurley is trying to help a friend," I said.

"Mr. Hurley," Connor replied with a pointed look, "is always on the side of the angels. That does not mean he is making wise decisions."

"I think it will be sufficient if the Hurley brothers make certain to consult with you before their next expedition downtown, don't you, Mr. Coughlan?"

He joined Gil's dry smile. "Quite sufficient indeed, Saint Audrey."

Connor bowed to us both and took his leave.

Even I was not optimistic enough to think we'd settled this.

After that, the leering patrons and their sneering wives were practically a relief. Nothing but the usual dressing room scene, in which the men looked at my legs and the women looked down on me. Things were a bit different this time, though, with my impeccably blue-blooded husband standing happily behind my chair, making neutral and appropriate conversation with our visitors, while delivering the sort of icily ferocious stare only a powerful British man can muster.

Every time a man flicked his eyes toward my tights, a subtle movement from Gil reminded him I was no longer simply a "theatre person," but a Peeress, with all the privilege and protection that implied. The women, who were often far more offensive, though less blatant about it, were thrown entirely off-balance by my new status, at once hoping to befriend me for social advantage, wishing to take me down a peg, and quite simply envying me. It's difficult when you can't choose which ignoble drive to follow.

After going through this little game with perhaps half a dozen of society's most important people (just ask them!), we had a true treat. Cabot squired Great-Aunt Cecily and, surprisingly enough, Lavinia Ten Broeck, into the room with great fanfare.

"Miss Ella, look who's staying out late!" Cabot crowed.

"We *invented* late nights, you whippersnapper," his matriarch said with mostly simulated irritation. "My dear friend and I were quite intrigued by the program when you discussed it last night…and certainly there's never a bad time to give to a good cause."

"And those poor unfortunates at the settlement house are always in need," added Lavinia Ten Broeck.

She wasn't really giving me a pointed look, I reminded myself. It was just the residue of the behavior of our earlier visitors. The Bridgewaters and Ten Broecks, at least the ones I've known, are so far up in the social firmament that everyone, be they a tenement skivvy or a Duke, is the whole atmosphere below. No need for snobbery, when literally the entire world is beneath you.

"You're quite right," I said. "But it's still very kind of you to come."

Great-Aunt Cecily took my hands and pulled me down to plant a kiss on my cheek. I managed to keep my amiable smile, but I was quite delighted. I knew it was a huge mark of favor; of course, women are often very demonstrative with our friends, but the fact that she considered me close enough for a display of affection warmed my heart.

"It was just the treat we needed, dear. Lavinia has been far too solitary lately."

Lavinia, whose mouth had tightened a little when her friend kissed me, now glared at her. "Indeed, I have not. But it is true, a night of good music is always balm for the soul."

"I agree," I said. "It was a great pleasure to put on the show."

"You were clearly enjoying every second in the finale," Great-Aunt Cecily said. "I rather envied Madame Marie when that great big blond tenor boy spun her around in the last chorus."

"Marc is a dear friend," I said. "And it's all entirely innocent."

I held Great-Aunt Cecily's gaze for just an extra instant. While Marc could have his pick of the coloraturas, his inclinations run more toward bassos.

"Of course it was innocent." Lavinia nodded. "Anyone who sees evil in a dance has a nasty mind."

"Absolutely." I nodded. "Dancing is a great—and harmless—pleasure."

Gil glanced over to us then. "I've always enjoyed a good dance."

"And you probably hold your own quite nicely," Lavinia said, giving him a surprisingly sparkly smile.

"I have heard no complaints."

"Nor shall you." I gave Gil a lightly flirtatious grin, enjoying the play with our two senior belles, as well as the memory of our little backstage spin.

"Lavinia, I think it may be time to host a ball again."

"That's quite an undertaking, Cecily," her friend said. "But I do know I would like to host a small reception after one of the Met performances, if our new acquaintances would be willing."

"We should be honored," I said, holding Gil's gaze.

It was one of the rare occasions I spoke for us both, and we shared a small smile.

"Good," said Lavinia. "My secretary will call yours tomorrow and we shall choose a day."

I nodded. Lavinia did not need to know that I was my own social secretary. Tommy handled performance schedules, but I kept my own calendar otherwise. It didn't matter; when the secretary called tomorrow, Rosa would take a message, and Tommy or I would call back.

In the meantime, we had turned in a very productive evening: a good show, a nice sum for the settlement house, and a chance to gather more information from Bertha Ten Broeck's circle.

If it meant I had to tolerate a certain amount of interference from Connor, there were worse things.

Really, there were, I reminded myself.

Chapter Thirteen: To the Morgue

A s is my habit, I fully intended to sleep late on the morning after the show.

But I woke with the dawn, and the uncomfortable sensation that someone was watching me.

Indeed, he was. Gil was awake, dressed except for his jacket, and making notes on a piece of house stationery.

"Ah. You are awake."

Yes, because you're staring at me, I thought irritably. I just nodded.

"I'm sorry, sweetheart. I'm trying to puzzle out some things." He sighed. "Would you ever be willing to run over to the *Beacon* morgue and see if Miss Hetty could help you with a bit of research?"

"Well, now that I'm awake." It came out as a growl, mostly unintentionally.

"I'm sorry. I'll owe you a late morning…and a favor of your choice."

"I'll hold you to that." I didn't want to smile, but of course, looking into those sparkly ice-blue eyes, there was nothing else to do.

"I hope you do." He leaned in for a kiss. "Now, why don't you get yourself assembled and pay a call on Miss Hetty?"

Gil started for the door.

"What shall I tell her?"

"About what?"

"About why I want to know about the Prince's visit?"

He sat down in the side chair. "We do have to concoct a story, don't we?"

"I'm afraid we must. What if we simply tell people a friend of the Prince wants to put together some reminiscences as a gift to him?"

73

"For a bad liar, you are quite good at shading the truth." A smile. "It's close enough to our actual motivation—and gives us a reason to talk to quite literally anyone about the visit."

"It does. I'm better than I thought I was."

"There is no one better than you, *mo chridhe*." He kissed the top of my head and once again turned for the door. "See you at the breakfast table."

Even after almost six months of marriage, that sentence was still a pleasure to hear.

After fueling myself for a busy morning with a simple but tasty traditional Scots breakfast of oatmeal and good coffee, I pulled a navy-blue jacket over my shirtwaist and grabbed my simple midnight-blue day hat. The airs of a Peeress do not sit well on a friend of the newsroom.

But baked goods do. I slipped downstairs and packed a nice basket of monkey-faces from the cookie jar, which turned out to be an excellent bit of timing, because Miss O'Hanlon was planning to make a new batch of snickerdoodles, a family favorite.

I resolved to invite Rafe over to enjoy them.

Nothing wrong with giving the course of true love a little nudge.

At the moment, though, I was involved in a different kind of adoration: Hetty's love of her work. Stories are her calling, the way music is mine. She's as happy in the rough and tumble of a newsroom as I am in a theatre.

And her work is every bit the magic and alchemy of a good performance.

Hetty can convince the most reticent heroine to whisper of her adventure or charm a hardened convict into bragging about his evil deeds. She spent her first years at the *Beacon* writing about clothes and furbelows, giving her a deep and sincere hatred of hats. Now, though, thanks to hard work, several high-profile stories, and an even higher-profile stunt drive to Chicago in a motorcar, she'd established herself as the writer the *Beacon* called on to cover "important and interesting women's stories."

When I arrived in the newsroom, Hetty was sitting at her typewriter, just one of many busy reporters banging away on their current story. I walked over to the editors' bullpen and put down the basket of cookies.

Loris, the impossibly ancient dayside editor and bane of Hetty's existence, looked up at me from under his green eyeshade. "Eh?"

"Brought cookies," I said. "Here for Miss Hetty."

"Over there," He grunted and grabbed a cookie. "Thanks."

"My pleasure."

With a growl, Loris took a deep bite and returned to his desk, where he'd been blue-penciling copy. Before he was quite finished chewing, he yelled: "MacNaughten!"

Hetty looked up and smiled, then bent her head back to the typewriter.

I knew what it meant. I started moving slowly and quietly toward her desk, and as I did, I heard a voice behind me. A most welcome voice.

"Hey, kid!"

Preston Dare, the dean of the sportswriters' corps, informal uncle to Tommy and me, and husband of our beloved former cook and current caterer Greta Dare, stood in the doorway, beaming.

"Caught you in the salt mines, eh?" I asked, walking over to him.

"I can't spend all my time backstage with you two miscreants." He took my offered hands, squeezed them, and took a look at me. "Marriage definitely agrees with you."

"And with you." It had become a bit of a joke between us.

"Indeed. It's quite possible to live a happy and fulfilling life without a spouse, but it's ever so much better with one."

"Just so," I said. "How are Greta and the children?"

"Boy's starting NYU—girl has finished her nurse's training." He stood a little straighter and beamed with pride. Greta's children were old enough to appreciate a benevolent male presence without any thought of him trying to take the place of their late father, and they'd developed a warm mutual affection.

Incredibly sweet for my crusty old friend, who'd spent most of his life mourning his wife and wee ones who'd died in a cholera outbreak decades ago.

"Good to hear. Jamie has started studying with a criminology professor there. They may cross paths."

"That's right." Preston nodded. "Maybe we make sure they cross paths.

You know Sam is a bit younger than the average college student. Could use someone to look out for him."

"I think Jamie would relish the opportunity to look out for someone," I assured him. "He's always been the younger brother and the baby."

"Well, then we'll have to give him something useful to do." He nodded to the basket on the desk. "Just dropping by to feed the troops?"

"Not quite," I admitted. "Hoping Hetty has time for a trip to the morgue."

"The morgue? What are you looking into?"

"Well, apparently a friend of Gil's is preparing some sort of birthday present for the Prince of Wales and wanted to find some newspaper accounts of his visit to the city."

"Wasn't that forty years ago?"

"Yes."

"Good luck, then." Preston shook his head. "The *Beacon* wasn't around then."

"It wasn't?"

"I know it seems as if it's been here forever, but no. The good news is, we took over *Trent's Illustrated Gazette* a few years ago, and we've got all of their archives. You should be able to find something useful."

"Excellent. Gil's friend will be glad to hear it."

Preston gave me a careful, assessing glance. I could tell him considering asking a question and thinking better of it. "Must be nice to have time to worry about things that happened forty years ago, eh?"

"I'll never know."

We shared a small, not entirely sincere laugh.

Preston finished with a shrug. "Well, send my best to the Barrister. Greta and I expect you kids–and Tommy and Cabot, too–will come over for dinner before you head off to San Francisco."

"We absolutely will. And we expect you at Washington Square some night soon."

"We'll take you up on that." He gave me a small bow, and his face took on a more serious cast. "Have to go knock out a few hundred words on that dumb and dangerous football game the college boys are playing."

"Pretty clear how you feel about it," I said.

"Packs of boys jumping on each other is far more dangerous than you'd think." He shook his head, patted my arm. "Anyhow, I'll see you tonight at the Colonel's."

"That's right," I said. "Looking forward to seeing him."

"They don't build 'em like that anymore. Wonderful old fella."

"What do you want?" Hetty asked, trying for a stern tone, given away by her eyes. She handed Loris the piece of copy she'd been writing and received a significantly less friendly growl than I'd drawn, then turned back to me. "Or is bringing cookies to the ink-stained wretches your good work for the day?"

"Not hardly." I returned her smile, as Preston nodded to us both and stepped away. "I was hoping you might have time for a trip to the morgue."

"Well, since I just turned in a piece and it'll be a while before Loris finishes the edits, why not? We don't have time for a velocipede ride."

"Not today, but soon."

"Definitely." She stepped back to grab a cookie. "All right, then, what are we looking for?"

"Preston tells me you have the *Trent's Illustrated Gazette* archives."

"We do." One of her brows twitched. "What on earth are you looking for?"

I offered the same explanation as I'd given Preston. It was a very good cover story—straightforward and simple, with no reason to question it.

"Really? My mother was a little girl when he visited, and she remembers being dragged out into the street by her mother to see his carriage go by. Papa always scowls when she tells the story and reminds her that good Americans have no need of Princes."

"Sounds like something my Aunt Ellen would say."

"She has more cause, though. Papa's from old Scots stock and has no personal grievance with the monarchy, other than a general opposition to them."

"The Scots aren't known for their desire to bend the knee," I reminded her with a grin.

"Isn't that the truth. And how is your half-Highlander?"

77

"Keeping himself busy with various things in between glaring at the patrons backstage." I shrugged. "Since it's the Met, we can't really close the dressing room, and it's been long enough that you'd think…"

"But it hasn't," Hetty said. "It'll always be there."

"I'd like to think not."

"Some version of it will. When terrible things happen, they leave a mark, and not just the one on your ribs."

"That's true. I suppose I should be more patient with his backstage prowling." I studied her for a moment. "Look at you, giving advice about how to manage a man. Anything you'd care to tell?"

"Indeed not. Rowan and I are enjoying a very pleasant courtship—and that's all I have to say."

"Right you are." I gave her a canny glance. "You know, I should send you two tickets for the dress circle. That's an entirely appropriate outing, isn't it?"

"Yes." A sigh. "Though I've taken to telling my parents I'm working late and slipping out to dinner once a week or so."

"Really?" I tried to look shocked, but I was actually quite pleased to know she'd found a way to get some time alone with her swain, noted defense lawyer Rowan Alteiss, who was every bit as head-over-heels as she.

"Really. They are treating me like some sort of romance-novel maiden, as if I somehow wouldn't know how to fend off Rowan's evil intentions… assuming he had any. Which he doesn't."

"None?"

"Not a one. Poor thing dines with us every Sunday after church and listens to Papa's ridiculous opinions as if they're the word from on high."

"Ugh." I shook my head. "There's very little uglier than trying to conduct a courtship as a grown adult."

"You're lucky. At least you had Tommy, who knows enough to give you a little room."

"Not too much. And don't forget I had a priest, Preston, and a full supporting cast of cousins, boxers, and stagehands ready to defend my virtue."

"True." A rueful shrug. "In any case, I think I do well to just enjoy what I have. I'm terrified Rowan will decide he wants an Angel in the House...and then where will we be?"

"Perhaps he's happy to have you—all of you."

"Well, he did cheer me on with the Chicago drive." She took a breath. "But if we start talking about marriage..."

"You'll find a way. If you truly love each other and it's truly right, you'll both bend." I held her gaze. "I know my situation is different, but that old Bible verse is right 'all things are possible with love.'"

"Good Lord, Ells, quoting the Bible on a weekday?" She smacked my arm. "C'mon. The archives are waiting."

No question this discussion was over. Which was fine—we had a great deal to do, and not much help doing it. The surly morgue librarian, a scrawny, ancient man who might well have been running the place when the Prince came to town, pointed to a bunch of grubby storage boxes and turned us loose, with a mumbled reminder not to track out any dust.

"Well," I said, "the good news is, we have a specific time period to search. Three days in October 1860."

We found the correct box quickly enough, and indeed, it was a bonanza. Even though the nation was not nearly as title mad as we are in today's era of dollar princesses, the visit was easily the most important and exciting story during its time...and for weeks before and after. *Trent's Illustrated Gazette*, like most of the papers of the time, had published souvenir editions before, during, and after the visit. And because of their importance, the archivist had saved close to a dozen of them.

The souvenir editions were amazing. Pen-and-ink drawings of rooms and people who no longer existed, and at the center of it all, a slightly pudgy, shy young man, clearly drawn to make him look more like a handsome prince than he actually was. The artist was a little too good to completely idealize his subject, though, and something of the boy's sad, droopy eyes and diffident posture came through in the sketches.

So did the excitement and lively beauty, of the women welcoming him to the city. In the drawings of the Academy of Music Ball, the artist captured the crowd flitting around the Prince and his entourage like so many lovely butterflies. I couldn't be sure, but in one illustration, the Prince was dancing with a dainty little woman whose impish smile distinctly reminded me of Great-Aunt Cecily.

The articles made sure to list all the local grandees who, as the writer put it, "Showed His Highness that a nation without royalty is not a nation without gentility." Hetty was looking over my shoulder, so I could only silently note the mention of Mr. John Ten Broeck and his daughter, Miss Ten Broeck. That was almost certain proof it was Bertha—she was the only daughter of John and Lavinia and would be referred to simply as "Miss Ten Broeck."

For Hetty's sake, I pointed to another name: "See? Mrs. Alexander Bridgewater led the Ladies' Committee who welcomed His Highness…"

"Is that Cabot's great-aunt?"

"I'm sure it is. There might be another Alexander Bridgewater—the Knickerbockers have very particular naming patterns—but Great-Aunt Cecily's stationery still reads Mrs. Alexander Bridgewater, even though he's been gone a quarter-century or more."

"That's the correct form," Hetty reminded me. "Once a wife, always a wife."

"True."

She looked at the article. "What do you mean about the Knickerbockers' names?"

"Well, some of the families have a very clear way of designating the direct line. I'm told the Ten Broecks name their sons Willem, Nicholas, and Alexander—in that order. So the current heir, Nicholas, is actually a second son who took over when another one died. I don't know the details—I've only met him once, at Cabot's."

"Cabot isn't a Knickerbocker name," Hetty observed.

"That's his mother's maiden name. And you know the Cabots of Boston…"

"Oh, heavens yes." Hetty chuckled. "The only people who are further up on the social tree than our Knickerbockers. So the Bridgewaters had to tolerate Mama's wish to give her name to her boy. And it probably came with her money, too."

"No, probably about it," I said. "I don't know the details, but I know Cabot has holdings in Boston through his mother."

"Amazing that he's so decent with all of that."

"He makes a deliberate and conscious effort. Tries to use his money for good, and to be just one of the fellows in company."

"And it works most of the time."

"It does. He and Toms do wonderful things for the libraries and poor children, and he's always good to see around the house."

"Probably more for Tommy." She smiled. "It's good to see them so close."

"Absolutely."

We shared a nod. All that was necessary.

Hetty gazed down at the papers, gently tracing the edge of one of the illustrations from the ball. "A world we'll never know."

"And don't really want to." I held her gaze. "I don't have much love for society—whether the British court or the American version of it."

"Well, too bad for you, Duchess, your life brushes up against it now." She shot me a wicked little smile. "And you probably have to get back to it soon. Loris is going to finish my edits and start looking for me."

"I probably should go soon." I looked at the pile of souvenir editions. "Do you sell the old copies?"

"We do. You'll have to ask Cobbin out there how much, but I doubt he'll mind. Probably be glad to get rid of them."

"Wonderful," I said, stacking up the souvenir editions. "Gil's friend will be delighted."

I fully expected Cobbin to demand a ridiculous price, but instead he merely charged me the *Beacon*'s current rate per copy, and even rummaged out a somewhat battered manila envelope to carry the copies.

Hetty was right—he did want rid of them.

Walking out into the main entrance, we wished each other well, and she enquired after Marie.

"Pretty well, considering." I held her gaze. "You know about the police raid."

"I do. I also know Alice LaJoy's place is generally considered the best of the lot there. And that Paul is one of the best men around. So, is it a blackmail

81

scam?"

"It sure looks like it," I said. "Miss LaJoy seems to have been current on her protection money, so there's no obvious reason for the raid."

"There's something about Miss LaJoy, though."

"What do you mean?"

"The fellows don't talk about her the same way they do the other women who run houses." She shrugged. "It's not like they sit around discussing houses of ill repute with me. But every once in a great while, when her name comes up, they speak of her with respect...and something else. I'm not sure what. I've never seen anything like it."

I nodded. It was not my secret to share. "Well, if you hear anything, please let me know. Tommy and I have asked some of our connections to see what they can see."

"Coughlan?" Hetty gave me a canny smile. She and Connor had a wary, but occasionally useful, acquaintanceship and mutual respect. "Of course you'd ask him. If there are bodies buried—or to be buried—he'll know."

"I'd think so—though he has nothing to do with that particular illicit business."

"I know. Odd, isn't it? Happy enough with leg-breaking, fencing stolen goods, and the occasional contract killing—but not that."

"Not odd at all," I said. "He has sisters, and had a mother, and he sees women a certain way."

Hetty nodded. "All men do."

"And how."

A shared smile, and I started to turn, but she put a hand on my arm. "You know,"

"What?"

"You might just be an important and interesting women's story."

"I might what?"

"The music collection dedication for you on Wednesday."

"Oh, that." A former backstage admirer of mine was endowing a music collection at the Bridgewater Library in my name as a wedding present. It was a shockingly appropriate gift, and honestly, I was more than a little sheepish about the attention for myself rather than my roles.

"Yes, that." Hetty smacked my arm. "It's a good story. I could attend, interview you, and get a little attention for the Library, the production—and the idea of women keeping their careers after marriage."

"Really?"

"Loris wants to send me to a wedding-gift display by some dollar princess that day. You could save me."

"Would you write my thank-you speech?" I'd been vexing about offering an apposite and graceful acceptance, and a professional wordsmith might be just the help I needed.

"Dear, I'll write you a song if you'll get me out of this."

"Well, in that case..." At least I was getting something for my trouble. "If it will spare you from one of those hideous shows."

"Ells, you are an angel."

"But not in the house." I returned the arm smack.

"Of course not. On a velocipede, maybe."

"When are we going to ride again?"

"Hope for a pretty day next week. In the meantime, I'll see you Wednesday."

"You and everyone else."

Chapter Fourteen: Dinner at the Colonel's

The evening brought a considerable pleasure: dinner with Colonel Vandergrift.

While he is an old Knickerbocker aristocrat like Great-Aunt Cecily, the Colonel has adapted to a somewhat more modern schedule, so the evening meal actually took place at a recognizable dinner hour.

Even so, I was quite sure the Colonel was not prepared for what constitutes appropriate dinner dress for women these days, and I chose a modest, higher-necked bodice with elbow-length sleeves instead of the scanty beaded top that also matched the amethyst cut-velvet skirt. The glittery bodice, with wisps of chiffon and strands of iridescent beads at the shoulders in a nod to the idea of sleeves, was entirely apropos for the Four Hundred or a British house party but would never have been comfortable for a dinner at my home table, never mind an old-fashioned gentleman's.

Poor Preston would not have known where to look...and Colonel Vandergrift might well have thrown a blanket over me.

Dressmakers often include a second bodice to address just this sort of situation, and as Rosa smoothed the sleeves, made in the new, slimmer style, I once again silently thanked Anna, my former dresser, for her wisdom in designing my trousseau. It had been a special consideration, because she's now much more in demand as a lyricist with her composer husband, Lewis.

Rosa clasped my pearls and pointed to my hand.

"Do you want to take it off?"

"No. One doesn't wear gloves at dinner anyhow, and Colonel Vandergrift will quite enjoy the famous jewel."

"You also want to make the Duke look good."

"Well, of course."

We had met Colonel Vandergrift shortly before our marriage, and he had taken a grandfatherly interest in both Gil and me. Not to mention forming a fellow Civil War veteran's bond with Preston. And Tommy? As one of the first Irish boxing champs, he was the darling of the Colonel's cranky but indispensable housekeeper, Mrs. Muldoon.

It all made for a most congenial evening, as the Colonel, quite old but not remotely decrepit, welcomed us in the foyer of his mansion, another revered Knickerbocker installation like Great-Aunt Cecily's home. Thanks to the Colonel's fondness for family portraits and historic artifacts, though, this home had a definite museum air.

"Well, I see marriage agrees with you two." The Colonel, who was in military evening gear, to which he had every right, complete with an impressive display of medals, greeted Gil with a handshake, and bowed over my hand, an acknowledgement of my new status as a married woman.

"Indeed, it does, sir," Gil assured him.

"Autumn appears to agree with you, Colonel," I said.

His still-sharp eyes gleamed. "I much prefer the cooler months, if only because oysters and apple pie are in season."

"That will do nicely, sir." Preston took his turn for a friendly handshake. "I never turn down a good fire or an apple pie."

"I hear your wife is quite the cook."

"She is." A modest bow. "She does a bit of catering here and there. Enough to keep busy."

"Well, if it isn't the Champ!" Mrs. Muldoon appeared behind us, clapping her hands and beaming at Tommy, exactly as she had before. The housekeeper, who was at least as old as her employer, was from the earlier generation of Irish folk who saw Tommy's title as a literal blow against the prejudice they had confronted as new arrivals.

"Mrs. Muldoon, as I live and breathe." Tommy turned to her and offered a warm handshake, accepting a bit of burbling admiration while Gil, Preston, and I exchanged more pleasantries with the Colonel.

There was an order to a visit here, disrupted at one's own peril.

We began with a cordial and light conversation in the drawing room, catching up on Gil's and my travels of the summer, Tommy and Cabot's charitable efforts through the Bridgewater Libraries, and Preston's latest columns on baseball. Then, Mrs. Muldoon rang the gong, the Colonel offered me his arm, and we proceeded into the dining room.

Dinner was solidly traditional and served traditionally: beef roast and accoutrements all laid out on the table and passed around. Service *à la russe*, the elegant procedure where footmen placed each dish in front of a guest, was far too new-fangled for the Colonel.

For me, too, honestly.

Even though the food was entirely beside the point, it was quite delicious; despite her age, Mrs. Muldoon had not lost a step in the kitchen. Or she had hired a very good cook. The beef was moist, the potato gratin rich and creamy, and the green beans boiled just enough, which is no guarantee when cookery-books advise one to leave them on the stove for hours.

Conversation, again, was interesting but not especially consequential, centered on opera and history, with a long and thorough discussion of General Grant's memoirs and the latest edition of President Lincoln's letters. At the Colonel's house, one practices the art of conversation, and one does not bring up serious situations or potentially distressing matters at table.

It was only as we demolished generous slices of Mrs. Muldoon's simple but perfect apple pie that Gil steered the conversation in a more fruitful direction. (Pun not intended, I promise!) Using a version of the same story I'd told Hetty, he asked the Colonel what he remembered of the Prince's visit.

"What an interesting time that was, son." A rusty chuckle. "My little sister and her best friend were so excited to see an actual prince."

"Did they go to the Academy of Music Ball?"

"I know my sister did not. Her friend Bertha may have done. I believe they managed to follow along on some visit or other. Philly—Philippa—and

Bertha came home just bouncing around in raptures. And they whispered and gossiped about it for months after. Right up until Bertha left."

"Bertha left?" I asked. Great-Aunt Cecily had said she died.

"Yes." The Colonel shook his head. "Terrible thing. She went to White Plains to help her brother and his wife with a new baby...and died of diphtheria or some such thing."

"Awful," Preston, who'd lost his first family in a cholera outbreak, put down his fork.

"That it was." The Colonel looked to me. "Philly was just crushed. You know how girls are with their good friends."

"I do." I sighed. "We rely on them so much. Even as grown women."

"Exactly. Philly saved every one of Bertha's letters. I think they're still here in a box—her husband had a very small house when they married, and when she was older, she was more concerned with her children and their traps."

"No doubt." Gil nodded. "I think my sister left her maiden correspondence at my mother's home, as well."

"Such things are terribly important for young ladies...and not as much later," I agreed.

"Until they are," Tommy said. Though he had not commented on Gil's and my excuse, I knew he had his doubts. Why, after all, would we be spending so much energy simply to gather a few mementoes for the Prince?

Preston caught something, too, glancing between us all.

"Would you terribly mind showing them to us?" Gil asked.

"Not at all. Why don't you adjourn to the drawing room, and I will bring them in just a few moments. Mrs. Muldoon would be delighted to serve you coffee."

I doubted Mrs. Muldoon had ever been delighted to serve anything. But it was a pleasant fiction.

Not entirely fiction when it came to Toms. She accorded him the adoration most Irish women her age saved for the saints in their shrines. The aging housekeeper bore the silver coffee tray into the drawing room with a scowl that melted when her eyes landed on the Champ. Then, she filled one of the cups, and handed it to him like an offering.

"Thank you," Tommy said, very politely.

"My pleasure, Champ."

She stood there, just staring at him, beaming.

Preston looked to Gil, who looked to me.

We didn't need the coffee anyhow.

The sound of footsteps and a cane broke the spell; Mrs. Muldoon, startled like a child caught with a hand in the cookie jar, scooted out. Leaving us sitting there with a tray and four empty cups.

I looked to the coffee pot. "Well, I'm certainly not above pouring, if no one minds."

"I'd actually rather like it if you did," the Colonel said from the doorway. "I've always thought it was one of the most graceful things a lady can do. Loved to watch my wife pour."

"Then, of course, I shall." I picked up the pot, the centerpiece of a glorious flower-painted set. These pieces were not as breathtakingly old as Great-Aunt Cecily's set, but they had still probably been in use for most of a century, and they were much fancier, extravagantly emblazoned with pink moss roses, fluted, and gilt-edged. It took considerable effort to keep my hands steady, but I managed it.

Unexpected advantage to the silver set I had at home: it wasn't breakable. Embarrassing if I dropped it, but it—and I—would live to fight another day. This set?

While I was quite happy to give the Colonel the pleasant echo of his wife, I was extremely relieved to put down the pot and worry only about not breaking my own cup. As I pulled back, Gil caught my eye and shot me an approving little smile.

"Lovely, just lovely, Duchess." The old man's face lit up with joy. "You are indeed an ornament to your husband."

From someone else, it might have been a veiled insult—or an expression of hidebound old-fashioned views. But the Colonel meant it with the highest respect, and I took the compliment as intended.

"Thank you so much, sir." I beamed right back. It is not only possible, but desirable, after all, to be both a working artist and an appropriate spouse.

The other gents just smiled. Tommy's eyes gleamed, giving me no doubt that I'd be hearing all manner of dry little comments about my status as an ornament.

The Colonel took a sip of his coffee, then produced a packet of papers, creamy with age, bound with a vivid green ribbon. "Here they are."

"Quite impressive," Gil said.

"Amazing," I agreed.

"There are quite a few of them," the Colonel said, holding out the packet to Gil. "If you'd like to borrow them for a few days, I would not object."

"Are you sure?" Gil asked.

"Absolutely. Perhaps you can use them to find someone who has pictures or other more useful artifacts. Or perhaps you could use Bertha's description of the Prince's visit. I suspect her family would like that."

"Her words would live on," I said.

"Exactly. If we cannot have our lost ones, at least we have their voices." A rueful smile. "On occasion, I read my wife's letters at night."

Everyone else simply nodded. There was nothing we could say to offer comfort, and it was more respectful of his loss to just sit with him and his words.

"At any rate," the Colonel resumed with just a trace of a smile, "I do hope you folks will not make me wait six months for another visit."

"No, sir," Preston said.

"You know you're always welcome in our homes," I offered. "We would be honored-"

"I'm an old man, Duchess. Set in my ways. I prefer people to come to me." He took a sip of coffee. "And I expect you to do so."

"And so we shall," Preston promised. "I'll make sure the young folks keep you on the calendar."

"Just what I like to hear. I hope the Duke won't mind if I ask his Duchess to pour on occasion."

"Not at all, sir." Gil grinned. "Though I may ask you to tell us a few of your best stories for the privilege."

"Quite fair, young man. Did I hear you are admirers of Mr. Lincoln's?"

"To a man, sir."

"Well, never mind that prince of yours, let me tell you what happened the first time our greatest President came to New York…"

Chapter Fifteen: Her Grace at Home

That Tuesday came another marker of my new status, an at-home. Society ladies are "at home" to friends and connections one afternoon a week, where they offer tea and little nibbles, and inane conversation.

As a working artist, I had never even attended one. Why on earth would I?

However, as the Duchess of Leith, it was an unavoidable necessity.

Gil's mother, the Dowager Countess, had convinced me I should hold a few over the course of the Met run, because, as the canny Scotswoman put it, "you want to keep those snobby women where you can see them."

Inarguable logic.

Equally inarguable, it's far easier to spin ridiculous stories about someone you've never met. So, if I were seen on a regular basis looking and behaving in an entirely appropriate ducal (duchess-al?) manner, it could only improve my social standing. And Gil's, not that he particularly cared.

All of which was in play when Rosa helped me into a lovely mauve dress with an open lace-trimmed Medici collar patterned on a style often worn by the Princess of Wales. She, too, is a bit slimmer than the current fashion, though because of fragile health rather than athleticism, and I often choose similar lines, knowing they will likely look good on me.

On this particular day, of course, I'd chosen a princess style quite deliberately. An echo of Her Highness could only add credibility to Her Grace.

"Very pretty, Miss," said Rosa, as she opened the jewel case.

The wonderful thing about the Tallach pearls is that they're so simple and perfect for all occasions, while also being incredibly old and valuable. As always, once settled in place on my skin, they took on a unique lit-from-within glow.

"They like you." Rosa, who hopes to write novels one day, sometimes makes unusual observations.

"Pearls just like to be worn. I happen to be the wearer of the moment, that's all."

"The color is especially good on you."

I looked at my hands, then to her. "Should I?"

"The rule about no diamonds before dark does not apply to wedding or engagement rings," she assured me. "I asked around a bit the last time I was at the park. And anyhow, most of the girls' bosses drape on the sparkle whenever they feel like it."

"They do?"

"Oh, do they!" A musical laugh. "Miss O'Hanlon and I see some of the other girls when we go marketing or to Mass, and they have stories to tell."

Having heard some of the matrons holding forth on the alleged servant problem—a funny little locution usually meaning servants who were insufficiently servile—I did not doubt Rosa. "Do they, now?"

Her amiable little face tightened a bit. "You know we'd never gossip about you-"

"Rosa, dear, you and Miss O'Hanlon are loyal, valued employees. If you occasionally complain to your friends about some rub or other, it is none of my business."

"Miss, after hearing what the other girls contend with, we haven't the faintest cause for complaint."

"That's very sweet, but entirely unnecessary."

"Entirely true." She grinned. "Now, do you want to hear some of the crazy demands the other girls get? No names, of course."

"Of course. I might meet them this afternoon, and I surely could not keep a straight face."

"I'd hate to be the cause of that." The laugh came back. "Well, the wildest one is probably the lady who decided the ribbons in her unmentionables were the wrong shade of pale pink and sent her maid out to buy new ones and re-thread them."

"No."

"Oh, yes."

"Now I'm going to be looking at every one of them, wondering if she's wearing the re-ribboned underwear."

We shared a laugh.

"So, the diamond stays." Rosa's tone brooked no argument as she smoothed my collar one last time.

"I agree. Nothing like a little extra sparkle."

"Miss, you sparkle quite enough on your own."

"Very kind." I stood.

Sophia knocked on the door and opened it. "Miss O'Hanlon is finishing everything. She'd like you to take a quick look before she goes back downstairs, if you could."

"Of course."

In the drawing room, Mary O'Hanlon stood at the coffee table, one hand holding a kitchen towel, the other at her chin, as she contemplated.

"What do you think, miss?" she asked, motioning to the display.

I suppose I have a small tendency to overuse superlatives when praising my staff, but this truly was perfection. She'd set out our silver coffee service— not a priceless antique, but the very best available from a good house—along with the floral bone china cups and plates I normally use when my female friends visit. This time, we were using the full set, instead of a few pieces, all carefully arranged so I could pour and offer dainties easily and gracefully.

And what dainties!

While Mary is an excellent cook, her great gift is in confectionery. She produces beautiful little masterpieces for us on any given day, but she had outdone even her own high standard today. No doubt knowing our offerings would be discussed and rated amongst the matrons, she had assembled thin, perfect lemon wafers with just a whisper of glaze, magnificently simple Scottish shortbread from the Dowager Countess' family recipe, and, for a fancy and colorful touch, fairy cakes embellished with mauve icing roses in precisely the shade and design of the decorations on the china.

The large crystal vase we kept on a pedestal near the door, as well as several smaller pieces, were filled with similar roses, delivered this morning from our favorite florist. They were spread out enough that the scent filtered through the room without overpowering it.

All in all, a delightful scene.

And a glorious setting for a duchess.

I still wished Gil's mother were here to support me. She had proudly adopted me as a second daughter and defended me against all comers. As far as she was concerned, I had saved her son from a sad and loveless life after his first wife's death, and as long as I made him happy, I could do no wrong.

She had even asked me to call her Mother, and I happily acquiesced; my own late parent had been Mama, so there was no conflict or uncomfortable echo.

As I took my seat on the settee, smoothing my mauve faille skirts, I knew the Countess would have been more than satisfied, but I dearly missed her calm, regal grace. Were she here, she would have patted my arm, re-settled the pearls, adjusted my collar a bit, and pronounced me ready for the show—with a wink and a smile that warmed my heart.

But her aunt's one-hundredth birthday took precedence, and I entirely understood. If I were so lucky as to reach the century mark, I would expect every single one of my beloveds to get themselves to my celebration. No question.

And thus, I was on my own.

On my own as the Duchess of Leith, but not alone. I reminded myself I was surrounded by a more than capable staff, with a loving family who would happily spring to my rescue if I needed it. I was, though, utterly determined not to need rescuing...even if the matrons quite honestly scared me more than any villain I'd confronted.

I would much prefer dueling a killer on a catwalk to making careful conversation with the cream of society. Especially since I had a chance of recovering from a misstep on the catwalk—but if I erred here, there were few ways to correct it, and no chance at all that anyone would forget.

What little I knew of society told me, unlike in the stage world, finishing with a good show would not cancel out any previous mistakes or problems. It's one of the things I love most about my profession: you can begin awkwardly and unevenly, even make a wrong entrance or forget the words early on—but if you end the show well, no one will remember the false start.

I had no reason to hope for such grace here.

Just before the appointed hour, Gil and Tommy stepped into the drawing room.

"Well, looky here," Tommy said with a grin. "Who are you and what have you done with Heller?"

"A vision of loveliness, my lady wife. But not so lovely as to spark jealousy," Gil added quickly. "We all know that, too, could be disastrous."

"So could any number of things," I replied with an irritated sigh. "Will I do?"

"More than do," Gil said. "You are graceful and appropriate. And you will absolutely stun them."

"And if you don't," Tommy added with a teasing gleam in his eyes, "you can just slug them with that big rock on your hand."

I put my right hand over the diamond. "You don't think it's too much-"

"Don't be silly, Heller."

"It is the ring your husband gave you on your wedding day, and it is therefore appropriate at any time you choose to wear it." Gil bent down and kissed my forehead. "Remember, this is a performance like any other."

"Only today, I am playing the duchess at home."

"Exactly."

I took a breath and smoothed the trim fabric of my bodice, pressing my hand to my stomach to calm it. "Her Grace at home."

"We'll bring you something good from the bookstore," Tommy said, patting my arm as he turned for the door. "Maybe even stop for candy."

"Ugh. I couldn't imagine eating right now," I said.

"In a few hours, *mo chridhe*." Gil bowed to me, one more deliberate reminder of who and what I am, and followed Tommy.

The door had scarcely closed behind them when the first contender arrived.

Mrs. Demeter Fisch is not quite of the 400, but she is also not bothered by this in the least, being the wife of an exceedingly prominent and wealthy store owner. A small, brown-haired woman of a certain age with sparkly amber eyes, she happily swims in between the inner and outer circles, helped by a friendly, no-nonsense demeanor and unerring observance of the social rules.

She also has a lively curiosity about quite literally everything that crosses her path, so of course, she was going to get a good look at the new duchess. Some of the other matrons would have made me feel like a freak, like one of those dressed-up circus animals, but Mrs. Fisch had an honest warmth.

"Aren't you looking wonderful, dear?" she said as she walked into the room. I stood, so we could exchange the friendly little hand clasp that is usual in these circumstances, bending down to her.

"Thank you," I replied, returning to my seat and smoothing my skirt.

"A lovely dress. The Princess of Wales favors that sort of collar, doesn't she?"

"Why yes. Thank you for noticing. My dressmaker will be delighted."

"And she should be." Mrs. Fisch's own seamstress was no slouch; her golden-brown floral jacquard day dress was a perfect fit, with subtle harmonizing embroidery around the neckline, cuffs, and hem. She, too, had fine but not ostentatious jewelry: a heavy, braided gold bracelet and chain necklace with an intricately worked locket.

All elegant but not remotely intimidating. Mrs. Fisch dresses to please herself, not to show off.

I offered tea and cookies. She accepted shortbread and a flower cake and praised the beauty of the cakes and the quality of the shortbread.

We exchanged a few almost comfortable sentences about the Met season and last Sunday's settlement house benefit, which she'd attended.

And then, it was over.

"Well, dear, I must be taking my leave. It's been just lovely to see you. I do hope you'll stop by when I'm at home sometime soon."

"Thank you." Victory. No other way to read that invitation.

When the door closed behind her, I let out a long breath. I had carried the day.

If I could do it once, I could do it again.

The next visitor was far less congenial. Mrs. Leonore Hightower, wife of a shipping magnate, was clearly here out of curiosity. And perhaps a sense of mission.

After she took a critical look at the drawing room, and me, clearly hoping to find fault with something, she accepted tea and a lemon wafer—perfectly suited to her sour expression—and began some of the most breathtakingly offensive small talk I've ever endured.

It started when I offered the cookies, describing them as "Miss O'Hanlon's excellent work," which set her right into the infamous "servant problem."

Never a favorite of mine, but even worse than usual with Mrs. Hightower.

"It's really quite awful, you know. So hard to find decent servants nowadays. You can't get a good Irish girl anymore—they're all working in factories or some such, so we're stuck with Italians, or heaven help us, those Russian or Polish girls with the weird long names."

Malka Steinmetz's daughter bit her lip and managed a neutral nod.

"Well, as you know, the world is going to hell in a handbasket."

"Hm." I nodded. Sipped my tea because I needed something to do.

"Well, you know, dear, society is simply falling apart. And it's all because of the…"

Here, she dropped her voice dramatically, as if to warn me she was about to bring up something very secret and terrible. I waited.

"Soiled doves."

I managed wide eyes and a nod, while I tried to figure out what on earth she was talking about. For a moment, I thought perhaps it was a reference to some disease among the pigeon population. And then I remembered a florid article about Five Points that had used the term as an allegedly delicate way to describe sporting-house girls. How those unfortunates could be responsible for the downfall of society was beyond me, but I realized I was about to get a good look at the logic.

"It's just terrible," Mrs. Hightower continued. "If those—places—did not exist, men would have to stay at home."

If it were her house, they'd probably go anywhere else. "I see."

"Unchastity is the great evil," Mrs. Hightower said, taking another bite from her lemon wafer. "Well, surely, you of all people should know."

I nearly dropped my cup.

"Of course, you would never have made such an advantageous marriage if you had not held onto your precious jewel. A woman without her precious jewel has no hope in the world."

Soiled doves, precious jewel. The weirdly indirect language made everything sound even dirtier than straightforward descriptions would. Perhaps that was the point.

And precious jewel, anyhow? As far as I'm concerned, my precious jewel is my family. And I would do anything I had to do to protect them. Whatever sort of dove I might be.

"Well," I began. "I've been very fortunate. But many others are not."

"And that's why we need to protect them. And protect our men from them. You may have heard that Assistant Police Commissioner Maitland is launching a public morals campaign soon. I hope we can count on your support."

"Public morals." I drank a bit more tea. Now, we're getting somewhere. A public morals campaign might explain the police raid at Alice LaJoy's...and might provide some fuel for the blackmail effort, too. "What is he planning to do?"

"Launch an all-out onslaught on iniquity. We must stop it at the root. Get rid of these cesspits of vice and clean up our fair city."

Talking about cesspits, even metaphorical ones of vice, was not exactly what I expected over tea. I let my eyes slide to the little ormolu clock on the mantel. These visits weren't supposed to go beyond twenty minutes or so.

We had to be close to the end.

"I'm sure the Assistant Commissioner has it well in hand," I offered,

"Indeed, he does. We're lucky to have such a fine upstanding man on our police commission.

Couldn't prove it by me. While Father Michael's detective cousin Andrew Riley was a regular visitor at our home, we had no acquaintance with the police "brass," as he referred to the higher-ups.

But we did have a visit planned to Cousin Andrew (as he was always known to family and friends) and his wife later in the week, so perhaps we could gather some insight. In addition to a pleasant time of catching up with good friends.

That was neither here nor there at this moment, though, as the supremely repulsive Mrs. Hightower continued her pontification on soiled doves and houses of ill repute. I found myself stifling an inappropriate giggle, as I tried to pretend I was anywhere but here, so I was not tempted to give my visitor a little lecture on the true evil in the world.

Which had nothing to do with unfortunate girls forced to make choices my visitor could never imagine.

Finally, at long last, Mrs. Hightower realized she had taken her time, and she swept out. I practically collapsed on the couch in relief, taking a generous sip of tea and wishing it were something stronger.

The next few women spent less time and took far less energy. They walked in, clearly expecting to find a den of iniquity or tenement hovel, and when welcomed to an elegant home by an appropriate hostess, were stunned into quick small talk and a quicker exit. The good news was, I had no doubt they'd speak well of me. The bad news was it would likely be framed as:

"I never would have expected it, but…"

The last guests, though, were unexpected and welcome indeed.

"Mrs. Bridgewater and Mrs. Ten Broeck," announced Sophia.

Not only was the visit an endorsement of the best kind, the company of these two excellent ladies was a joy in itself.

Both were dressed in day dresses in currently fashionable lines, but fabrics that had been in style a long time ago. Clearly, the Knickerbocker ladies do not get rid of a good dress if there's still wear in it.

Lavinia Ten Broeck was once again in black, as she'd been on the other occasions we'd seen her, clearly a follower of Queen Victoria's mandate for widows to wear black for life. Not Great-Aunt Cecily, who was in the jewel blue she favored, with her own priceless pearls.

"What a lovely home you keep, dear." Great-Aunt Cecily held out her hands. "And such a pretty dress."

"Thank you."

"No one would know you grew up in a tenement," Lavinia said.

I chose to take it as a compliment, nodding and smiling. Mrs. Ten Broeck, being of the older generation, probably assumed she had the right to say whatever she liked, hurtful or not.

"May I offer you some tea and cookies? My cook, Miss O'Hanlon, has outdone herself."

"Well, she certainly has," Lavinia said. "I do favor shortbread. My mother was Scots."

"How fascinating," I said. "My husband's mother is from the Highlands."

"That's right," Great-Aunt Cecily said. "Cabot tells me she's rather formidable."

Pot, meet kettle, I thought. "Indeed, she is, but in the kindest possible way."

"My mother was born in Edinburgh. I wanted to name my daughter Maud for her, but my husband insisted on Bertha for his aunt."

"Bertha's still a lovely name," I offered as I poured. Perhaps I could get her to slide into Bertha's story without interrogating her.

"It is. And she was a lovely girl." Lavinia smiled. "Dark hair, the Ten Broeck blue eyes, and a smile...such a smile."

Great-Aunt Cecily put a soothing hand on her friend's arm. "She was a dear girl."

"Lively and spirited and happy," Lavinia continued, slipping into her memories. But then her face hardened. "With no idea what the world could do. What men could do."

"Men can be just awful, dear." Great-Aunt Cecily said, casting a glance to me.

"Oh, indeed they can," I agreed, trying to match her somewhat lightened tone. Probably hoping to start the conversation about the foibles of opposite sex men think women are having whenever two or more of us are alone.

Lavinia was gazing at the shortbread, but apparently seeing something we could not. Her pain and loss clearly went deep, even after forty years.

I wasn't one to talk, considering a cold day or a prick from a sewing needle could send me straight back to the tenement room where I had awakened one February morning with my mother's body. Not a thought I needed right now.

"What would you like in your tea?" I asked Lavinia, keeping my tone smooth and polite, as if it were entirely normal for a guest to just disappear into another world for a moment.

"Oh, yes, thank you." Lavinia returned, stared at me. First without recognition, then understanding, and finally with something else. Hostility.

How could I possibly have offended her?

If my own upsets were any indication, probably simply by being here when it happened. I was always mortified. Fortunately, my upsets are very rare, and I'm usually able to avoid things that cause them.

Something had caused Lavinia's upset.

"One lump, please," she said.

I added the requested sugar and handed over the cup. Then passed the shortbread. Lavinia took one, and a bite, as Great-Aunt Cecily watched her closely, wanting to be sure her friend was all right.

As I poured the second cup, Lavinia contemplated the shortbread.

Once Great-Aunt Cecily was settled with her cup and one of the lovely fairy cakes, Lavinia turned to me with a smile.

"There is definitely a real Scot in this house. Petticoat tails and the perfect texture."

"Thank you."

"Good for you, dear," Lavinia said. "So many people pretend at being Scots now, like the British Royal Family. Germans, really, you know."

I did. I'd heard similar comments from Gil's mother, but only as a matter of pride. Lavinia's tone did not suggest pride in being better than the Britons... but hatred, the same animus she'd shown the other night when talking about their accents. And I thought I knew why.

"Oh, Lavinia, not this again," Great-Aunt Cecily scowled at her friend.

"Let's all just agree the Queen is a fat little hausfrau and find a more congenial topic."

"Very well." Lavinia turned her scowl on me. "You did much better to marry a Scotsman than those nasty Germans. Can't trust a word they say, you know."

"Well," I said, hoping to pour oil on the waters, "I'm quite fortunate in my spouse."

"That you are." Lavinia said, the hostility still in her tone. "A girl like you should be grateful indeed."

Great-Aunt Cecily shot her friend a squashing glance. "The Duke should be grateful, too. It's not every day such an accomplished artist decides she wishes to marry."

"Well, thank you. We are quite well matched." Suddenly, the air in the room felt very thick and warm.

I took a deep breath, carefully hanging on to my demeanor.

"You're luckier than you know, Miss Shane," Lavinia said. "Britons are a very untrustworthy lot."

"I'm half-Irish, Mrs. Ten Broeck," I replied. "We know what the British are capable of."

"That you do." Great-Aunt Cecily gave her friend a sharp glance. "Now, on to more pleasant topics. These bone-china cups are the sweetest things. Were they a wedding gift?"

"No, actually. A housewarming gift from my mentor, Madame Lentini, when I set up my own household."

"That's right," Great-Aunt Cecily said, "you learned from Lentini."

"Really?" Lavinia asked, her eyes suddenly sparkling with interest. "Did you perform with her?"

"We toured with *Capuleti* a number of times," I assured her, relieved to have found a happy topic of conversation.

"How fascinating." The old lady took another piece of shortbread and settled in for a friendly interrogation.

And one I didn't mind a bit.

When the matrons finished their mandated twenty minutes, I saw them to the drawing-room door to exchange farewells. And then, Great-Aunt Cecily offered me the ultimate endorsement:

"Dear, please do come by for tea some afternoon soon."

"I'd love to."

"Are you performing Friday?"

"No—I'm booked for Saturday and Sunday this week."

"Then perhaps you would come over for tea Friday?"

"Of course. I would be honored."

"Delightful!" She clapped her hands like a happy child. "I will see you Friday afternoon, then."

"I shall look forward to it."

Despite our earlier chat, Lavinia Ten Broeck seemed sad and distracted again as she murmured an appropriate farewell and headed for the carriage.

"Don't worry, dear," Great-Aunt Cecily said. "She's had a very difficult life, you know."

"Of course. I cannot imagine."

After the ladies left, Sophia closed the door. "Are we done?"

"You bet we are." I smiled. "And here's the good part."

Sophia waited.

"You and the girls get the rest of the cookies!"

Chapter Sixteen: Return to Five Points

Cookies were not in the plan for me, since Tommy and I were planning a trip back to Five Points before dark.

Tommy had returned a few minutes after I sent the ladies on their way, and after I told him about the impressively unpleasant Mrs. Hightower and her theories about soiled doves, we decided it might be better to talk to Miss LaJoy if we could. Since it was only mid-afternoon, we could take advantage of the last couple hours of daylight and make a quick, but hopefully enlightening, visit now, and learn what we might.

There was nothing in our situation to suggest delay was helpful or desirable.

A quick change—a theatre career proves useful at the most unexpected moments—later, we set out for the dangerous side of town.

As Tommy and I turned the last corner, a man suddenly fell in step with us. It would have been extremely menacing had he not immediately shot us a wicked grin. A grin that did not, however, dilute the chill in his shamrock-green eyes.

"Well, Eddie Hurley as I live and breathe." Connor's grin widened, and his eyes narrowed as he shook my hand. "Thought I'd never see you again."

"He's not supposed to be seeing you, Connor," Tommy said pointedly. "Eddie just got back from upstate."

"And he's not to be consorting with the criminal element." Connor chuckled. He was enjoying the game. At least as much as Tommy. "Well, as it happens, I've been asked to keep an eye on Eddie here. Make sure he stays out of trouble."

"Keep an eye?" I asked sharply.

"A mutual friend, who's perhaps a bit closer to Eddie," Connor said, not even trying for a straight face, "has asked me to take an interest. A protection racket's a protection racket, after all."

"Protection?" I asked. "I was going to ask you to look to my husband's safety."

"Ah, but as it happened, already asked me to look to yours."

"I knew it," I muttered.

"You know I keep an eye on both of you at any given time, more or less." I did.

"And it's just as well he asked me to step in."

"It is?"

Connor's amiable expression faded, and his gaze sharpened on me. "Let's just say you're lucky you belong to him and not me. If I caught you wandering around Five Points, I'd strangle you myself."

"That's hardly fair," I said. "I'm not wandering around Five Points. I'm investigating a potential blackmail threat against a friend."

"Your man told me what you're doing. I still think you should leave it to Tom." Connor's expression softened just a bit. "But I have cause to know you aren't capable of standing by when a friend is in trouble."

He meant, he would probably have died at the hands of a backstage murderer a year ago if I didn't have a habit of jumping in when friends are in danger.

No need to belabor the point. I met his gaze squarely. "I'm not looking for trouble. We're simply going to have a quick word with Miss LaJoy."

"You're going to that house?" Connor sputtered.

"The Hurley brothers are going to the house," I said calmly. "And it's in broad daylight, and we won't be there long enough to suggest...anything."

"Well, I don't like it." Connor scowled.

"Your annoyance is duly noted," I said.

"Connor," Tommy said, "this really is just a very short, above-board conversation with Miss LaJoy."

"We're just trying to get a sense of her in hopes of getting a direction on the blackmail matter," I added.

"Ah." Connor slowed his pace a bit. "You think the raid was a setup."

"We do," Tommy agreed. "We understand she's up to date on her bribes to the coppers."

"So no obvious reason for the raid," I added.

"Other than the proprietress's brother," Connor nodded. "And who might have known he was there?"

"Perhaps we can figure that out today," I said. "I suspect Miss LaJoy keeps matters very close to her vest."

"She seems to be the best of a very bad lot," Tommy said.

"Best of my knowledge, she is. Probably the only honest one in Five Points." Connor put his hands in his pockets, as the three of us fell into a comfortable pace. Just three fellows walking around the neighborhood. "Understand, I'm not endorsing it, and I'll have no truck with it."

"Of course." I nodded.

"But I've never heard a word of trouble about the place. And I know some of her girls have gone on to marry good men."

"They have?" Tommy blinked. While women "with a past" often did marry, it was extremely unusual for anyone other than the husband—and often not even him—to know about it.

"I think she may keep an eye out for ways to help them move on to better lives, but I don't know enough to know." Connor shrugged, and his next sentence was in the key of closing the subject. "At any rate, she seems to really care about them, and that is quite unusual."

"I imagine it is," I agreed. "Well, now that you've looked to my safety, might I make a humble request?"

Connor tried to scowl but couldn't hold back a laugh. "Very well, Master Hurley."

"Ah. Well played."

"Better be nice to my little brother, Connor," Tommy joked.

"Oh, he's a scrappy one." Connor flicked him an eyebrow, then turned to me. "So?"

"There's a Scotsman who popped up in Morrissey's the other day," I began.

You never knew who might hear what in Five Points, and it could create all manner of trouble for Eddie Hurley to be just walking down the street talking about his husband.

"A Scotsman?" Connor asked.

"One Robert Stewart," Tommy said. "Tall, dark-haired, distinctive light-blue eyes."

A canny nod from Connor. "Ah, that Scotsman."

"Yes." I returned the nod. "And I'd like you to put the word out he's under your protection. Just in case."

"Easily enough done, as long as he's not meddling in anything he shouldn't be."

"I'm reasonably sure he's only looking for information…though I'm not sure how he'd find anything related to his current area of interest here."

"Area of interest?" Connor asked, as Tommy watched me closely.

"I can't say much, you understand, but he's doing a favor for a friend."

"As he often does," Tommy said.

"No doubt." Connor was aware of at least some of Gil's activities, because they had joined forces on more than one occasion, when their interests coincided. Every once in a while, even a murderous gangster takes an interest in seeing justice done.

"This particular matter is extremely sensitive, but it should be mostly a matter of research. And I'm not at all sure what he might be looking for down here."

"Ah, well, I imagine I can help you with that." Connor grinned. "You know, the city took shape down here and moved uptown. If it's research, and he's seeking records of some kind, they might well be at a church or city office down here."

Well, one matter easily explained, at least.

"That might be it, at that," I said. "In any case, if you happen across Mr. Stewart…"

"I'll keep an eye on him." Connor nodded. "And I'll see that he has a safe-conduct, for lack of a better."

"Thank you."

107

"You didn't have to ask, you know." Connor punched my arm lightly. "Any friend of Eddie Hurley's is a friend of mine."

"Thank you," I said.

"Very good of you, Connor," Tommy added.

"Not good at all." The dangerous scowl returned. "I'm doing my part. So you do yours and get Eddie Hurley back where he came from as soon as you can."

It was not a request.

Chapter Seventeen: Alice, Not in Wonderland

I t won't surprise you to know I'd never been to a sporting house.

Not that I was in the habit of judging women who did what they had to do to keep body and soul together. I'd seen too much suffering, and want as a child in the tenements to blame anyone for trading so-called virtue for survival. And I was well aware of how fortunate I was to have been able to put off that part of life for a marriage bed and a man of my choosing.

To save my "precious jewel," as the repulsive Mrs. Hightower would have it.

Yes, Marie was right. I did have a rather low opinion of chorus girls who charmed their way into work that should have gone to more talented but less compliant performers, but the women who ended up at a place like Alice's house were not social-climbing soubrettes. These were tenement girls who'd found work they considered easier and safer than the factory or the laundry.

And as Tommy and I stood awkwardly in the elegantly appointed foyer of the unremarkable townhouse, I would have had a hard time arguing the point.

"We're here to see Miss Alice," Tommy told the maid, a girl in her early teens in an utterly plain black dress and white apron. The fabric and make were good, but the style entirely unremarkable. Someone wanted this very young girl to look simple and decent, and attract absolutely no notice.

It spoke well of the proprietress.

"Who shall I say sent you?"

"Her brother Paul. I'm Tommy Hurley, and this is my brother Eddie. We're friends of Mr. Coughlan."

At the names, the girl's eyes widened a bit. More when she took a look at Tommy. As young as she was, she clearly recognized him as the Champ. He's a bit of a legend in some Irish circles. She dropped a little curtsy. "I'll tell her."

In the time it took for me to ascertain that at least two of the paintings on the walls appeared to be real works by famous French artists, the girl disappeared and returned.

"Please come back this way. Miss LaJoy will have tea brought."

"Thank you." Tommy and I returned her bow as she conducted us down a short hall to a pocket door and opened it.

Inside a parlor that appeared to be inspired by—and was a worthy homage to—Empress Alexandra's famed Mauve Sitting Room we saw a woman sitting in a large, cream-colored wing chair. In an *eau de nil* crepe de chine tea gown, frosted with fine lace and ribbons, she looked slim and elegant. Framed by a few soft chestnut curls escaping from a loose knot, her features were sharp like Paul Winslow's, but with a pretty delicacy that was no doubt a problem in her former life, and a considerable advantage now.

If Marie had not told me Alice LaJoy was once Allen Winslow, I would never have entertained the thought.

At the sight of us, she gave a friendly smile. "Tommy Hurley? As in the boxing champion?"

"Yes, ma'am," Tommy said, bowing over her extended hand. "And my brother Eddie."

As I took my turn, the slim but strong white fingers closed a bit more tightly over mine and her clear amber eyes focused on me in sharp appraisal. "Eddie, is it?"

"It is."

"Hm." She motioned behind us. "Tea, please, Teresa. Unless the gentlemen would like something stronger."

"Thank you," I said, "but best not."

"Not a social visit, ma'am." Tommy shot me a look. Of course, he was right; the less I said, the better. If anyone would know Eddie Hurley was not as he seemed, it would be Alice LaJoy.

"Ah." Rueful smile. "I didn't think so. You wouldn't invoke Mr. Coughlan."

"I'm sorry about that," Tommy said quickly. "We wanted to be sure you'd see us."

"And Connor Coughlan opens every door in Five Points," she replied. "Even the ones he finds abhorrent."

"Coughlan doesn't have truck with your line of work, but he says you're probably the only honest person practicing it."

"It's simple enough, Mr. Hurley. I treat my girls the way I'd want to be treated. And I treat this as what it is: a transaction. Nothing more, nothing less. Honest work."

Tommy and I offered non-committal nods. What could one say to such an extraordinary comment?

"Whatever you think of me, I only hire grown women who choose this life freely, pay them their fair share, and make sure they're as protected as they can be."

"It's not my place to judge, ma'am." Tommy shook his head. "We're not here about that. We're here about the raid the other day."

Teresa, the maid, arrived at that moment, carrying a tea tray with a silver pot that could have been the twin of mine, fine bone china cups with pale-blue roses, and a plate of what looked like thin ginger wafers.

Alice poured and offered the cookies, which Tommy and I both declined. Our hostess put them aside and took up her own cup, a small furrow at her brow making clear her concern.

"Now, what about the raid? Part of the cost of doing business. I'll just make a bigger payoff to the precinct next time."

"Not for Paul," I said quietly.

"You know."

"We know enough," I replied, keeping my voice low, but probably not as rough as I should.

Alice LaJoy's gaze sharpened on me. "I think I know enough, too. What

111

are you about?"

"Trying to help Paul," Tommy said. "We're cousins to his wife's singing partner, Miss Shane."

"Are you, now?" Alice LaJoy nodded to me. "Eddie, is it?"

"It is," I said, careful to add a bit of rasp for the masculine effect. "Miss Shane would never come to Five Points."

"Never." Alice gave a faint smile and nodded to Tommy and me. "So you have an interest."

"Judge Winslow and his wife are good people," Tommy said. "And we want to protect them."

"Protect them from me?"

"Of course not," I said before I thought. I took a quick sip of tea.

Alice's faint smile widened. "You two seem to be good people, too."

"Do our best." Tommy shrugged, and then his gaze sharpened. "See, we're reasonably sure the raid was a blackmail trap."

"Of course it was." Alice sighed and gazed into her cup. "I suspected as much, but only too late. What do we do now?"

"Figure out who's behind it and stop them," Tommy said.

"I agree. Paul's gone out very far for me, and I don't want it to cost him his career." She ran her finger around the rim of her cup. "We were very close as children, and it's been so wonderful to have my brother back. Selfish of me, I suppose."

"Surely everyone needs and deserves a loving family." I wasn't careful with my tone when I spoke and sounded far too much like my normal self.

Alice LaJoy gave me a warm and rueful smile. "There are those who would say I don't deserve my next breath."

"There are foolish, ignorant people everywhere, Miss LaJoy." Tommy shook his head. "We can't stop them from existing. We can only minimize the damage they do."

"And we'll do our best for you," I assured her, not even trying for Eddie's tone.

"I appreciate it." She managed a tiny smile. "So what happens now... gentlemen?"

"We go home, and you keep your eyes open." Tommy drank the last of his tea.

"And your guard up," I added.

"With all due respect, Brothers Hurley, I don't need you to remind me of that."

We arrived back in Washington Square just as the afternoon light was fading, to find a quiet house and an envelope from Hetty. I grabbed it, ignoring Tommy's puzzled expression, and ran upstairs to change.

By the time the rest of the household arrived for dinner, I was back to my ladylike self, ensconced on my chaise in a mulberry crepe dress, with my current book. Tommy was in his wing chair, similarly occupied.

Butter wouldn't melt in our mouths.

Chapter Eighteen: Songs Unheard

The next day brought a very pleasant and unexpected duty: attending the dedication of the Ella Shane Music Collection at the Bridgewater Library's Manhattan branch. Grover Duquesne, Captain of Industry, who had once been the worst of my grubby backstage admirers, was endowing the collection as a wedding present. The simple fact of writing that sentence is bizarre enough, considering the man waged a years-long campaign to make me his mistress.

And yet.

After an unbalanced admirer attacked Gil and left me wounded, and we announced our engagement, Mr. Duquesne apparently had a change of heart. It's still unclear to me whether the insane actions of his fellow stage-door johnny, or the fact that a man at least as powerful and important as he had decided I was worthy of marriage, or perhaps some combination of the two, worked the magic. But magic it was, because now, my former nemesis had become one of my greatest supporters, telling anyone who would listen how much he respected me, and how impressive it was to see a poor but virtuous (!) young lady elevated to such a position of importance.

The Lord truly works in mysterious ways.

In any case, Gil and I, as well as Tommy, Cabot, and Jamie, proceeded over to the library together for this still rather stunning turn of events. Even more stunning, Hetty was covering it, because, as she had said dryly a few days before, the dedication—and I—were an important and interesting women's story.

If she said so.

I was just glad she'd be there. My Aunt Ellen flatly refused to attend, saying a nice Irish woman didn't belong in the room with all those society types. She might well have braved it, if Gil's mother had been in town. They had become close friends, and often worked in tandem for matters involving Gil and me, like hens supervising their chicks.

And Marie, my other close and dear friend, was avoiding public engagements at the moment, preferring to avoid any awkward questions or notice in view of the sporting house raid. I didn't blame her a bit, but I missed her.

At any rate, the timing of the event created a bit of a conundrum for Rosa and me. Despite the time of day, an evening or recital gown would have sent precisely the wrong message, with the glitter and exposed flesh of a diva in concert. But a suit was too masculine, and a day dress not elegant enough for such an important moment. In the end, we settled on a lovely violet faille afternoon dress. With intricate floral embroidery across the high neckline, bodice and cuffs, it was suitably fancy, while not conflicting with the Tallach pearls.

Much easier for the fellows, who wore their best dark suits and simple ties in the colors they favored: Gil blue, Jamie yellow, Tommy green, and Cabot deep red. Had I not been a bit nervous about all the attention, I would have found the display quite amusing.

But I was, in fact, nervous.

It's one thing to walk out onto the stage as someone else. That's a very specific experience, and I've trained for it most of my life. While the usual woman would be terrified by a house filled with thousands of patrons, it's a day's work for me, and I welcome it.

A room full of people who are here to see me, a live woman rather than a stage boy, though, is much different, and I had to admit, just a bit scary. Especially since my name is on it.

Mr. Duquesne had offered to put both Gil's and my names on the collection, or to describe it as the Ellen St. Aubyn Collection, since that was, after all, my actual married name. But Gil, in one of those moments that told me he really does love me for who I am, said it should be the Ella Shane Collection, because that was the name associated with my professional achievements.

Which Gil had added, were mine, and not his, even if he was my husband.

I was hoping to find a way to work that particular comment into Hetty's story...because for my money, a man who understands his wife is a professional and an artist in her own right is important and interesting indeed.

And all too rare.

So, as I draped a harmonizing cashmere paisley wrap over my dress and took Gil's arm for the walk to the cab, I couldn't quite keep down a very unaccustomed case of the jitters. Even so, a small part of me was amused to be experiencing something like stage fright.

Certainly Tommy found it more than a little funny, teasing me about being afraid of a couple dozen people when I'd sung for thousands just days before.

By the time we arrived, Tommy's jokes had done their work. I was more annoyed with my cousin than unnerved as Gil handed me down in front of the building.

The library was rather amazing. A gorgeous old mansion, whose owners had donated the building before moving further uptown with their fancy friends, the place was a real temple of reading.

Tommy spent a good deal of time there, with all the work he and Cabot were doing to bring books to poor children, but I visited infrequently enough to be more than a little awed when I walked into the foyer. Just as it had been as a private residence, the entrance was still elegant and expansive, with the fading sunlight shattered into colored bits by lovely stained-glass windows...though now dominated by a charging desk with a pair of rather beleaguered-looking librarians.

The dedication was planned for early evening to make the morning papers, but also so as to not disrupt the children who go there after school. Nothing we could do is as important as their studies.

Tommy and Cabot strode confidently forward, trailed by Jamie. I hesitated a bit, and Gil took my hand, squeezing my fingers before presenting his arm. I took it, and we proceeded ahead. Their Graces in full steam.

While the music collection would be kept in an upstairs room, the dedication was in the former ballroom on the main floor, normally a large, beautiful reading room with the sides lined with shelves and shelves of books. The reading tables had been moved and the chairs rearranged to face a little stage-like area where orchestras had once played. There, a podium and a half-dozen chairs awaited us.

"Miss Ella!" a booming voice proclaimed. Grover Duquesne, Captain of Industry, walked toward us, beaming, his tone and aspect showing nothing but the most respectful admiration. A sizable man with an equally sizable beard, he was the very picture of a prosperous industrialist.

"Mr. Duquesne. How delightful to see you," I said, holding out my hand.

He bowed over it, without making any attempt to kiss it, in perfect propriety. "Lovely as ever. And the Duke."

The Captain of Industry turned to Gil, who gave him a slightly wary glance, then extended his hand for a genuinely friendly shake.

"I am given to understand the Dowager Countess is not in attendance?" Duquesne asked.

"I'm sorry,\ no. My lady mother is attending her aunt's centenary celebrations in Edinburgh."

"A pity. She is an amazing lady." A surprisingly wistful note in the Captain of Industry's voice.

"That she is," I said. "She will be back in the winter, after joining us on our San Francisco stand."

"I shall look forward to it."

He sounded almost as if he were nursing a crush. Gil shot me a glance, as the head librarian came over to us, while Tommy, Cabot, and Jamie walked out of the stacks with a junior staffer, a young lady who was clearly enjoying Jamie's company. He, much like Cousin Rafe, gave no indication of anything other than amiable politeness, but that was quite enough.

"Your Grace, Miss Shane—ah—" the head librarian began, clearly slightly confused as to how to address me.

"Miss Shane is fine," I said. "At least when we're just talking."

Gil added with a smile: "The collection is named for, after all."

"Standing behind your wife, Saint Aubyn?"

Gil turned at the sound of the voice. It was the man from the window at the Consulate.

"I am delighted to see her so honored," Gil replied, taking the man's arm and walking off toward the tea table without so much as a backward glance.

I didn't have time to think about it, because I had more than enough of my own fish to fry.

The librarian smiled at me, straightening her back and coolly taking command. "Thank you. Now, Miss Shane, let's talk about how the dedication will go…"

Soon enough, we took our seats for the short, but quite delightful ceremony. I looked out over the audience, truly amazed to see reporters, socialites, and Duquesne's fellow robber barons, all gathered to celebrate something in my name. Better, my family and dear friends, including Preston and his wife Greta, as well as Lewis and Anna Abramovitz, my former accompanist and dresser, now building their names, as a composer and lyricist. I resolved to have them all over for tea soon. As I studied the audience, I also noticed the man who'd approached Gil was no longer there. Interesting.

The head librarian welcomed us, turning to Cabot for a few words about the importance of offering learning to everyone, and his happiness at expanding the library to include a music collection. He handed off to the Captain of Industry, who said some very flattering things about me and my career, and how glad he was to celebrate my new joy with a gift for aspiring musicians.

Two adorable children presented me with a lovely bouquet of autumn flowers, and then it was my turn to say a few words. Fortunately, Hetty, per our deal, had written me a perfect paragraph of thanks in return for the exclusive interview, which I'd mostly memorized, though I held the paper for security. She beamed from the front row as I thanked the good people in her crisp and graceful words, finishing with:

"…and I sincerely hope that someday this collection will help the next young person with more talent and determination than resources to gain a foothold in his or her musical career. I can only offer my deepest gratitude for this honor."

All absolutely wonderful.

And then, the evening took a turn.

As the applause for me died down, the head librarian turned to Gil. "Anything to add, Your Grace?"

Gil blinked for a moment. "No, indeed. My lady wife has summed it up nicely. And this is her sphere, after all."

Her sphere. Two dismissive and damning words. Speaking of my career as if it were setting tables and pouring tea. I stared at him.

He bent and kissed me on the cheek. Patronizing.

Then held my gaze.

Something was going on here.

There was no time to think it through, because we immediately moved into a little reception, forcing us all into a receiving line of the sort usually reserved for weddings.

We shook hands, offered and accepted light embraces, and exchanged bits of cheerful talk about opera, music, and the importance of education. While my body went through these happy motions, my mind was spinning. Why would Gil speak of me in such a dismissive way?

He always treated my work with great admiration and respect. Without exception.

Good heavens, he often addressed me by my (stage) last name the way men do among equals. To then brush off my work as my "sphere," a very specific term of art usually used to describe the home as a womanly domain? Why on earth would he diminish me and my career in that way?

Of course, other than Tommy and Hetty, both of whom shot me concerned glances, no one else in the room understood what had just happened. They thought the Duke had sweetly deferred to his wife.

"Oh, look who's here," said Mr. Duquesne in the midst of the crush. "Colonel Vandergrift. I'd hoped he might come—he told the librarian he would like to make a special donation."

"Colonel!" I exclaimed as our dear friend moved towards us, a green ribbon-bound sheaf of sheet music in hand.

"You don't think I'd miss this, do you?" he asked, taking my extended hand. "It's quite good of Mr. Duquesne to honor you in this way. And I have something for the collection."

"Oh, let's go look!" Grover Duquesne, Captain of Industry, sounded like an eager child.

"Please," added Gil, motioning to an empty study table.

"So," began the Colonel, untying the ribbon and spreading out the pieces. "I thought, in view of our conversation, that you might like my sister Philly's music from the Academy of Music Ball."

"What?"

The sharp voice made us all turn. Lavinia Ten Broeck, looking tired and impossibly tiny, seemed to appear out of thin air.

"You know your sister wasn't at that ball, you old fool. My daughter went in my place, and she was almost the only young girl there."

The Colonel shot us an exasperated glance and offered a soothing tone to Lavinia. "Bertha and Philly went out a few days after the ball to buy the music that had been played. As souvenirs."

He pointed to one piece with a hastily printed label slapped on the front: "Played at the Academy of Music Ball for the Prince of Wales."

"Really historic pieces," Duquesne said.

"Indeed, they are," the Colonel said. "And that's why I want them in a collection instead of moldering in my attic."

"Thank you." I picked up the waltz. "Incredible, isn't it? They danced to this forty years ago."

Lavinia's mouth tightened as she spoke: "I wish I'd been there."

Her tone wasn't wistful...but guilty.

"Everyone, everyone!" the head librarian called, clapping her hands. "We have a lovely tea laid out over here. Please do enjoy it."

The tea, I hardly need tell you, was not as lovely as Miss O'Hanlon's, but it was an absolute requirement. And so, we all, under that duress, trooped into the line. The odd moment with Lavinia passed, and she joined in the amiable small talk and minor chaos of obtaining refreshments. Later, I would wish I'd kept a close eye on where everyone was as cups were handed out...and who handled each one.

At the time, though, I was just grateful to get some tea, even if not especially well-brewed, and take one of the really rather nice gingersnaps so I had something to nibble. I was so busy shaking hands and accepting congratulations I didn't have a chance to talk to any of my dear ones, but I was sure they'd understand—and be happy to chew over everything later.

As often happens at these events, the whole thing became a whirlwind with many people coming up and exchanging a few words before the next person spun through.

All rather dizzying.

I had, as I often do at such times, started to just let it all wash over me. Murmuring appropriate responses while my mind was elsewhere…yes, still on that comment from Gil.

I was puzzling over it, yet again, when I heard the crash.

"Mr. Duquesne!" the head librarian cried. "What's wrong?"

Grover Duquesne was on the ground, insensible, his jaw clenched, his back arching as if he were having some kind of seizure.

"Call an ambulance!" Cabot ordered, his usual easygoing demeanor giving way to sharp command in the crisis.

Tommy, who'd seen more than one man unconscious on the floor in his boxing career, dashed up and knelt beside the victim, trying to calm him. He wasn't able to stop Duquesne from thrashing about, but he was able to keep him in one place. Jamie stood behind him, clearly ready to pitch in, watching with sharp concern.

Gil and I were a bit further away but quickly moved in.

"He's alive," Tommy said, looking up at us with a grim face. "But I don't know what's wrong."

I knelt on Duquesne's other side, speaking to him in a soothing and comforting tone, trying to calm him. And there I stayed until the ambulance surgeon came. Whatever he'd once been, he was a decent man now, and no matter what, he did not deserve to be at death's door alone.

Chapter Nineteen: An Unsettled Evening

A tired and enervated group returned to Washington Square an hour or so later. I walked right over to the decanters and started pouring whisky. After I'd served Tommy, Cabot, and Gil, I reached for a fourth glass, as Jamie glanced to his father.

"Medicinal," Gil said, nodding.

I met his gaze as I poured. My husband needed to know I had not forgotten the slight in the disaster that followed.

"Medicinal indeed, Belle Starr." Jamie took his glass with a slight bow to me.

The gentlemen properly tended to, I looked to my own needs, pouring a generous sherry.

"Medicinal?" Jamie asked, a glint of humor in his gaze over his glass.

"Absolutely."

"After that, you'd be justified in swigging from the bottle, Heller," Tommy said.

"So would you," I replied, taking a pleasant sip.

"I might yet."

"A hell of a thing, sorry, Ella," Cabot said.

"Simply a statement of fact," I assured him. "It was indeed like something out of the Inferno. How sad that Mr. Duquesne is finally doing good and decent things, only to be struck down in such a shocking fashion."

"Shocking," Tommy echoed, with an odd note in his voice.

"I think it was something worse than that." Jamie looked into his glass. "Pater, how familiar are you with strychnine poisoning?"

"Nasty stuff," Gil replied.

"Very nasty." Jamie took a breath. "But the clenched jaw and arched-back spasms made me wonder."

"How does one give it?" Cabot asked.

"It has to be ingested," Gil said, looking at his son. "You think someone put a dose in his tea?"

"I do. It would be easy enough—the stuff is everywhere. Medications, rat poison—stimulants."

"Stimulants?" Gil asked.

"Some students take tiny doses of it…and some men who are looking to, er…" Jamie trailed off, beet-red to the roots of his ginger hair.

Gil tensed. *"You* are not one of those students, James?"

"Good Lord, no, Pater. I know much too much about poison for that."

Gil's posture relaxed a bit, and he took a sip of his whisky. If I hadn't still been more than a little furious with him, I would have put a calming hand on his back.

"But I've heard tales," Jamie continued. "If someone gets the dose wrong, it's very easy to become desperately ill."

"And higher doses are just plain fatal," Cabot said.

"Precisely." Jamie took a sip of his drink. "I don't know if there are natural illnesses that look like what we just saw…"

"You're right, James," Gil said. "The jaw-clenching is considered a distinctive sign of strychnine poisoning."

"But who would want to kill Grover Duquesne?" Jamie asked.

"Two years ago, I would certainly have had motive," I admitted.

"And so would I, in your defense." Tommy nodded, took a sip of his whisky. "There could easily be any number of other offended women and their protectors who might still wish him ill."

"Poison is a woman's weapon, after all." Cabot's comment had a particularly sharp resonance with us, since one of his relatives had tried to poison him, and we'd suspected a woman, when the real danger was a man. "Or usually is."

"That event was one of the few places it would be easy to get to Duquesne—

and the rest of us," I said.

"The rest of us?" Gil asked, his aspect sharpening.

"There was a good bit of chaos at the tea urn," I reminded him. "I don't know we can say with certainty that he was the intended target."

My observation was a stopper.

For me, too.

We were all staring into our glasses when Sophia dashed in, skidding to a stop as she often does. Poor girl picked up on the general upset in the house.

"Miss Hetty is here!"

"Thank you, Sophia." I nodded, keeping my voice calm and gentle. Then I turned to Hetty.

"Whisky or sherry?" I asked.

"Oh, whisky, please. I'm a newswoman."

The reply gave us a much-needed flash of comic relief as we all smiled at our reporter's beleaguered condition. At the reception, Hetty had looked crisp, pristine, and professional in a neat gray suit and white broadcloth shirtwaist so sharply pressed as to be dangerous. Now, the jacket was unbuttoned, her little black tie loose, and her hat askew. To say nothing of the red curls attempting an escape.

"Any word from the hospital?" Tommy asked as I handed over the glass.

"It's the strangest thing," Hetty replied, taking a dainty little sip. "I called his personal secretary, expecting to hear he was near death after that horrible collapse…and instead, I'm told he's holding his own."

"Really?" Jamie said.

"Nothing definitive yet, but he's hanging on and not getting any worse. So there's hope."

"Hm." Gil put down his whisky glass. "We should probably leave you ladies to your conversation, since you still have an important and interesting interview to do, do you not?"

Hetty gave him a little scowl. "Yes, we do."

"Come along," I said, taking her arm, "you and I can take the parlor for ourselves and leave the gents to the checkerboard and the drinks cart."

"And I know which one they prefer."

"Wouldn't you?"

We shared an entirely inappropriate smile as we crossed the foyer and went through the open pocket door, which I closed.

"All right, so what's going on with you?" Hetty asked as she sat.

"You mean that odd little comment about my 'sphere,' and practically throwing us out of the drawing room?"

"That's it."

"I have no idea." I shrugged. "He's concerned about—or involved in—something, and I'm darned if I know what."

An absolutely true statement, there, even if not a complete recitation of the facts.

"Well, I'm getting bored with the lot of you," Hetty replied, with an irritated edge in her voice. "Marie's barely speaking to me right now, and now you're acting weird, too."

"Well, you know why Marie is lying low," I said. I could at least help both of them with this. "The police raid."

"We generally don't cover such things, you know. We're a family newspaper." She took another sip of whisky and shook her head. "And I'd be happy to nose around and see if there's any way to help her and Paul, you know."

And wasn't that the absolute last thing any of us needed?

"I know, dear." I put my hand on hers. "Marie's terribly ashamed and upset by the whole thing and probably doesn't want to talk to much of anyone right now. That's why she didn't come today. I haven't even heard from her in days."

"All right. I just hate seeing a friend in trouble and not being able to do anything."

"I know. Why don't you send her a quick note, then. Just let her know you're around and able to help if she needs anything."

"Good idea."

"Even a stopped clock…"

We shared a smile.

"All right, Miss Duchess, let's get to that interview. I'm sure all our lady readers would like to know about your new life…"

Perhaps half an hour later, Sophia knocked on the door.

"Mr. Alteiss is here, Miss."

Hetty's face lit up for an instant, and then she frowned in surprise. "Rowan?"

In the foyer, Alteiss, a tall, spare man renowned as a force in court, was standing by a side table with a shy smile. "Henrietta!"

The way he said her name told us everything we needed to know.

As did the way she said his.

"Rowan, what a surprise."

"I stopped by your house to see if you might have time for a short walk, and your mother told me you were here, finishing up after something—untoward—at the dedication?"

"Untoward is one word for it," I said.

"Mr. Duquesne collapsed," Hetty told him.

"Is he-"

"Alive and holding his own," she replied. "That's all I know."

"All any of us knows," I added.

"Oh, Miss Ella." Alteiss turned to me. "I'm so sorry. I should congratulate you on the honor…"

"It's quite all right. After what happened, I hardly remembered the reason we were there."

"No doubt." He turned to Hetty. "May I see you home?"

"Well," she demurred, "I have to go file my story at the news office…"

"I can wait. It's always a pleasure to talk with the writers and perhaps pick up a little inside information from the sports desk."

Hetty looked to me. "Are you…"

"I would have happily invited you both to dinner, but clearly you have a deadline." And something better to do, I didn't say.

"I do."

"Then we shall expect you two for dinner on another night."

"I'll look forward to it, Miss Ella," Alteiss said.

I saw them out, smiling to myself at the prospect of providing the lovebirds with an entirely appropriate evening activity. Much easier said than done, considering Hetty's parents behaved as if their adult professional daughter were a wayward teenager in need of chaperonage.

Not unexpected, even in our new century, but quite maddening for the couple.

They would have been a very positive addition to our table that night, considering the events of the day. In the event, dinner was a depressingly quiet affair. Tommy and Cabot took off together for an evening reading session at a different Bridgewater Library, leaving Gil, Jamie, and me.

After such a trying day, I decided in favor of a hot bath and a tray upstairs, leaving Gil and Jamie to enjoy a father-and-son evening. Good for them to have time together—and excellent for me not to have to sit opposite Gil, studying him and wondering what on earth he'd been thinking.

A few hours later, I was warm, relaxed, and smelling of tuberose bath salts, curled up in bed with a book and a little bowl of meringue kisses, an extra treat Miss O'Hanlon had added to my simple plate of bread, cheese, and fruit. The book was one of Miss Austen's delightful novels, a perfect escape from a day of drama and danger. I was quite absorbed in the misadventures of our Regency heroines when Gil knocked on the door and walked inside.

I moved to put a marker in my book, and Gil winced.

"Are you going to throw it at me?"

"By rights, I should."

"I do not disagree." He leaned on the door, giving me a sheepish expression better suited to Jamie than a grown man. "I did not do well by you today."

"No, you did not." I put the book aside. "I'm assuming there was a good reason."

"There was."

I waited.

"I spoke with Aldrick yesterday, and he made a comment about the way I treat you as an equal. Asked if I told you everything...and suggested it might not be wise in these particular circumstances."

"Ah. And the other fellow?"

"Just a functionary from the Consulate, but an unpleasant one. And his

127

presence reminded me of what Aldrick had said."

"I see."

"I cannot bear the thought of endangering you."

I took a breath. "So…"

"I am attempting to protect you."

"By treating me dismissively."

"By treating you as an ordinary wife. That way, anyone who might be observing my behavior will assume you have no knowledge of my activities."

"Just shielding the little woman."

"No one would describe you as a little woman, Shane."

I glared. "Add *that* to your account."

"I mean, *mo chridhe*, that no one would dismiss you." He walked over to the bed and took my hand. "I'm simply trying to protect you. I don't know any better way."

"Is this your plan for the future? To treat me like an angel in the house when we're in public?"

A sheepish shrug. "At least for the moment?"

He laced fingers with mine.

I growled.

"Surely we can have a private understanding that I must play a role for now. And perhaps you can even play along a bit, if it's all in the interest of a good cause?"

"You mean your mission?"

"No. Your safety. There is no better cause, in my opinion."

His concern was so sincere I could hardly argue.

"Oh, all right. I'll try to tolerate it."

"And try to show no public interest in my efforts?"

"I shall be terribly absorbed in my Met run," I assured him. "Entirely unable to spare a thought for my husband's activities outside of my…sphere."

Gil winced slightly, taking the last word as the slap intended. "I deserved that."

"You did, *mes epinards*."

The nickname made him smile as always. And he knew what it meant.

128

"Would your hair ever need a brushing?"

The Northern accent and phrasing told me my Highlander was still in there somewhere, even if he was playing the role of a hidebound British Peer. I took the ribbon out of my braid. "I suspect it might…"

Chapter Twenty: Sisters and Others

The old wives would have us believe that everything looks better in the morning.

This new wife had her doubts the day after Mr. Duquesne's unfortunate collapse.

While it was a near-perfect autumn morning, one of those sunny, clear blue days where it seems nothing untoward can happen, most of our world did not seem to have taken notice.

Hetty's story was above the fold, with a large headline: *Captain of Industry Collapses at Dedication*, and of course focused mainly on Mr. Duquesne, who had at least still been among the living at press time. My interview was relegated to the "women's page," though there was a note directing readers to it at the bottom of Hetty's article.

I didn't really mind.

If nothing else, Gil would not have to worry about anyone confusing me for an equal partner, since my praise of him had ended up buried amongst the fall fashions.

What I minded was the distinct and disturbing feeling that there were other shoes left to drop, on any number of fronts, from Gil's search for the truth about Prince Albert and Bertha Ten Broeck, to the blackmail plot around Alice LaJoy—and who knew what else.

I decided to try for a productive morning, heading upstairs to the studio, opening a window, and taking a good vocalization session with Montezuma. The parrot happily sang along and then sat on the piano watching me as I ran through a few simple movement exercises.

I was enjoying the breeze and the feeling of gently stretching my muscles when a voice cut through the quiet.

"I don't suppose you're in a fencing mood."

' Gil was standing in the doorway with a shy smile.

"I'm always in a fencing mood," I assured him, turning for the cabinet where I keep the foils.

"I am sorry about last night, Shane."

"Over and done," I said, handing him a foil. "You're trying to protect me."

"Trying too hard, perhaps," he admitted.

"Well, don't let it happen again." I tapped my foil on his. *"En garde."*

We fought to a draw, as we often do, and the pleasure of the match might well have led to other pleasures (we are newlyweds, after all!) had Sophia not knocked on the door.

"Miss?"

"Yes."

"Madame Marie wonders if she might come over for tea and a chat. Says she's visiting her booking agent and…"

Living in Brooklyn, Marie was in the habit of telephoning before leaving the house if she hoped to drop by, since the travel time was just about enough, for Miss O'Hanlon to brew tea or coffee and set out cookies while Rosa got me into a suitable dress.

"Of course," I told Sophia. "Please tell Miss O'Hanlon so she can prepare."

"Right, miss." Sophia dashed off.

Gil took the foil from my hand, managing to work in a little caress on my wrist and a rueful smile. "Give my best to Madame Marie. I have an engagement."

Even for Gil, the curt description was unusual. But I knew it was part of his protection campaign. Not that I was happy about it.

"I shall."

"I'll be home in time for our dinner engagement."

"I'd expect nothing less." I gave him a warm smile.

By the time Marie arrived, I was neatly turned out in a lovely aubergine shadow-stripe day dress with a harmonizing cutwork embroidery collar and cuffs. She and I are close enough friends not to need to show off for one another…but we both enjoy a good outfit, and we often wear things just for the shared pleasure.

Today was no exception. Marie had on a smoky-blue cashmere coat with swansdown trim, and a matching dress with a wide, steel-buckled ribbon belt. The turnout was a sign she was feeling better.

After our greeting, embrace, and a few words about the denouement of the dedication, we spent a very happy few minutes admiring each other's sartorial splendor. I exclaimed over the beauty of the swansdown, and she complimented the workmanship of my collar and cuffs.

Then, the pouring of coffee and passing of treats.

And finally, only once all our regular formalities were covered, did we get down to the more serious matters at hand.

"So, have you learned anything?" she asked.

"We went to see Alice. She's quite nice," I said.

"I agree. If I didn't know, I would think she was any other lady. Certainly not a sporting house owner…or—"

"Exactly. She seems like a truly decent person, trying to run her business, such as it is, as ethically as one might."

"Just so. She's made a life for herself. Not a conventional one, and admittedly, one that would horrify many women just like us. But it seems like she's found a way to manage." A small furrow at Marie's brow emphasized the extent of her concern.

"And she should not fall victim to a blackmailer, any more than Paul should."

"Precisely. Do we have any indication who is behind this?"

"So far, nothing. Everyone we've spoken to in Five Points agrees the raid was oddly timed, and Alice said she paid her protection money in full, on time, as usual."

Marie shook her head. "We are discussing police corruption as if it were any other bill to be paid."

"And it's a simple fact of life in that world."

"I know. It just—"

"Wrong. Yes. But unfortunately, we cannot right all the wrongs of the world."

"I know." Marie's mouth took a rueful twist. "We right the ones we can and try to do better in the future."

"Has there been a blackmail approach?" I asked.

"No. And it's driving me mad."

"I don't blame you. How is Paul?"

"Working late and wandering around the house like a bad dog when he's home. He thinks he brought all of this down on us by standing by Alice." She ran her finger over the edge of her cup. "There's nothing I can say to convince him; I don't blame him. It's his narrow-minded family and the world we live in, not him."

"True," I said. "I suppose Alice could have lived as a maiden lady in some modest home in the city if her family hadn't completely cast her out."

"Well, exactly. But she had only that little bit of money from the grandparents—and thank God she did. Otherwise…"

"Far worse." I nodded. "It's tragic that the family prefers a dead brother to a living sister."

Marie took a breath, let it out slowly. "I would like to think that if one of my boys told me he had this—problem, we'd find a better solution than this. I cannot imagine casting out a child."

"Neither can I…and I don't even have one. Yet."

She held my gaze over her cup.

"I am taking Dr. Silver's advice and not thinking too much about it."

"Smart girl. Just let things happen."

"Easy for you to say with a full nursery."

Marie put down her cup. "It took Paul and me a year. Once, I was really, really sure…and then it wasn't. I cried for a week."

"Oh, honey. I didn't know. I'm sorry."

"Of course you didn't. Once the children are here, the struggles to get them tend to recede. But just about everyone has some kind of cross to bear here."

"I guess."

Sophia walked in just then, actually managing to move at a relatively slow pace. "Miss Hetty."

"To be continued," Marie said, lifting her cup to me.

"Thanks."

"Well, looky here, not one but two divas." Hetty held out her hands to Marie, and the two embraced.

"Good to see you, Hetty," Marie said.

"And you." She joined Marie on the settee. "Look, you need to know right now, I know about the police raid, and it's not a story I'd ever have anything to do with."

"Oh." Marie managed only the one stunned syllable.

"It's none of my business what happened, but it would never be a *Beacon* story." She patted Marie's arm. "And whatever the truth of the matter is-"

"Thank you," Marie cut in. "Thank you so much, Hetty."

"Of course. I'm telling you honestly, it's not the kind of thing we'd ever print. And if the yellow papers do anything, everyone knows what they are anyhow."

"That's true, at least."

"Anyway," Hetty said as she sat. "I have news."

We all sat, Marie and I looking eagerly to Hetty.

"Grover Duquesne is going to survive. He's awake."

"Awake?" I asked.

"Yes. Very confused but awake."

"Amazing," said Marie. "Your story suggested he was in grave condition."

"He was." Hetty grabbed a cookie as I filled one of the extra cups my very prepared Miss O'Hanlon always included. She took the cup and continued: "Police are said to be taking a very hard look at this. I was too far away to see what happened when he collapsed...but a few people who were closer thought they saw signs of strychnine."

"Maybe more than a few," I said.

"The Barrister?" Hetty asked.

"Well, his son first. Jamie's studying criminology, you know."

"And his father's allowing him?" Marie asked.

134

"You've met Jamie. I don't think anyone *allows* him to do anything."

"True," said Marie. "He seems to be a very determined fellow."

"He is," I assured her.

"Like his pater," Hetty allowed herself a small smile as she reached for another cookie. "I suspect you two will have to keep an eye on him."

"We do," I admitted.

"I did not know they taught criminology in New York," Marie said.

"He is studying with a professor at NYU. I suspect he could get just as good an education with someone in London."

"He might," Hetty said, finishing her first cookie and reaching for another. "There are a number of very good criminologists there."

"But his father isn't in London very often," Marie said. "I imagine that's the deciding factor."

"It is." I joined their smiles. "It's wonderful to see."

"He wasn't so wonderful last night," Hetty said. "That comment about your sphere?"

I should have known Hetty would not let it go.

"Oh, yes, sphere." Marie misses less. "I read that. That seemed-"

"Even worse than it sounds," Hetty said as I stared in surprise. "He was talking about her like she was some little angel in the house."

I sighed. "It was bad, but not-"

"Oh, it was," Hetty said with a scowl. "I thought it through again this morning, when I was reading my piece. I couldn't help remembering just how dreadful it was. And I was honestly furious on your behalf."

"It does seem out of character for the Barrister," Marie offered.

Hetty met my gaze with a sharp glare. "Perhaps he's one of those men who change once they have a woman under their control."

"He is not." I assured my defenders, "He's simply over-protective at the moment because of everything that's going on."

"He'd better not be scared by his woman's success," Hetty growled.

"He's not," I assured her. "I promise he's not. He just gets—stupid—at times."

"Well, that is undeniably a masculine failing." Marie reached for another cookie, then pulled back. "But *he's* always been so good until now. What's changed?"

I could not tell either of them everything that had changed, of course. I shook my head. "Well, you should know," I turned to Marie. "Is it some kind of marriage thing? Or some kind of—hope—thing?"

"What kind of —" she began, then broke off as the realization dawned. "Oh, that sort of hope."

"Right. Is he treating me as if I'm already in a delicate condition because it's possible I could be at some point soon?"

"It's a man," Hetty said with a thundercloud face that made me worry for Rowan. "Anything's possible."

"Well," Marie contemplated. "I do think there's something to this. Paul has always been solicitous of me, but he practically wrapped me in cottonwool when the first one was on the way."

"Ugh," Hetty said. "If that's what marriage and family do to perfectly good men, I don't think I want anything to do with it."

Marie and I exchanged glances.

"Oh, stop. Both of you. I suppose she told you Rowan came after me last night."

"I did not, in fact," I said. I took a cookie. "But clearly, he will follow you to the ends of the earth."

Hetty blushed. "Returning to the topic of the Duke."

"I think we've addressed him quite adequately," I said. "Marie's insight gives me the answer I needed."

"Good." Marie shot me a little smile.

"And we have far more important matters to discuss right now," Hetty said.

We waited.

"Well, who would want to harm Grover Duquesne, of course."

Marie and I nodded.

"You'd have had motive a year ago, Ells," Marie said.

"So would any number of other singers," I reminded her.

"Dancers, actresses, and the occasional restaurant hostess," Hetty added.

"But he's definitely backed off Ella."

"He has," I said.

"Any indication as to why?" Marie asked.

"My guess is the marriage and everything that's led up to it." I took a sip of tea, then continued: "He seemed to completely change his behavior toward me after the theatre fire, which of course coincided with the public announcement of the engagement."

"Makes sense," Hetty said. "You're now the wife of a powerful man, and he doesn't want you holding grudges."

"I suppose." I shrugged.

"In any case, you're absolutely right," Marie said. "It could very easily be a jealous or protective man tied to any of the women he's insulted."

"And that's not a short list." Hetty shook her head. "And then there's business dealings. He's said to be pretty fair—but drives a hard bargain. So it could be a money matter, too."

"It *could* be anything," I said, taking a sip of my coffee.

"Or nothing," Hetty said.

We stared at her.

"Well, it was a pretty mixed-up scene at the tea table. He might have gotten a cup meant for someone else."

I shook my head. "Please, no. If that's the case, it could have been meant for anyone in that room…and we'll never figure it out."

"Well, anyhow, please do keep your ears open and your guard up, ladies," Hetty said.

Marie grinned. "When do we not?"

Chapter Twenty-One: A Visit with the Rileys

We had a wonderful treat that evening: dinner with Cousin Andrew the Detective and his wife Katie. She had just started her first school year teaching a primary class at a private school on the West Side, and they were settling into married life in a nice but not fancy apartment near Andrew's precinct house.

The private school was one of the few that allowed married women teachers, and Andrew had found the job for her before he proposed, to show the college-educated Katie he would not stand in the way of her work. Between the excitement of a new job, and the joy of a new marriage, Katie was absolutely glowing.

Not, I hasten to add, glowing for any other reason.

While the expectations of the Rileys' two Irish families were, if anything, more obtrusive and annoying than those of Gil's and my clans, these newlyweds were in no hurry to welcome a little stranger. Katie wanted at least a year at her school, Andrew was working for a promotion, and both were hoping to save up a bit of money to make the happy event more comfortable.

So far, their plan was unfolding as hoped. If the delay in a baby was more than hope, it was none of our business—and more to the point, none of their priest's business. Father Michael is wise enough not to ask questions, he does not want answered. But there are others of his calling who see matters differently.

In any case, they were happy and proud to welcome Tommy, Father Michael, and me that evening. The small size of their apartment prohibited large dinner parties, which was perfectly fine, since Gil and Jamie had taken off for some kind of crime discussion with Hetty's swain Rowan Alteiss.

Probably better that way. No matter how unpretentious and ordinary the Saint Aubyn men are—and they truly are—poor Katie would still have been uncomfortably aware she was hosting two titled aristocrats in her small apartment.

Not fair to her.

Small the Riley home might be, but it was welcoming, cozy, and prettily decorated with Katie's eye for detail. It was clear she'd envisioned it as a haven from Andrew's difficult and dangerous world, not because she aspired to be an "Angel in the House," but because she loves her man and enjoys taking care of him.

A very important distinction, and one I completely support.

Dinner was simple and delicious, roasted chicken, potato gratin, and vegetables properly and gently cooked, showing Katie had far more sense than many young brides who blindly follow the books. With, of course, bread from Katie's family bakery. Not to mention a cake for dessert befitting the baker's daughter.

The evening was warm and wonderful, a return to the comfortable world we had known before a British peer and a Knickerbocker upset all apple carts. We lingered long at the table, happily listening to adorable tales of Katie's students and less sweet ones of Andrew's stupid criminals.

"...and he walked right into the shop wearing the watch he stole two weeks ago!" Cousin Andrew's big finish brought the house down.

Katie topped up coffee cups, beaming the same way I did when I poured at my home. I exchanged a smile with her. "I love doing that, too."

Shy shrug. "It's such a small thing, and yet such a big one."

"I know."

"My sisters are the same way," Father Michael offered. "If I didn't think one of you would throw coffee at me, I'd say women have a special need to rule in their nests."

Katie and I glared.

"Heller's a secret homebody," Tommy added. "If she didn't have all kinds of social obligations, she'd stay in the parlor and fuss over all of us."

The redheaded detective looked at me. "You and your husband don't have much to do with the Consulate, do you?"

"We've been there for tea, and he has a few friends there," I replied, returning the gaze with appropriate suspicion. "Why?"

"One of the officials died in a fall there a few weeks ago. Always hard to investigate in those places, and my pal just had a really bad feeling. But he couldn't do anything about it."

"Not with that crew," Tommy said.

Father Michael scowled. "We all know about the British Crown."

"We do," I took a breath. It wasn't fair to leave it there. "But it's also fair to say their representatives are not necessarily terrible people."

"They stand for any number of terrible things," Father Michael reminded me.

"They do. But all Britons aren't bad."

"No one's saying they are, Heller," Tommy said. "And we aren't talking about your husband. We're talking about Consulate officials, who are specifically charged with carrying out the wishes of the Crown."

"True," I said. "And those wishes are often terrible, if you are not from the privileged class."

"I'd guess class was part of my friend's problem," Cousin Andrew said with a rueful grin. "Damon O'Donaghy still has a trace of his Ma's County Kerry accent."

"The Consulate officials heard his name and voice, and hackles went up," I agreed.

"And unless he's a very unusual Irish man, when their hackles went up, so too did his." Tommy took a sip of his coffee. "I'm sorry, Andrew, but I doubt very much you'll ever find out what happened."

"True," the detective said. "It's a shame. And too bad for Damon, because everyone's under the magnifying glass right now."

"How so?" Father Michael asked.

140

"One of the Assistant Commissioners is trying to make his reputation with crime-solving and public morals. And leaving a mysterious death at a prominent place is not in line with his plans."

"I'd guess not," I said.

"Wait—you mean that Maitland fellow?" Tommy asked. "Pudgy, sanctimonious, always jawing about the decline in the city's moral fiber."

Cousin Andrew grimaced. "You've met him."

"Showed up at one of Cabot's library reading groups last week. Spent a good half-hour yapping about masculine purity and staying away from cesspits." My cousin allowed himself a grim chuckle. "Cabot and I were bringing some new books and caught the end of it. One of the fellows asked me if he was telling them not to train for the plumbing trade."

Everyone at the table laughed.

"Well," Father Michael began, "There's no doubt a great deal of sin is in the city. But I'd argue that the biggest sins right now are allowing people to starve and sleep on the street. Once everyone's fed and safe, we can start worrying about the other things."

"Ah, but that will make it a better place," Cousin Andrew said, "not advance Assistant Commissioner Maitland's career."

"Which is the true point of the exercise." Tommy shook his head. "Seems like a nasty sort."

"He is." A scowl. "And he's going to be trouble for the Department."

"Think so?" Tommy asked.

"Look at it this way, Tom. If we're raiding what he calls cesspits…" the detective broke off and coughed, taking a nervous glance at his wife. An Irish man, no matter how modern, would never openly discuss a sporting house in front of his wife. "Raids take us away from other things we could be doing. Protecting people who actually need it."

"Not to mention sending you into danger for no good reason." Katie's definite tone left no doubt she knew exactly what he was talking about. She shot me a glance, Irish women have probably exchanged for centuries.

Our men protecting us. Whether we need it or not.

Not worth arguing. But nothing wrong with changing topic.

141

"So," I said, raising a perennial problem for the newly married, "have you decided whose family you'll go to for the holidays?"

Katie put her head in her hands.

Her husband whistled under his breath. "Why don't we just talk about the cake?"

Chapter Twenty-Two: An Invitation from Great-Aunt Cecily

Walking alone into Great-Aunt Cecily's home the next afternoon was a bit intimidating. It was probably my first solo social event outside my immediate family circle as a duchess, and certainly my first time sitting down with a society woman as an equal in her own home. Just a note: those who suggest a peeress outranks a Knickerbocker aristocrat have never met the latter!

A blank-faced footman opened the door and motioned me into the drawing room, and again, I was flatly amazed at the incredible treasures just casually displayed on the shelves. Not to mention the tea set—more of that breathtakingly thin, impossibly old china.

Great-Aunt Cecily was on the settee, elegantly arrayed in a lovely deep blue cashmere gown frothed with antique lace. Draped around her neck was an elegant long pearl strand, likely at least as old and precious as the Tallach ones, and she was wearing a large sapphire ring that I had not noticed before.

Was she trying to intimidate me? Or simply parallel me, because she had to know I would be wearing the Tallach pearls and my lilac diamond? From her warm smile, I had reason to hope for the latter.

She clapped her hands when she saw me. "Aren't you looking just lovely."

"Thank you. Yourself as well. That's the perfect shade of blue for you."

"I'm blessed with a good dressmaker—as I see you are, too." An approving nod to my lilac-and-gray shadow stripe day gown, chosen to set off both my complexion and the pearls.

"Did you choose your trousseau for the pearls?" she asked with a smile, gently touching her own strand. "I swear I did not marry Alexander for these, but it was not a disappointment that he came with them."

"Actually, I didn't even know about the Tallach pearls until weeks after we married." I laughed. It was a rather amusing story, and I gave Great-Aunt Cecily the short version: Gil and I, and his mother, spent a few weeks at his family seat in the North of England toward the end of the summer. The Dowager Countess was a great one for long walks on the heath, which were lovely, but a bit exhausting after a while. Late one afternoon, she'd called me aside, and I'd been terrified we were going for our third walk of the day. Instead, she guided me to the library and a hidden safe, and happily presented me with the pearls, urging me to wear them for dinner—and apologizing for not handing them over before.

My hostess gave a musical laugh. "So instead of yet another trudge across the moors, you got those lovely jewels. You're right, that is quite a tale."

"Please understand, I was quite happy to grab my walking stick and follow the Countess the next morning. She has truly become like a second mother to me."

"Of course." Great-Aunt Cecily motioned to the chair by the settee. "Please do sit. I like people to be comfortable in my home."

"Thank you." I sat, and carefully arranged myself.

"How do you take your tea?"

"Black, if you don't mind." No need to tell her I associated the taste of sweet tea with the day of my mother's death; my teacher had found me with the body, and taken me to school, where she and the other teachers brought me cup after cup, just loaded with sugar, because it was all they could do. That February morning was my first taste of sweet since a few stray bits of Christmas candy.

"Of course." She caught something from me but was too polite to acknowledge it. "You know, I do have lovely fresh lemon slices today, and they go well with this particular orange pekoe."

"That would be lovely indeed," I agreed. "I do enjoy lemon, but I don't like to ask, since everyone doesn't have it."

"Dear, you're a duchess now. If you like lemon in your tea, then you may absolutely insist upon it."

She poured the tea, then picked up a pair of delicate silver tongs and expertly floated a perfect lemon slice in the cup.

"I suppose so." I took the cup and inhaled the marvelous, complex scent of fine tea and tart, slightly floral, lemon.

"May I tell you one of my favorite little stories?"

"Of course."

"I heard it first from that dreadful Mrs. Astor, and it involves those awful British royals, but it makes a useful point, so indulge me."

I waited.

"The tale goes that Queen Victoria and Empress Eugenie were at the opera during an Imperial visit." She took a sip of her own tea—which was also garnished with a lemon slice. "The national anthems had been played, and it was time for everyone to sit. Empress Eugenie, born an aristocrat but not a royal, looked back to see if the chair was there. The Queen sat right down, knowing it would be—or else."

"Oh."

"Now, as I've said, I don't hold much with the British. We broke away from them for a reason, after all. But the idea that you are so confident the chair will be there you simply sit down without troubling to look—it's a very good thought."

"It is," I agreed.

"So you, my dear, need to start assuming the chair is there. You say calmly that you like lemon in your tea. You walk into any room as if you belong there, and they're grateful to have you. When someone says 'Your Grace,' you believe they mean you."

I remembered how I'd looked behind myself when Great-Aunt Cecily addressed me so. "You caught that."

"I did." She smiled. "I had a bit of a row to hoe when I married Alexander."

The agricultural expression caught me off guard. Cabot had described his great-aunt as a Knickerbocker matriarch, which led me to believe she'd been from the same social circle as the family. "How's that?"

"Of course, my dear nephew would never tell you, but I grew up on my family's farm upstate. Back then, even in good families, children were free labor. I picked peas, sewed sheets, and hoed weeds until Mama's cousin invited her to bring me and my sister to New York 'to meet some other young people.'"

"Matchmaking?"

"Precisely. As it turned out, innocent farm girls of good family were quite a commodity. I probably could have married the governor's son, but when I met Alexander, it was all over. Not only was he the best dancer I'd ever met, we'd read the same books...and of course, there was that smile."

"The smile always helps, doesn't it?"

"Indeed, it does. You would have married your Duke if he were the handyman, wouldn't you?"

"I would."

"I would have married Alexander if he'd been a simple yeoman farmer." A rueful smile. "At any rate, it was quite an adjustment for me. We were from a very good family, and had some very nice things, not that we were showy about it. And of course, I knew how to behave." A sip of tea. "Still, I often felt shy and awkward. Eventually, you must remind yourself that you are every bit as good as anyone else in that room. And that the chair will be there."

"It will, won't it?"

"Well, either it will, or the person who's just made the Queen fall on her bottom will be looking for work." She gave a naughty laugh. "So keep it in mind."

"I will."

"Good girl." She nodded to the tray. "My cook has made a nice little batch of *speculoos* cookies. Have you ever had these?"

"No—I've heard about them, but no. Our cook makes delicious snickerdoodles, in addition to her good Scots shortbread. Perhaps you'll have them at our house one day?"

"I would be delighted. I'll look to my calendar." She grinned. "Now try these. I used to take any kind of house or yard work to get Mama to give me an extra one."

When I tasted the cookie, rich with butter and spice, I entirely understood. "Delicious."

Great-Aunt Cecily took one and bit into it with relish. "When I no longer enjoy one of these, it will be time to pray for God to take me back to Him."

"Lord willing, a long time from now."

"Indeed." She took a sip of her tea and contemplated for a moment. "It is a much different world these days."

"It must seem so," I offered neutrally. Being in the middle of a production, I really should not have another *speculoos*.

"Not always for the worse, though," she said. "Old people always say the world is going to hell, and things were much better when we were younger. That's not true in everything, you know."

"I do." I nodded. "In many ways, it's a better and freer world than it was forty or fifty years ago."

I didn't know whether this was just the musings of a matriarch, or some kind of deliberate message, but there had to be at least a chance of some insight on Bertha Ten Broeck. Even if not directly, perhaps I could glean some useful direction for Gil.

"Freer for sure. Alexander and I sent money to the abolitionists for years, and his family's old house was a stop on the Underground Railroad."

I blinked at her.

"Just what decent people do, child." She smiled. "I bet you and yours know a bit about this. If there's a wrong, we do what we can to fix it."

"We've never been tested to that extent, but we certainly try to do good." I nodded. "But you must be very proud of the lives you saved."

"It's not to be proud of, dear. It's to know you did what you could. It was a different time. We knew there was a great evil, and we were called on to fight it." A sigh, a sip of tea. "It's hardly the same thing, but I do send the occasional check to the suffragettes. I'm not sure the vote will cure everything, but it certainly won't hurt."

"Please tell that to my husband," I said with a dry chuckle. "The man was willing to sign a marriage contract guaranteeing me full rights over my property and person—but he still believes women should not vote."

"Men are the funniest creatures."

"Isn't that the truth. Even the best of them have odd quirks."

"They do. Alexander was similar—had a protective streak that showed up at the strangest moments." She smiled, clearly reflecting on her long-gone spouse. "But we were blessed. At that time, there was no guarantee that one would be able to marry for love."

"Even then?" I was a bit surprised. She would probably have married sometime in the 1840s, the height of the Romantic era.

"Parents, of course, wanted their children to be happy, so they provided a circle of suitable matches, hoping lightning would strike in an appropriate place."

"As it did for you."

"Yes. Good luck for us—and very sensible on the part of our parents. We did the same thing when it was our turn, of course. And our children were lucky, too." Another sip of tea, and again, the contemplative expression.

Probably thinking about her late son. I hoped the happy memories gave her some comfort.

"The Ten Broecks, though, weren't as lucky."

"No?"

"Poor Bertha got into that whole mess when the Prince came to town."

"You said she danced with him, too."

"Yes. I was actually surprised it was allowed." She scowled. "And more than danced, I suspect. She was good friends with the Vandergrift girl, and I think they ran about after him on his tour."

"How? Weren't girls closely supervised?"

Great-Aunt Cecily snorted. "*My* daughter was. The Vandergrift girl was the youngest, and the parents were too old to notice much. And Lavinia's son was ill that year."

"Oh, no."

"Poor woman has suffered a great deal. At least the boy recovered—it was a bad riding accident, and an infection in his leg—I think he was still in sickbed when the Prince came to town. That's the whole reason Bertha came to the ball instead of Lavinia."

"So Lavinia wasn't really watching her daughter, either."

"Not at all. And of course it was not my place to meddle." A breath, a twist to her mouth, and then she picked up another cookie. "But I doubt very much that Lavinia had any idea what her daughter was up to—or where she was. I think they were both running wild and chasing the Prince."

"The Colonel showed us a few letters that suggested Bertha had a crush," I offered cautiously.

"I'm sure. For weeks before the visit—and of course once he was in town, all the girls were royalty-mad. Fortunately, my girl was already engaged, and the only thing she was in love with was her trousseau."

"Really?"

"Heavens, yes. Philly Vandergrift and Bertha Ten Broeck got bored with shopping and cataloguing and such, and started dashing off on their own, a few weeks before the visit.

"And then when the Prince came to town..."

"Oh, they trailed him like camp followers." She took a nibble of her cookie and sighed. "You know, that really is not a fair way to put it."

"No?"

"No. They were just excited little girls, chasing around hoping to grab a bit of stardust. It was dangerous, I suppose, but they didn't have any bad intentions."

"Just girlish fun?" I asked.

"Exactly." She contemplated for a moment. "And really, considering what happened to Bertha, it was probably some consolation to her parents."

"What..."

"Went up to White Plains to help her brother and his wife with a new baby a few months later—and then died. I don't know exactly what happened. Lavinia was just crushed, and no wonder. She'd just seen her son through that horrible accident, and then she lost a daughter. It's not that we all didn't lose children, you know. Back then, there were all kinds of terrible illnesses."

Like the consumption that had killed my mother, I thought. I nodded.

"But by the time you're ready to marry them off, you think they'll bury you, not the other way round." Great-Aunt Cecily put down her cup. "Something broke inside Lavinia that year, and I don't think it's ever healed."

"It wouldn't, would it?"

"No." She took a deep, careful breath. "I miss my son every day, you know. I live for my daughter and grandchildren, and of course, Cabot…but my heart is in the grave."

In the overwrought prose of a romance novel, the words would have been excessive and faintly ridiculous. In Great-Aunt Cecily's matter-of-fact tone, they were a devastating statement of fact.

"I'm sorry," I said, gingerly reaching over to pat her hand. I wasn't sure it was appropriate for someone of her standing, but I've never been comfortable allowing anyone to suffer without trying to help.

She took my hand and squeezed it for a moment. "Thank you, dear. It's a terrible thing, to bury a child. I pray you'll never know how terrible."

I nodded. Nothing I could say—especially since I was offering precisely the same prayer.

After a moment, she took a breath, straightened up, and met my gaze with a bit of her sparkle returning. "Cabot is not here to tell me to back off, so I am going to ask. Do you and your Duke have expectations?"

"Not yet, but we have hopes." It seemed a diplomatic reply.

She gave a small, musical laugh. "A very graceful answer. I will pray for you."

"Thank you."

"And when you are blessed, expect something special for the little stranger."

"Oh, thank you."

"Well, one of the great benefits of being an old bird is being able to play fairy godmother." The wonderful, wicked grin. "And so I shall."

"I hope you shall soon have cause to do so."

"Well, since you're not performing tonight, why don't I pour you another cup of tea and tell you about the first time Alexander took me to the opera?"

"That would be delightful…"

Chapter Twenty-Three: A Fine Performance...And After

Friday night passed without drama, and with an unexpected delight: dinner *à deux* for Gil and me. Everyone else had their own interesting plans: Jamie's mentor had invited him to dinner at home, and Tommy and Cabot were up at the Bridgewater mansion, quite possibly to give us some privacy...or to have a bit of quiet themselves. In any case, Gil and I lit Shabbat candles, enjoyed a simple and delicious dinner of his favorite shepherd's pie, and sent Rosa and Miss O'Hanlon home early before adjourning to our room.

Enough to say a good night was had by all.

Most of the cast reassembled at a late breakfast at Washington Square, all of us enjoying the treat of family time before the busy performance weekend ahead. When it was time to head for the Opera, I was rested and ready.

At that exact moment, it would have been terribly easy to forget all the dark and dangerous matters swirling around us. But, I knew from grim experience what a terrible mistake it would be. Like losing track of the blade in a knife fight.

That said, I did still have a show to do. Two of them.

While it may seem I spent no time whatsoever performing that autumn, thanks to the Met's far less arduous schedule, when I actually did take the stage, it mattered far more. In many ways.

For close to a decade, Tommy and I had resisted various overtures from the Met, because of the limitations and demands the premier company placed on its artists. Now, though, with my new family life to consider, it was a perfect fit. Just as it was for Marie, though her particular gift for the Queen of the Night gave her value—and freedom—in a way I would never have.

Not that I envied her, I hasten to add. I know how lucky I am, and I'm quite happy with my own talents.

Besides, a gifted trouser role specialist is also an unusual and valued performer. Any number of mezzos and some sopranos can hit the notes in the major roles. But only a very rare singer can also meet the other requirements, including fencing skills and physical presentation. My mentor, Madame Lentini, had started my training when I was a tomboyish teenager, and all these things were second nature to me now.

The fraught pleasure of the stage was second nature, too.

From the first time I stepped in front of Madame Lentini's friends in her drawing room, I'd known I enjoyed performing. Loved vaulting out of my drab tenement life into the bright new world, going from being just one more child in a crowded home to the center of attention. Becoming a fanciful character in a story instead of merely another disposable poor kid.

I was too young and too desperate to have any fear of the audience. Honestly, it wasn't until years later that I even thought about the possibility: one morning when I was out for a velocipede ride with Hetty, and she asked me if I ever had stage fright. I almost wrecked my cycle because the thought was so stunning. Fear, like most other things in my early life, was for people who could afford it.

Before going onstage, I always felt a little tug in my stomach, but it wasn't stage fright or nerves, as people describe it. No, I just wanted to do it right. At first, to make Madame Lentini proud. Later, because my name is on it.

At the Met, though, I'll admit a little awe mixed in with the usual respect for the work. Stepping out onto that renowned stage, before an audience filled with the most important people in the world (just ask them!) was a touch intimidating, even for an old hand like me. Fortunately, I was playing a role uniquely suited to my gifts, surrounded by an excellent cast, and all the luxuries a Met production could offer.

Before I made my first entrance that night, I ran a hand over my deep-purple silk velvet robe. Literally cocooned in luxury.

My diamond ring was in Gil's waistcoat pocket. He was in the Diamond Horseshoe tonight, very unusually for him, hoping to gather more insight on the Prince's visit. By now, forty years after the fact, most of the Met's patrons are either too old, or too nouveau riche, to be of use. But he might find a stray patriarch with a long memory, and so, it was worth the effort.

I prefer having him backstage. When Gil is in the audience, I'm often aware of his gaze and wonder what he thinks of my work—and me. Even now, with our deep bond and successful transition from acquaintances to courting couple, to husband and wife.

At any rate, before the show, I'd peeped out to see where he was, so I could avoid looking at him, and seen him talking to a familiar older gentleman in the row behind him. Colonel Vandergrift was in attendance, but would never come backstage, having informed us ages ago that his mother raised him not to lurk about young ladies' private accommodations. I wished the rest of society shared his mother's views. In any case, I knew I could expect—and enjoy—a full report on the conversation later.

As soon as the opening bars of the overture began, however, I was a working artist.

The star of the show.

Performers will tell you the work carries its own weight. Once you're onstage and into the show, it is the only thing that matters, shaping notes, hitting marks, taking and giving cues. Nothing like it.

Even better, this was a good night.

Most audience members probably can't tell the difference between a decent night and a very good one. Even observant and regular patrons generally don't know what it's actually like to be on stage, and the way it's possible to either feel like you're flying gloriously from peak to peak...or struggling to get off the ground. Only when it's a very bad night and the struggle shows—or an extraordinarily good one, and the audience is flying with us, do they notice.

This wasn't quite one of those extraordinary nights, but it was certainly very good.

By the time my last big aria came up, I was confident enough to allow my eyes to stray to the Diamond Horseshoe. Even from the Met's huge stage, I just barely recognized Gil's tall form.

And the way he was sitting, transfixed.

Absolutely frozen in admiration.

It mattered far more than it probably should have.

I knew, because we'd discussed it any number of times, that he was aware I tried not to look at him while performing, and probably believed I couldn't see him from the stage anyway. So this reaction was honest.

Heartwarming.

Despite his explanations and very good reasons, the "her sphere" nonsense had hurt. Had made me doubt his respect for my work, just a tiny bit.

Not the time for this.

I pushed Gil and his expression to the back of my mind, to bask in it later.

After the show, basking was pretty much the last thing on my mind, with the usual procession of society folk, though my status as a married woman generally and duchess specifically did seem to knock down the worst of the stage-door johnnying.

The stream of visitors was winding down when a whirlwind blew through the door.

"Clear out! You've gotten your chance to see her...now it's time for family!"

Gil and I exchanged glances, then looked to Tommy.

"She said she wanted to come tonight, and we always make room for family."

"We do," I said.

I had just a moment, because Aunt Ellen first grabbed Tommy and gave him a big hug.

"Well, son of mine, when are you and your friend coming by for dinner again?" she asked.

"Soon, Mama."

"Good. He's a very nice fellow for one of those society people. And the girls loved the books he brought."

"What books?" I asked.

154

"And hello to you, too," she said with a sniff. "Too fancy to hug your auntie?"

"Of course not." I crossed to her and enjoyed a generous embrace.

When she released me, Aunt Ellen turned to Gil.

He hesitated for a moment, and so did she, as was their habit. And then, it was the same warm hug as the rest of us got.

"So," I asked. "The books?"

"Most improving ones," Aunt Ellen said with a smile. "Abigail Adams—did you know she suggested John should try to get women the vote?"

"I did," I said. "It would have saved a lot of trouble."

"He was no more interested than any other man, respect her though he did." Aunt Ellen shook her head. "The other one was about Dolley Madison. Did you know she was a Quaker originally?"

"Yes," Tommy said. "No surprise that didn't last."

Aunt Ellen's eyes, the same blue-green changeable shade as the rest of the family, narrowed. "Don't be disrespectful to our First Lady."

"I just meant those bright turbans, Mama." Tommy wilted a little. No matter how full-grown or accomplished a man, when his mother reproves him, it hits home.

"Anyhow," I said, pouring oil on the troubled waters, "it's so good to see you. Did you bring the girls?"

"Of course not at night. Mr. Hanrahan from the parish was kind enough to accompany me."

"Mr. Hanrahan?" Tommy asked.

"Don't you get any ideas, young man. No one will ever take your Da's place."

Tommy and I stared.

The simple fact that Aunt Ellen felt the need to make the declaration was suspicious.

"Poor man's been keeping to himself for years since his wife died of consumption, and I needed a chaperone, so I thought it might kill two birds with one stone."

"Fair enough, Ma," Tommy said.

All three of us nodded as if it were entirely normal for Aunt Ellen to go out at night with a man. Which it most certainly was not.

"Whatever you're thinking, stop it." She glared at us. "I had to come out tonight to give you a warning."

"Warning?" I asked.

This was not going to be good.

Aunt Ellen firmly believes she has the Second Sight. What she actually has is a family who tolerates her occasional fancies…and a certain amount of luck in predicting things. I firmly believe that is all.

Yes, she has occasionally had visions that came true in unexpected ways. But no, I do not think there is some supernatural explanation. Science is, after all, constantly discovering simple explanations for things that used to seem miraculous.

Aunt Ellen, though, never sought us out with happy visions.

"Yes, a warning." She scowled at us. "I know you don't really believe, but you know I've been right more than once."

"We do," Gil said. As the son of a Highland Scotswoman, he was at least as familiar with unnatural determination as Tommy and me.

"So there." She took a breath. "This isn't anything terrible—like that fire I saw last winter."

Tommy, Gil, and I all tensed. The madman who tried to kill Gil and stabbed me instead had burned down a theatre in the attempt.

"It's not like that," she repeated.

"All right," I said, pulling my hand away from my waist, where I'd unintentionally rested my fingers on the knife scar. Gil and Tommy moved closer to me, protectively.

"So what is it, Ma?" Tommy asked, his tone unexpectedly gentle.

"Just a little picture I can't get out of my mind. You two—" She pointed to Gil and me. "Sitting in a carriage looking unhappy."

"Unhappy."

"Unhappy," she repeated. "So I just wanted to come and make sure everything is all right with you two."

I smiled. Gil chuckled. Tommy grinned.

"That's all?" Tommy asked.

"That's all." She shrugged. "I needed to be in the same room with you two to see you're doing all right."

"We are," I said.

"Absolutely." Gil took my hand.

Tommy chuckled. "They actually are, Ma."

"Anything I should know?" she asked, glancing down at my waist. She'd taken my touching the scar as a different kind of sign.

"Nothing," I assured her. "But Dr. Silver says everything is fine and I should just let nature do its work."

"You should spend less time talking to your doctor and more time-"

"Ma, maybe I should get you and Mr. Hanrahan into a cab." Tommy took his mother's arm and shot me a glance.

I would have owed him a favor for sparing me, if I hadn't known he wanted to get a look at Mr. Hanrahan. And at Mr. Hanrahan and his mother together.

"Home, Shane?" Gil asked.

"Indeed."

I moved to duck behind my changing screen, but he grabbed my hand. "I did not get a chance to tell you. You were amazing tonight."

"It was a good show."

He squeezed my hand. "It was a wonderful show. And you are incredibly talented. In any sphere."

"I love you, *mes epinards.*"

Chapter Twenty-Four: Cookies for Cousin Rafe

That Sunday, I admit I was derelict in my obligations to God and man, by sleeping into the midday instead of going to Mass. Tommy went to the late Mass and made my excuses to Father Michael, who certainly understood and forgave my very rare absence. I can't speak to the good father's Boss, but I have reason to hope He also gives a tired performer the occasional indulgence. If not, well we'll just add it to my account in Purgatory.

When I finally awakened, I slipped into a simple violet silk crepe tea-gown, planning to spend the day relaxing on my chaise to restore my strength for the show. Downstairs, however, I walked right into an extraordinary scene. Actually, not an extraordinary scene in any house where Rafe Coyne is a visitor.

My cousin was ensconced in the parlor, with the tea tray and a wider selection of treats than we'd offered the society matrons, with my entire household staff surrounding him as if he were an exotic potentate. Nothing but the usual when Rafe is around: Sophia enjoys looking at him, Rosa likes his colorful stories of his wealthy employers...and Miss O'Hanlon, of course, is the true object of his affections—and he of hers.

Rafe, though, is one of those men who is utterly irresistible to women...and utterly oblivious to this fact. He thinks he's merely having friendly and polite conversations, when the ladies—of all ages and classes—are drawn like bees to a flower patch. It's not looks, though Rafe is tall and presentable enough, with dark hair and the same greenish blue eyes as most of the family. But then he smiles, and the angels sing.

Thus far, Miss O'Hanlon does not seem to mind the effect her man has on other women. Not surprising, since it's abundantly clear he only has eyes for her. When I walked into the room, Rafe was finishing a story of a society matron who'd asked him to knock down a wall to create a larger dining room...and did not care that the wall was holding up the second floor.

"...so I said, I think the ceiling falling in might ruin the dinner party."

The girls laughed, and so did I.

"Hello, Rafe."

"Ellen! I dropped by to see you, but..."

"You were a bit distracted," I said, as Sophia pulled a dust cloth out of her waistband and dashed toward the drawing room, and Rosa pulled a bit of embroidery out of her apron pocket and slipped out behind her.

"I was. I'm sorry. I know the girls have work to do." Rafe's sheepish expression would have melted a far harder heart than mine. Miss O'Hanlon sent him a sweet glance as she picked up a couple of empty plates, then turned to me.

"Sorry, miss."

"No apology necessary from either of you," I said firmly. "I'm quite sure no one's work suffered because of a short break for treats."

"I should check the roast," Mary said. "Thank you, miss."

I smiled. "Of course."

After the door closed behind her, Rafe turned to me. "I don't mean to upset the applecart, Ellen, but I just couldn't resist stopping by to see her."

"It's quite all right. Just tell me you're also running a proper courtship."

"What do you mean?"

"I know you've been taking her walking out on her half-day, but don't you think it's time for a little more?"

"More?" Rafe asked, his brow furrowing in concern. "Am I doing it wrong?"

"No, no." I held out the nearest plate of cookies, some of Mary's tasty snickerdoodles. "You're behaving perfectly."

He took a cookie. I topped up his cup, and started pouring my own.

"Then what?" Rafe asked.

"It's all right to try for a bit more. Take her to the matinee. Perhaps even a dance."

"A dance." His face softened. "I would love to dance with her."

"So maybe you take her to a wedding. There's always a cousin's wedding if you look."

"Isn't that the truth." Rafe's eyes met mine, terrified. "But if I take her to a wedding, everyone will think she's my girl."

"Isn't she?"

"Well, I want her to be, for sure, but…"

"Have you told her that?"

Rafe's amiable face flooded bright pink. "No…I don't want to give her the wrong idea. I won't finish my accounting course until-"

"You may be giving her the wrong idea now. You haven't suggested anything beyond walking, or made any reference to your future hopes, have you?"

"I don't want to scare her."

"If anyone's scared, it's you."

He laughed. "Probably so. But she told me a little about what happened at the Waverly Place Hotel, and I don't want her thinking I'm that kind of man."

"Dear cousin of mine, no one with a working mind could mistake you for that kind of man." I raised my teacup to him. "Miss O'Hanlon is in no hurry to wed, but you might do well to let her know your intentions are honorable. Perhaps even have a word with her aunt."

"I had to pass muster the first time I took her walking."

"Good. Just let the aunt see you a bit more. You could even ask if Aunt MaryKat could save her a spot at dinner after Mass."

"No! I'm trying not to scare her away."

"Good point." His mother my aunt MaryKat's cooking was only slightly less terrifying than her piety. Let's just say she put her faith in boiling and the Rosary, and Sunday dinner was an endurance test on both counts. "You're right. I would avoid that particular family scene as long as possible. Perhaps you can arrange a meeting in more soothing circumstances."

"That would be smart." Rafe drank a little coffee. "So what you're telling me is…"

"Let her know you're serious. Don't push, but don't let her wonder about you."

"I can't propose for almost a year."

"So? You can buy tickets to a matinee now."

"Good thought."

"There's nothing wrong with moving slowly, Rafe. But you have to move."

"I understand." He took another cookie. "Thanks, Ellen."

"Of course."

"I didn't come here to see Mary, though."

"Really?" I asked.

"Really." He reached in his satchel. "Here. I saw Miss Hetty's article on the Ella Shane Music Collection, and I thought this would be good."

He held out a small book. The cover was deep green Morocco, so old it was almost black, embossed in a language I didn't read. For a moment, I had to stare at it, and then I understood. Irish Gaelic.

Carefully, gently, I took the volume.

"It's a hymnal from one of the convents. My mother's aunt gave it to her when she married and emigrated, so she could bring the sacred Irish music with her to a new land."

"It's amazing." I held it gingerly, awed by the realization of the generations of people who must have used this for worship.

A sheepish shrug. "Your fancy library folk may not want our Irish songs, but it's important sacred music. Some of the songs go back to the medieval days."

"I know. And we'll accept with thanks. One of the great things about having a collection named for you is that you can add anything you want to it."

Rafe smiled. "Good."

"I appreciate it."

"That must have been quite a scene at the dedication."

"It was. And we invited you-"

"No, no, Ellen. I'm not offended. I wouldn't have come to your fancy thing anyway." He chuckled. "But Miss Hetty wrote a very nice account."

"Apparently, I am now an important and interesting women's story." I shook my head at Rafe's puzzled expression. "It's how Hetty's editor describes her work. And rather maddening."

"All of the fancy folk came out, though."

"A lot of them did. I was surprised."

"Even the old Ten Broeck lady."

"Yes. She's apparently close to Cabot's Great-Aunt Cecily."

"She's also a bit odd."

"Really?" I asked.

He squirmed. "It's that whole weird widow thing."

"What..."

"You know, where they try to make time stop at the moment the husband died. The house has to be maintained exactly as it was, things have to be repaired into the precise configuration they were, all of that."

"I've heard of it," I said. "I've known a few society matrons who do sort of freeze in time. But I thought only Queen Victoria actively tried to stop time."

"No," Rafe shook his head. "More people than you think do this. And it's always weird. But the Ten Broeck lady is weirder."

"Weirder how?"

"It's not her husband, I think it's a lost child, but she doesn't give any details to riff-raff like me."

"That's not-"

"It's exactly how it is, Ellen, and very soon I won't care." He reached for another cookie and thought better of it. "She's had me over any number of times to repair little things that fall apart—curtain rods rusted out, a cracked window, worn-down floorboard in front of a door. Most of the repairs were in that room, which looked like it belonged to a girl."

"She did lose a daughter," I said.

"Well, if it was the girl's room, she's trying to keep every scrap of her life intact. Once she had me put new bristles in a brush, and then thread the hair from the old one back into it."

"That's a bit much."

"It's a lot much..." He trailed off, and his face took on a reflective cast. "She never said so, but I'm sure it was her little girl. And if I'd had a child and lost her..."

"Unthinkable."

We were both silent for a few moments, thinking of Lavinia's terrible loss.

"Probably more so for you, now." A faint gleam in his eyes and the start of a teasing tone in his voice. "Especially now, hey?"

"Rafe! I've no news for Aunt MaryKat, and you're not going to worm it out of me."

"That's fine. You know my mother. She'll ask me if I asked, so I had to."

"I know." I sighed. "And I'll blame her for this, not you."

Rafe gave me the grin. "Good. Will you tell her to stop nagging me to go to the early Mass?"

"I'm not that brave."

Chapter Twenty-Five: Blood on the Stage Floor

S unday night found me back on stage, enjoying the routine of a working artist again.

When we'd been touring heavily, I'd done seven or eight shows a week, including a two-performance matinee day, for months on end. We'd followed, an only slightly easier schedule during the New York and London runs of *The Princes in the Tower*, adding a few extra dark days so Marie could spend time with her children.

With that experience, the Met run was actually far too slow. It was an immense relief to have two performance nights in a row. I practically bounded backstage, excited to return to work with the triumph of the previous night fresh in my mind.

Every show is different, and you learn from each one. But with a long gap between performances, it's too easy to miss ways to improve.

So this night, all of the little subtleties and changes I'd noticed in the previous performance were easy to remember, leading to an even better show. Most of the people in the audience would never know what we did—they'd just think it was an extraordinary performance.

Which it was, from start to finish.

It was one of those nights that reminded me of my true calling, that rare moment when you know you are exactly where you should be, doing exactly what you're meant to do—at the absolute best of your ability. Since I met Gil, I've had a similar feeling when I'm with him, but it's not the same, and one does not replace the other.

When I have a show like this, I wonder if other people feel this way when they're doing what they're meant to do. I don't think it's just the thrill of being on stage. It's more the deep certainty of being exactly where I belong, giving the world exactly what it needs from me.

The applause is only a part of it.

I made sure to enjoy every note and bar of the performance. It's always wonderful, being onstage, but sometimes it feels so good you don't want to leave. This was one of those nights. I soaked it up as we gave our final encore, and bravas and bouquets flew at us. The young soprano ingenue was generously showered with praise and floral tribute, and finally, it was my turn.

If I ever get tired of the diva's final bow, it will be time to close my piano and put away my sword. As I've said, acclaim is not the reason we do this...but anyone who tells you it doesn't feel good to be applauded and celebrated is lying through their damned teeth.

That night, I scooped up my flowers and headed for the dressing room, a couple of large bouquets under my arm, and a few more bunches of roses in my hand. Surprisingly, not red ones. Red roses are the standard offering for the diva, and I do not fancy them, after seeing so many in the hands of stage-door johnnies with the worst of intentions.

For this run at the Met, though, the red-rose bouquets had been almost uniformly replaced with yellow, white, and pink. I wasn't sure if it was my new status as a married woman, presumably off-limits to the johnnies, or if someone at the Met had put out the word about my preference. Either way, it was a pleasant surprise.

Back in the dressing room, Tommy, Jamie, and Rosa were waiting.

"Was it as much fun as it looked?" Jamie asked.

"It was." I grinned back.

"Everyone was in really wonderful form tonight." Tommy beamed too—Jamie's enthusiasm is infectious.

"We were," I agreed, as Rosa removed my headdress. I left on the velvet robe, mainly because of a certain married-lady modesty—but also because it was beautiful and felt so good to touch.

I put the bouquets down on my vanity and turned to Jamie, waving a hand. "So, how do you like backstage life?"

His face went pale. "Belle Starr…"

"What?"

Tommy's eyes followed Jamie's horrified gaze, and so did mine.

The palm of my left hand was bloody.

"Oh, it's probably just a thorn," I said lightly, reaching for one of the little towels I kept for wiping off cold cream.

"Looks pretty messy for a thorn," Tommy said. "Wrap it up while I go find the medical kit."

"Toms-"

"You were carrying the flowers, right?" Jamie asked, looking at the two bouquets I'd dropped on the vanity. He pulled a pencil out of his pocket and poked around at them. "Hm."

"What?"

"Remember, I went to a boys' school, with lots of nasty little fellows who were always on the lookout for an unkind joke."

He said it coolly, but my heart went out to him as I had a sudden picture of a small redheaded boy still mourning his mother. Probably an easy target for the bullies.

"All right," I said, tightening the cloth around my hand. It did hurt a bit.

"I've seen a trick with a bouquet," he continued, poking at the ribbon binding a particularly nice sheaf of large candy-colored roses. Gingerly, he ran a finger down a few stems. "Not a thorn, Belle Starr."

"Well, perhaps the other one."

"I don't think so." He picked up the bouquet, careful not to touch the bow, and moved it back and forth a bit. "See?"

"What's that?"

"A bit of broken glass, probably a piece of a glass or bottle, tied into the bow. Somebody did that to me after a school chorale. It's quite diabolical—you're actually lucky to come away with one ugly cut."

As the door slammed open, I nodded to him. "Kindly tell it to your da."

"What's happened?" Gil asked as he stomped in, trailed by Tommy with the medical kit. "Who attacked you?"

"Pater," Jamie began. "It's bad, but not that bad."

"James, any attempt on my wife is *that* bad by definition."

Later, I would wonder why he immediately defined it as an attempt on me. At the time, I was more interested in tamping down his overreaction, and honestly, bandaging up my hand before it became more than an annoyance.

"Toms, please bring over the kit. I may need a bit of help bandaging it up."

"I'll take care of this." Gil grabbed the box, and Tommy put his hands up, shaking his head. He knew as well as I did there was no point arguing.

"While you're patching me up," I said calmly, "why don't you allow Jamie to explain what it looks like?"

"Excellent idea." Gil set the box down and loomed over me for a moment, then tossed a single syllable over his shoulder: "Speak."

"Thanks kindly, Pater." Jamie shot me a sympathetic glance. I realized he'd probably been on the receiving end of one of Gil's overprotective displays at some point. Likely more than once, as the baby of the family.

"Someone tied a piece of broken glass in the bow of the bouquet, so Belle Starr would cut her hand."

"Save the bouquet, James. It's evidence."

"I'm well aware of that, Pater. I'm studying criminology, if you don't recall."

Gil sighed, and our Imperial Lord High Protector bent just a bit. "I'm aware."

"Perhaps you can just dab a bit of iodine on it and wrap me up so I can meet my guests?" I suggested.

"Guests?" Gil turned his ire on me. "You are actually going to entertain guests after an attack on your person?"

"Some fool slashed my hand. It's unpleasant, but not incapacitating." I glared right back. "This is the Met. There are people expecting to greet the leading lady."

"Not when she's injured."

"It is a cut on the hand. And these are the Four Hundred."

"Never mind the Four Hundred. You are the Duchess of Leith."

"At the moment," I said irritably, nodding to the medical kit, "I am still bleeding into a towel."

"Oh, terribly sorry."

The tops of his cheekbones went light pink, as they do when he's embarrassed. It's actually rather adorable, most of the time.

By the time my hand was painted with iodine and wrapped in gauze, the guests had begun to knock. And Gil had realized we would do better to have any potential enemies where we could keep an eye on them, so he agreed to allow the people who'd already arrived to come in for a brief talk.

We left the bouquet out on the vanity, turned so the glass did not show, hoping to see our visitors' reactions.

A useless endeavor, as it turned out. While there had no doubt been regular patrons in the Diamond Horseshoe, a Russian Grand Duke was in town, and he and his entourage completely overwhelmed the backstage area. They inspected the flies and lights, prowled among the ingenues and chorus girls, and just generally disrupted everything. I spent what seemed an incredible amount of time attempting to keep up with a very fast and loud French conversation before the Grand Duke and his minions gave up and decided their prospects were better with the ingenues.

"Did you understand anything they said?" Gil asked as Rosa handed me my coat.

He and Jamie both speak French, but they don't sing in it regularly, so my skills are a bit better. Not that much better, though.

"Only enough to know they were very impressed by the show, and wondered if they might buy the entire chorus."

"Did they mean..." Tommy asked.

Jamie blushed.

"Nothing like that," I assured them. "They want to take them back for the St. Petersburg Opera. All of them. I told them to talk to the conductor."

"That will be a fascinating conversation," Gil said.

"And good luck to them," I said, reaching for my bouquets.

"No, Belle Starr." Jamie scooped up the flowers, including the sabotaged one, which now had one of his handkerchiefs tied around the glass. "We'll keep these, just in case."

"Fair enough."

I suspected it was going to end up in the bottom of a drawer somewhere, because I had a hard time imagining how he'd match it to anyone...but who knew?

At the end of a very long night, I honestly didn't have the energy to wonder.

Chapter Twenty-Six: A Quiet Day at Home

"Shane, sweetheart?"

I opened one eye to see a fully-dressed Gil silhouetted by the morning light in the window. He was in a neat day suit, settling his tie into place. Clearly, he was not planning to spend his Monday recovering from the performance.

"What..." I muttered, putting a hand down to raise myself, wincing at the pain from last night's cut, and lying back on the pillows.

"I'm sorry, *mo chridhe*. I have to go to White Plains to look for Bertha Ten Broeck's records."

"Records?"

"At the very least, the town should have a death certificate for her. It's a relatively short trip by train now. Forty years ago, it was an upstate town where one might go to start a new life."

I nodded, as my mind awakened and I began to follow his logic. "Or to hide one."

"Precisely. Deaths—and births—are registered. And there might be more from the coroner."

"Definitely worth a day on the train."

He bent and kissed me. "And for you, a restful day on the chaise."

I sighed. "I would fight you, but I'm too tired. No promises when I wake."

"You may promise, or not promise." Wicked little smile. "I have delegated a very capable surrogate to keep an eye on you today, and he will not fail in his mission."

"Oh, no."

"Oh, yes. Rosa is also doing her part. She has strict orders to dress you in a tea-gown so you can't leave."

"I can entertain friends, I assume?"

"I am not walling you up in a tower, sweetheart." His tone was petulant, hurt. "I'm only trying to make sure you take a bit of time to rest and heal. Surely that is not unreasonable."

"No," I sighed. "I'm going back to sleep."

"A wonderful idea. I will see you at dinner." He bent down for a more comprehensive farewell embrace. "Sweet dreams."

"Well, they will be now, *mes epinards*."

A warm, shared smile. I slipped back under the covers, and Gil smoothed the counterpane over me. My last thought before I fell back to sleep was how nice it is to have a loving husband.

Several hours later, my thoughts were far less rosy.

By midday, I was awake and swathed in another of my favorite tea-gowns, sweet lilac crepe de chine with a generous froth of lace at the neck and cuffs. As ordered (admittedly, Gil would call it a request), I was on the chaise, with a delightfully lurid Gothic novel on my lap, and a rose china teapot and cup set on the side table.

Miss O'Hanlon had apparently also been briefed on my semi-invalid status because the pot was filled with mint tea generously laced with honey, my usual remedy for vocal strain. She had offered a light breakfast when I wandered downstairs well after eleven, but understood completely when I simply asked for tea at my chaise.

Unless I missed my guess, she was probably relieved. On the coffee table, several plates that had once borne various baked goods were cleaned down to crumbs, and an empty cup sat beside the silver pot. We did not have an invasion of locusts, but merely one hungry nineteen-year-old, now lounging on the settee, properly fed and reading a thick scientific tome.

"Good morning, Belle Starr!" Jamie crowed, beaming up at me. "How is the hand?"

"Sore but all right. I see you've had breakfast."

"Oh, that was hours ago. This was a snack."

"Of course it was. Are you spending the day with me?"

"Pater asked if I had class today, and since I don't, I was happy to study here. Especially now I know Miss O'Hanlon is baking."

Probably baking in self-defense.

"Well, you're quite welcome. Is Tommy about?"

"He was meeting Mr. Bridgewater to buy books. At least that's what I heard. They seem to go out buying books more than anyone I've ever seen."

"Not for themselves, Jamie," I said gently, "for the Bridgewater Libraries and poor children."

"Oh. Well, that makes sense." He picked up his coffee cup, gave it a hangdog expression, and continued. "How does it work?"

"Well, this time of year, they buy a lot of books, so teachers can send students home with their very own." I smiled at Jamie. "Libraries are wonderful, but there is something magical about the first time you actually have a book of your own. Madame Lentini gave me mine, and I've never forgotten how I held it and stared at it. I could hardly read it—I could not believe it actually belonged to me."

Jamie was staring at me. "I didn't know."

"Know what?"

"Know how poor you were. Pater never told me—I mean, I thought you lived with your Aunt Ellen over on…"

"That's the house Tommy and I bought for her when we started making money. We grew up in the tenements. My late mother and I lived in a single room, survived on piecework." Suddenly, I felt a chill, and my hands began to shake. I took a breath. "I won't belabor you with the details."

Just about the last thing I wanted to do was have an upset in my stepson's presence. On very rare occasions, usually when I am very cold or otherwise distressed, I find myself back in the tenement room with my mother's body. I was eight when she died of consumption on a February night, and I awakened cold and alone. If not for Aunt Ellen, I would have gone to the orphanage and probably followed my mother to Potter's Field soon after.

"She died there?" Jamie asked.

"She did." I took another breath. Poured myself more of that good, hot, black tea.

Jamie put his book down and sat up. "You know my mother barred us from her sickroom at the last."

"I do." I took a sip of the tea let it warm me. I was not the only bereaved child here. "She likely saved you from the Russian flu."

"I know." His voice was thick, his eyes full. "But I never got to…"

He dashed a hand to his eyes as he broke off.

I reached for his other hand. "I'm sorry, Jamie. If there's one thing I know about mothers, it's that she knew you loved her. And that she loved you—and still does."

"That's what the vicar says." He took a ragged breath, patted my hand, and released it. Still very much a boy who doesn't want to embarrass himself by accepting affection. "But he's such a stick it's hard to believe him."

"Even a stopped clock is right twice a day," I reminded him.

He managed a small smile. "Thanks, Belle Starr."

"Glad to." I drank more of my tea. The shaking and cold were subsiding. Perhaps the best way to avoid an upset, was to help someone else. "Now, you and I are apparently spending the day together. Whatever shall we do?"

"I suppose Pater will be furious if you give me a fencing lesson."

"Well, I do need to vocalize and do a few basic exercises to stay in trim. A bit of practice with you would do no harm."

Jamie grinned. "So…"

"Meet me in the studio in ten minutes. Now, we must be back down here by early teatime—without a sign that we've left."

"Naturally. I won't melt the butter."

"The expression is 'butter won't melt in my mouth.'"

"Ah. That makes much more sense." He laughed. "You can school me on slang, too."

"One thing at a time, my dear."

My stepson is not a particularly good fencer, but he is improving slowly but surely as we practice together. On this day, since I was tired and my hand sore, even if it was not my sword hand, I spent more time instructing than actually fencing. That was quite all right, because Jamie needed plenty of guidance.

Fencing practice with Jamie is far different than sparring with Gil. The young man can barely keep up with me, and of course, it lacks the fillip of excitement Gil and I enjoy. Still, it's definitely fun, much the way I used to love chasing my young cousins around when I watched them for Aunt Ellen.

Perhaps I will make an acceptable mother after all.

We resumed our places in the parlor just in time, with a rather substantial afternoon tea provided by Miss O'Hanlon. I was back in my tea gown, nibbling a scone, when the door opened.

I expected Tommy, Cabot, or both, since it was too early for Gil, but instead, Sophia announced Marie. An elegant, but very troubled Marie, in a neat cornflower blue wool suit, topped by a plain navy coat and hat, an umbrella in her gloved hand.

"What a treat!" I exclaimed as I rose, before I noted the furrow at her brow and tightness of her mouth. "Oh, dear."

"Oh, dear indeed." Marie looked to Jamie. "Would you terribly mind leaving us? This is a delicate womanly matter."

Jamie's eyes widened. "Womanly?"

"Yes," Marie sighed. "I really need to speak with Ella, and I simply cannot discuss these matters with a man in the room. I'm so sorry."

Jamie blushed to the roots of his hair. "Of course, I'll go. I'll see how Miss O'Hanlon is doing on dinner."

"A wonderful idea." For me. I doubted Miss O'Hanlon really wanted to see our eager, hungry puppy sniffing around her cookery. But he was so kind and sweet he would make himself tolerable—and Marie definitely needed a private chat with me.

I poured Marie a cup of my tea as she took the settee and smoothed her skirt.

"All right, so what's really going on? Poor Jamie probably thinks you're about to have kittens on the rug."

"I'm rather a mess, if not that kind of mess," she said, taking a small, calming

174

sip. "It looks like we've gotten the blackmail demand."

"It looks like it?" I echoed her odd phrasing. "Surely you'd know."

"Well, how else would you take it if the Assistant Police Commissioner let it be known that he wants to come to dinner at our house tomorrow?"

"He's got something to say to Paul that can't be said at the courthouse...and he wants to menace you a bit."

"Meaning..."

"It probably *is* the blackmail demand." I drank a bit of my own tea. "You're right. Have a scone."

"I could not eat if my life depended on it."

"Well, in the larger sense, it does." I pushed the plate of thin ginger wafers toward her. "Ginger is good for settling the stomach."

She took one. "Perhaps."

While she took a grudging nibble, I returned to our topic. "So, you're expecting something to happen tomorrow night?"

"I am. I don't know what Paul is expecting. I think he's so busy feeling terrible that he got us into this mess, he can't figure out much."

"You are probably right."

"So what now? We obviously have to host the Assistant Commissioner...."

"You do. But you don't have to do it alone. I am not performing tomorrow night, so if you would like some moral support..."

"And a Barrister?"

"Yes, but probably not the Champ. Tommy is too well known in Five Points for that to be safe."

"Likely true. The Barrister will probably be enough."

"He certainly thinks so."

Marie joined me in a rueful chuckle. Then took a larger bite of the ginger cookie. "Thank you, Ells."

"Of course. We've survived worse together—and will again."

"Probably true." She held my gaze. Remembering, as I did, the night when Paul had reached the crisis with scarlet fever, and we sat in the spare bedroom waiting and praying together. Not to mention a long list of other, less desperate scrapes. "We will survive this, won't we?"

"Indeed, we shall. Now let me top off that cup, and let's bring Jamie back in here. He's probably hiding in the foyer in absolute terror."

"We can't do that to the poor sweet boy."

"He is a sweet boy," I said.

Marie's eyes sharpened on me. "You are not picking out a suitable young lady for him, are you?"

"He's nineteen. He should not be thinking of suitable young ladies for at least a few years."

"I don't want my boys thinking about them until they're forty."

We laughed together.

"Jamie!" I called. "The woman talk is over."

I was not surprised to see him bound right back into the room. I was a bit surprised to see him followed by Tommy and Cabot, but not really shocked. They'd been out all day doing good works, after all, and it was quite time for them to return.

"Well, look here. A truly pleasant surprise." Tommy proclaimed. "Good to see you, Marie."

"Mrs. Winslow." Cabot took her outstretched hand. "Lovely as ever."

"Thank you."

"Are you staying for dinner?" Tommy asked.

"Sorry, no. I just came to talk with Ella," she said.

"About something private," Jamie contributed.

Everyone glared at Jamie, and then Tommy shot me a scowl.

"Well, I must get home to supervise my own dinner," Marie said.

"I will see you to a cab," Tommy offered.

I knew she'd bring him up to date, answering at least one of my concerns for the day.

I also had an answer for the rest of my day: serving as the quiet center while the fellows sparred, play-fought, and played games. At least until Gil returned from White Plains.

I knew far worse ways to spend an evening.

Chapter Twenty-Seven: Deep in the Night

One of the best things about marriage is the quiet nighttime conversations in the bedroom. I don't discount the other marital pleasures, for sure, but the simple and wonderful intimacy of honest talk, in the wee hours, is almost enough reason to marry all by itself.

That night, Gil arrived just as we sat down to dinner, and we were in company—admittedly very jovial and beloved company—all evening. It wasn't until we were alone in our bedroom that we had a chance to talk.

"How was White Plains?" I asked, allowing myself an appreciative glance as he undressed. While Gil is old-fashioned in many regards, in sleeping gear, he is quite modern, preferring simple blue cotton broadcloth pajamas to the nightshirts or union suits favored by previous centuries of men.

Sometimes, as now, he took his time buttoning the shirt, allowing me a generous view of his manly chest. I'm sure he's aware I appreciate it. He may even bask a bit in my admiration.

"Well, it was a useful trip." As he walked over to the bed, he took a glance at me. "Too bad your hair is already braided."

"Do you want to brush it?"

"You don't need to get out of bed…"

"It's quite all right," I said, sitting up and reaching for my peignoir. "I've done almost nothing but lie about today. If you want to brush my hair, I can certainly get out of bed for a while."

"I'll make it worth your while."

"Will you, now?" I tied the ribbon of my peignoir and sat down at the vanity.

He followed and loosened the bow on my braid. "I shall do my best to repay the pleasure."

I smiled at him in the mirror. "You never disappoint."

Rueful return smile. "I like to think I make a good effort."

"So, White Plains?" I asked, knowing he was far more interested in talking right now.

"More questions than answers." He gently unbraided my hair, slowly running his fingers through the locks. "You know, I would have married you on the spot that day your hair fell down during our fencing match."

"It wasn't *marrying* me you were thinking about just then."

"No, it was. My intentions have always been honorable." He held my gaze in the mirror, very seriously.

"I know. And unlike many other men would have, you never saw me as the kind of woman one doesn't marry."

"That is an unfortunate social construction." Gil picked up the brush. "I'm not entirely certain there is such a thing as a woman a man does not marry."

My eyes widened.

"As far as I'm concerned, love and marriage go together. And everything that entails. You're aware I had a bit of an adventure before we met, but I loved her, too. Not as I loved May, or you, but…"

"You would have married her if she'd been willing." I did not point out that the lady in question was a Landgravine and would have probably been a more appropriate choice than I.

"Yes." He took another stroke. "Of course, I'm aware of the unfortunates involved in — commerce, if you will, and I know for some men it's a simple physical need, no different than a glass of water. But I also know I am not one of those men."

"It would be a better world if more men were like you, love." I leaned back as he brushed, met his eyes. Even before we married, I was aware that my sensible barrister is a bit of a romantic, but I didn't realize until we started having these late-night conversations just how deeply, perhaps even unrealistically, romantic he is. All manner of alleged experts on the sexes like to pontificate that men are driven by their physical needs and women by their feelings, but Gil definitely prizes the connection of the heart and mind as much as the body.

"The one thing I hope for Charles and Jamie is that they have the good fortune to find a true companion." He toyed with the ends of my hair. "We have gone far afield from White Plains."

"A bit," I agreed.

"Not that far. This whole affair did, after all, begin with two young people in love."

"Or infatuation—or lust."

He began another stroke, met my eyes in the mirror. "You surely do not think a girl would risk her entire future and life for anything less than true love."

"I'm sure she believed it was true love. And, certainly, the flush of infatuation can lead to true love."

"It did for us." Shy smile.

"True indeed." I realized Gil was seeing the Prince's adventure as some sort of tragic first love, perhaps an echo of his marriage to Jamie and Charles' mother, May. Probably best to just let him see it as he would. "And who knows what might have happened between these two young lovers if they'd had the chance."

"Exactly. It's fair to say they were doomed from the start. Whatever premium Her Majesty places on true love—and she was lucky enough to marry for it—the Prince Consort had a definite idea of an appropriate wife for his son."

"And an American girl, even one of the most impeccable Knickerbocker lineage was undoubtedly not it."

"They had probably been combing the *Almanach de Gotha* for German princesses since the Queen was still in confinement." Dry smile as he took another careful stroke. "So this was always a forbidden love."

"Which only adds to the pleasure."

"Of course. Especially for a rather contrary young man. I don't know how much you know about the Prince in his youth…"

"I've heard rumblings. He was quite a caution, wasn't he?"

"Very much so. Hence, the possibility that quite literally anything might have happened."

"Everything we've learned about Bertha suggests she was no delicate flower, either."

He put down the brush. "I suspect that's why it was so sad to see the death record today."

"So there is a death record."

"Yes. She died in July of 1861." He paused, held my gaze. "Of a hemorrhage."

"No other description?"

"I looked for the coroner's records. They don't go back that far. The doctor involved is twenty years dead. The current coroner took suddenly ill a few days ago and is apparently recovering. But the one-word description of death makes one wonder."

"So does the timing. You can't be unaware that it's just about nine months since his visit to New York."

"No." He took a breath, and his voice dropped. "I looked for birth records as well. There were none for her."

"Would there be?" I asked. "A friend of my mother's died in childbed in the tenements, and they took them out together and buried them together. I'm not entirely certain how that would be recorded."

"Especially if the mother were an unmarried girl, and they were trying to preserve her—and her family's — honor." He nodded. "It's a very good point. Particularly since the full report on the girl's death was gone. Only the entry in the record remained."

"I see what you mean about more questions than answers."

"It could simply be the passage of 40 years."

"Or it might not." I nodded. "One cannot help wondering."

"One cannot." Gil took a breath. "There is more. I also looked up the brother and his family.

"And?"

"The sister-in-law had a baby whose birth was registered in early August."

"Meaning either she nursed a dying girl in the final stages of an interesting condition…"

"Or that baby was Bertha's."

"Girl or boy?"

"Girl. Still living in White Plains, married to a respectable factory owner and the mother of five children."

"Perhaps a perfectly happy life."

"And perhaps at least six lives that could now be turned completely topsy-turvy." He put down the brush and handed me the ribbon.

I started braiding my hair. Early on, he had attempted to handle that part of the evening, only to make a complete hash of it. So it was easier for me to do the braiding. "No wonder you're troubled."

Gil turned down the lamp and climbed into bed.

I followed him, leaving the peignoir on the chair and climbing under the covers in my nightgown. The sheets were a bit chilly—it was late September, after all!—but Gil's waiting arms were warm, and I snuggled into him.

"I know less now than I did when I rose this morning," he said, kissing the top of my head.

"And have more questions."

"Precisely."

"There is one good thing, though."

"What's that?"

I turned to face him. "We're here, and together."

His eyes glittered in the moonlight, and he smiled. "I love you, *mo chridhe*."

"I love *you, mes epinards*."

Chapter Twenty-Eight: Trouble on Two Wheels

The next day dawned clear and bright, the sort of autumn day no one who enjoys outdoor pursuits could resist. When I came down after a good night's sleep, I found a message from Hetty and three snickering fellows enjoying coffee and muffins in the parlor.

"Better stay out of the park for a while, gents," Tommy said, raising his cup to me. "Looks like the ladies are taking a spin."

Gil simply chuckled and sipped his coffee.

Jamie put down his muffin—which I'd be willing to guess was at least his second—with a shocked expression. "Belle Star rides?"

"My dear friend—you know Hetty MacNaughten of the *Beacon* — and I enjoy the occasional run around the park on our velocipedes." I sat and poured myself a cup. "How could one resist such a lovely day?"

"Do you have another cycle?" Jamie asked eagerly. "I'd love to go."

"I'm sorry, dear one," I said. "We don't have another velocipede, and more to the point, this is a strictly feminine event."

My stepson blinked, shocked. "What?"

"Ladies' sports are for ladies," Gil said rather stiffly.

Tommy reached for another muffin, smiling to himself.

"My esteemed husband is expressing it in a rather antediluvian fashion, but it is true, Hetty and I prefer to ride without masculine companionship."

Jamie looked hurt, like a little boy who wasn't invited into the playground game.

I patted his arm. "This is a special thing between Hetty and me. But there's no reason you can't get a cycle of your own and join me separately one of these days."

"A capital idea." Jamie beamed. "I'll go shopping for one after class today."

"In the meantime, I only have half an hour to get into sports costume, check my tires, and meet Hetty." I rose, carrying the coffee with me. "I leave you to your pleasure, gentlemen."

I can't speak to the gents' pleasure, but my ride with Hetty was a considerable joy.

We didn't accomplish a great deal in terms of our various concerns, aside from establishing that Grover Duquesne was going to survive, though he would likely not be out in the world anytime soon, and that Assistant Commissioner Maitland was giving every sign of moving ahead on his public morals campaign.

Also, the Assistant Commissioner had accumulated precisely no goodwill among the newspaper folk. Apparently, his strident temperance campaigning stopped at the door to Delmonico's, where he'd been seen partaking of the best of menu and cellar—provided someone else was paying the tab. There's nothing journalists hate more than a hypocrite.

As Hetty and I finished our final spin and wheeled toward the park gate, we drew the usual attention. It's not because of me, but because of the velocipedes. Some people still aren't sure what to make of a woman on wheels, and they stare, or whisper, or glare.

Usually, the glares come from older people, but every once in a while, it's a younger lady who feels she's missing out. We also get the occasional cheer, sometimes from fellows who are probably Jamie's classmates at New York University...and sometimes from older ladies who love the idea of the next generation of women being freer than they were.

In any case, none of it was especially interesting and concerning on a given day. That day, though, I had an odd feeling as we approached the gate, like "eyes on my back," as Aunt Ellen might put it. A look around the path turned up nothing unusual, but just outside the iron fence, I saw movement. A dark, bulky shape, possibly a man in a homburg hat. Too fast and far away to get a good look.

But if a man had been watching me, he'd behave in exactly that fashion.

And if someone was watching me, why?

No good answers there, considering it could be related to my career, my private life, any of Gil's efforts…or someone else entirely.

Or it could be nothing at all.

At the moment, the best strategy was to simply shake it off and keep going. I made my farewells to Hetty, with the promise of another ride soon, and steered my machine toward the townhouse.

On the way inside, I unpinned my hat and turned to find Gil standing there, with a note and a stunned expression.

"What?" I asked. His mother was in Edinburgh. Bad news would come in a telegram-

"Colonel Vandergrift," he said.

"Oh, no. What's happened?"

"He collapsed after having tea with an old friend this morning. Mrs. Muldoon thinks it could be a stroke. She asked Preston, Tom, and me to come over."

"Of course we'll go. Just let me change—"

Gil shook his head. "No, sweetheart. This is for men. If he sees you, he'll assume it's the worst. If it's not the worst, he'll be scandalized by the sight of a woman in his private quarters."

"You are absolutely right."

"Sweeter words never spoken by a wife." He managed a tiny smile. "I am very sorry to hear this. The colonel is an excellent old man, and we shall not see his like again."

"Indeed, we won't."

"But that said, he has had a very good run, and if he is truly making his farewells, we must give him all the comfort he needs."

"True. A good death, as they say."

Gil sighed. "I have a hard time accepting those two words together, but yes."

"Well, you will bring my regards, and who knows, a few baseball stories from Preston, a good argument with Mrs. Muldoon about Tommy's boxing career—and perhaps a brisk legal discussion with you could help."

"Indeed." Gil's tone did not match the words. "Mr. Dare is on his way, and Tom is changing his tie. I'll be back in time to squire you to dinner with the Assistant Police Commissioner."

"Thank you. You will need all your perception for this."

"The Assistant Commissioner is somehow mixed up in the Judge's arrest at the sporting house?"

I nodded. I had told him as little as possible, of course, but it might well be time to bring him further into the case, if only for his observational skills. Though I was quite uncertain how he would handle the issue of Alice LaJoy.

"You believe this is some sort of blackmail scheme?"

"We do. There is a great deal going on here, and a few unusual matters hanging fire."

"Really?" His eye sparkled with interest. "I should love to delve into someone else's intrigue. Especially, if there's a possibility I might do some good."

"Well," I sighed. "If nothing else, you may be able to supply a bit of insight on some of the players."

"Come along, Barrister!" Tommy called from the landing as he straightened the new tie in question. "Preston will be here any second."

Gil planted a quick kiss on my cheek.

"Give my best to the Colonel," I said.

"Hopefully, you'll do it yourself, soon," Tommy replied.

"I will pray for it."

Gil looked back at me. "Would not hurt to light a candle, love."

Chapter Twenty-Nine: With a Green Ribbon

D ressing for a quiet dinner at Marie's, especially one where I did not want to draw attention to myself or my outfit, took only a short time. Once appropriately turned out in lavender, I wandered back downstairs to see who might be about.

No surprise, the gentlemen were still out, whether providing comfort to Colonel Vandergrift in his extremity, or perhaps comforting themselves with a wee dram afterward, who knew? But Jamie was in the parlor, at the small corner desk he'd taken over for his studies.

When I walked in, he beamed and pointed to Bertha's letter.

"I've got it, Belle Starr."

"You do?"

"Absolutely."

I walked over to the desk, as Jamie carefully smoothed out the letter on the blotter and picked up the magnifying glass.

"You see," he said, happily setting up as the professor with a class of one, "there are a number of ways to authenticate a letter."

"No doubt." I leaned in for a better view. "What are we looking for here?"

"Well, first, we determine if the pen, paper, and ink match the time at which the letter is supposed to have been written."

"And?"

"Heavy handmade cotton rag paper, maker's watermark, simple engraved address, exactly what you'd expect."

"Only the best, but not fancy," I said.

"Precisely. Does that fit with the—Knickerbockers?"

I smiled at his stumble. "It does. The Knickerbockers are the old Dutch aristocracy. They'd already been here a while when those scruffy Pilgrims landed at Plymouth Rock."

"I'm rather weak on my American History, I'm afraid."

"Probably not much reason to learn, considering our rather acrimonious separation."

He grinned. "That's mostly forgiven by now, I hope. Not forgotten, though."

"Of course not. But you might think of the Knickerbockers as the equivalent of the very oldest British families: unassailably certain of their importance and bloodline, and so high in the firmament they have no need of airs. So this sort of stationery is exactly right."

"Good, then." Jamie picked up the magnifying glass. "Now, we need to think about the pen and ink. This was clearly written with a quill pen. Which seems a bit old-fashioned, but…"

"Probably right for Bertha. Steel pens were available forty years ago, but not as widely used as they are now."

"Some people still use quills. My great-aunt Caledonia insists nothing is as precise."

"I've met her. I'm not surprised."

The grin flashed back, but he quickly returned to studying the paper. "Now as far as the ink, the color and texture suggests a homemade blend. That seems like a lot of work, even for these folks."

"Perhaps, but some cookery books still have ink recipes."

"Oh, that's just for the people going West in covered wagons, isn't it?"

"Maybe now. But forty years ago, it would have been more common."

"And we're talking about a girl from a family that clung to the old ways."

"Exactly."

"So the ink is good, too." He nodded. "This all fits, then."

"I think so."

"Excellent." Jamie had exactly the same expression his father did when he was parsing a case. "You see, when verifying something, it's not always any one thing. It's the combination of facts, and most importantly, the absence of any false notes."

"Because a fake almost always gives itself away."

"Precisely." He studied the blotter for a moment. "And, Belle Starr, look at this."

He used his pencil to point to the ribbon that had tied the letters.

I reached for it.

Jamie pushed my hand back. "Sorry, no. Better not to touch at all. Even tiny amounts of arsenic can be absorbed through the skin—and Pater will never forgive me if I let you poison yourself."

"Right. Arsenic Green. No one uses it anymore because it's so dangerous."

"Exactly. The ribbon places this in the right time—and not after." He looked at it. "But this is odd."

"What?"

He gently poked at a wrinkle in the ribbon. "See these marks? It looks like the ribbon had been tied one way for a long time...and was then re-tied."

"Recently?"

"I'd say so. See how the old marks are so deep? And how this new bow looks barely wrinkled?"

"You're right. What does that suggest to you?"

"I think someone took a letter out of the bundle and then re-tied it."

I looked at the small stack. "A missing letter."

"It's at least possible. What do you think was in that letter?" Jamie asked.

I met his gaze. "I think we should not speculate on that."

"No?"

"No," I replied firmly. "Let's just wait and tell your father what you found."

"He'll like this, won't he?" Uncertain expression like the little boy he still was in so many ways.

"I'm sure he will. Well done."

"I'm glad to help Pater. I wish he felt he could trust me with why we are looking into a forty-year-old junket."

"It's not that he doesn't trust you." I held his gaze. "It's that he doesn't want to endanger you. He's protective."

"Too protective," Jamie said with a scowl. He folded up the letter and placed it back in the envelope, set it on the pile, then used his handkerchief to move the ribbon on top of it. "I'm going to wash my hands and then go see if perhaps Miss O'Hanlon might have an extra cookie or two. Would you like one?"

I laughed. Couldn't help it. Suddenly, the very serious criminologist was a little boy seeking cookies. "No, I'm quite all right. We're going to Madame Marie's for dinner tonight, and she will murder me if I don't do justice to the meal."

Jamie gave me a rather wistful look. "I'd love to have dinner with the Winslows."

"And they would love to have you. On a happier night." I held his gaze. "This is not a joyous social night."

"It's not?"

"I would tell you the story if it were mine to tell. Suffice to say, we are helping Marie with a matter requiring the utmost discretion. And that I would trust you with it if I could."

Jamie sighed irritably. "I suppose that will have to do."

"It probably will, if I add a plate of Miss O'Hanlon's cookies."

Boyish grin. "You know, Belle Starr, it's entirely possible it will."

Chapter Thirty: Around the Table

Gil and I were both quiet and concentrated on the cab ride, after exchanging just a few sentences. He assured me that Colonel Vandergrift was holding his own, apparently well enough to complain that Mrs. Muldoon and his visitor, Lavinia Ten Broeck, might be the last women he ever saw. For my part, I told him he needed to speak to Jamie about the ribbon, without further explanation. We made a quick agreement to be as unobtrusive as possible without trying for incognito, because that was clearly out of the question, and spent the rest of the trip to Brooklyn alone with our thoughts.

Though he took my hand and laced fingers, the sort of subtle small gesture a husband has every right to make, even in public. Not to mention a direct reminder of the deep and true bond between us.

The moment of warmth and unity was likely the most enjoyable part of the entire evening.

Not for lack of trying on the part of our hostess, I hasten to add.

Marie takes her time in the domestic sphere very seriously and works very hard to be Paul's "Angel in the House" when necessary. Because it gives her great pleasure, I hasten to add, not because some advice author or society at large is ordering her to do so.

An evening at Marie's is never less than convivial and elegant. She carefully chooses her guests, selects a meal, catered whenever possible by Greta Dare, and presides over cultured and clever conversation.

Or at least, that is the ideal.

On this particular evening, the presence of the Assistant Police Commissioner changed the pleasant balance of the night beyond recognition. With the knowledge that the evening was likely to end in a blackmail demand, Marie could not help replacing her comfortable charm with the cut-glass calm of a diva in concert. Paul, though married to a performer, was not one himself, and managed only to radiate a nervous upset entirely at odds with his usual easy confidence. Gil and I were well aware we were the extras, in addition to observers, and we likely read as a bit reserved.

And then there was the Assistant Commissioner.

With thinning dark hair and a Van Dyke beard and mustache probably intended to hide his extra chins, an awkwardly tailored suit in expensive dark wool, finished with a heavy gold pocket-watch and chunky signet ring bearing some religious school insignia, Duncan Maitland was the very picture of a particular sort of New Yorker. The Scots-Irish arrived more than a century after the Knickerbockers, and they very quickly set about putting an end to the party, such as it was.

Duncan Maitland was clearly a proud follower of family tradition. Proud of other, less savory things, too, we quickly learned.

When Gil and I arrived, he was already settled in the drawing room with Marie and Paul, holding forth about policing the "lesser orders." Gil and I, catching that phrase, exchanged glances. I suspected the Assistant Commissioner was going to really enjoy us.

"The Leiths," Marie's maid gave us the very simple announcement, as she would on any quiet night at home.

"Well, isn't this an unexpected pleasure!" exclaimed the functionary, rising with an outstretched hand.

Marie offered smooth introductions, and Gil and I took a seat on the other settee, where we could observe the Assistant Commissioner...and he could observe my dinner dress. Just as I'd done for Colonel Vandergrift's dinner, though for entirely less pleasant reasons, I had chosen a very modest gown, in this case, a grayish lavender silk with a lovely lace overlay. The Assistant Commissioner gave me the distinct impression he was trying to see through the lace. When he was not giving similar attention to Marie's gown, blue-gray with pleated chiffon sleeves and high collar. Much later, Marie and

I would share a good laugh over the fact we'd both gone for grayed-down colors in hopes of drawing less attention.

Right then, his gaze was not especially amusing.

After the introductions, the Assistant Commissioner returned to his ruminations on policing, warming to the topic of the "dirty immigrants in the tenements."

Marie shot me a glance.

I wasn't the one who should cause her concern.

Since my stage name was chosen specifically to carry no echo of my Irish or Jewish forbears, and my official biography makes only brief mention of my early life in "a working family," it was just barely possible the Assistant Commissioner truly had no idea with whom he was speaking.

Equally possible, since Gil was always described by title and our officious official did not strike me as someone with a deep comprehension of British affairs, that he did not understand Gil's status as a border lord and the half-step of independence it implied, or Gil's complicated family history, including a great-uncle who had tried to help his tenants during the Great Hunger.

"...and I bet *you* know, Duke, those Irish are animals."

A muscle flicked in Gil's jaw. If it had not been followed by such an incredibly insulting remark, the Assistant Commissioner's addressing Gil as if his title were his name would have been hilarious. As it was, though, my husband's ice-blue eyes took on a sharply frigid cast, and when he spoke, it was with crystalline Westminster diction.

His Grace had had enough.

"Mr. Assistant Commissioner, I am not in the habit of describing *any* humans made in the image of our Creator in that fashion."

For a long moment, the only sound in the room was the crackle of the fireplace.

Marie's eyes met mine, imploring.

She need not have worried.

Duncan Maitland was so enraptured with himself and his rightness he heard only the words to start a new disquisition.

"Quite right, Duke. We really need more religion. Muscular Christianity, now that's the ticket."

Marie's maid gave us a temporary reprieve by ringing the dinner bell, but as soon as we assembled at the table, to be served with fine little game hens, duchesse potatoes, and an assortment of delightful accoutrements, the Assistant Commissioner returned to his topic.

None of us at the table had any problem with the idea of Christianity in general, of course. Not even me; I follow both my mother's and father's faiths as I can, though I am not unaware that I am technically a Jew as the daughter of a Jewish woman. The problem was the particular variant of Christianity our new acquaintance espoused.

Muscular Christianity is apparently some sort of new-fangled practice among the Protestants. At least I assume it's the Protestants. I had never heard of any such thing from Father Michael, and if it were in currency for Catholics, a priest who enjoyed the occasional boxing match would likely have known and had thoughts on the subject.

As far as I could tell from the Assistant Commissioner's commentary, the idea was that the Lord wants men to be manly and march bravely into the world doing manly things in His name. These manly things apparently include activities like exploring, fighting wars, claiming land, and, of course, putting the lesser orders in their place.

I need not tell you women are the ones most in need of being put in their place. Or that the place in question is the home—or, as described, "the feminine sphere."

By unspoken agreement, everyone at the table who was not the Assistant Commissioner became very interested in the food and restricted our responses to the occasional nod of acknowledgement. No question, the best way to handle this ignorant vitriol cloaked in the language of a perfectly decent religion was to simply let it wash over us...and wash it off later.

It was truly a pity, though, because the dinner was probably delicious.

None of us managed more than a few bites.

Only after the Assistant Commissioner had thoroughly ruined our meal, did he rise for what he assumed would be a masculine redoubt: the infamous brandy and cigars in the parlor. Paul fastened a nervous glance on Gil as he followed the Assistant Commissioner's lead. Gil looked to Marie, then to Maitland.

"Please forgive me, Mr. Assistant Commissioner. My wife and I need to discuss an opera company matter with Mrs. Winslow before I join you."

"Certainly." The Assistant Commissioner offered an oily smile to Marie. "Then, if you will excuse us."

As the pocket door closed, Marie and I muttered in unintentional unison: "There is no excuse for you."

Gil allowed himself a chuckle.

For a long moment, we stared at the door in silence.

"What *is* he?" I finally asked Marie.

"A very particular sort of functionary." She sighed, reached for the wine decanter. "Can I interest you in another drop?"

"I probably should not, but after that dinner..."

She poured. "Precisely. Barrister?"

"Yes, please. I assume I am to stay here while the Assistant Commissioner can make his approach."

"If that is the play," Marie said. "Of course, he didn't give Paul an explicit declaration of intent when he suggested he would like to come for dinner."

"Naturally not," Gil took a sip of the offered wine. "So, shall we discuss plans for the December run in San Francisco?"

"Tommy's booked everything?" Marie asked.

"Yes," I agreed. "At this point, there is no reason not to make the trip."

Everyone at the table understood what was not being said, and everyone also understood it was better for Gil and me to stay busy while we waited for the situation to change.

"I quite agree," Gil said. "I am looking forward to seeing the Paris of the West."

"As am I." Marie smiled and took a sip of her own wine. "It will be a delightful holiday. The children will be out of school, so they will join us."

"And the Countess will be back from Scotland," I added.

"Will Jamie be joining us, too?" Marie asked.

"He will be on school holiday, too, so I would assume he will," Gil said, a proud smile warming his face.

"Then," I said, raising my glass. "This little tour will be a true family affair."

"I'll look forward to it." Marie raised hers and drank.

"Not yet, we won't."

Paul.

His face was gray.

"What happened, darling?" Marie asked, rushing to him. The fact that she used the endearment in company told me just how concerned she was.

"It was indeed the blackmail approach. He said it would be too bad if anyone found out I had an abomination for a sister who was running such a disgraceful business. That it was a good thing only someone as trustworthy as he knew this horrible secret."

Marie patted his arm as Paul took a long, shaky breath.

"And then he told me that he owns me."

"Well, Judge, there he is wrong," Gil said. "That war was already fought and won."

"Not my version of it, sorry, Barrister. What am I going to do?"

"You are going to remain calm. And we are going to find a way to stop this man."

Either of us might have made the reassuring declaration, but in Gil's supremely empowered Westminster tones, it carried the ring of absolute certainty.

We could only hope it was true.

Chapter Thirty-One: Body and Soul

Deep in the night, I woke to find Gil staring at the ceiling.

He was always too kind to wake me, but somehow, I knew when he stirred. Whether it was the sound of the change in his breathing, or some small movement, I could not explain. No matter, I welcomed the late-night conversation.

"Gil?"

"Awake, *mo chridhe?*" A chuckle. "Of course you are."

"So what is troubling you?"

"Any number of things." He took a breath. "Just reflecting upon the last few days. I have the oddest feeling that I am a step behind someone as I investigate. A strange sensation I have never had before."

"Behind someone?"

"It is as if another person is looking into the same matter, but so subtly as to leave few signs."

"Ah." I remembered the fellow who seemed to be watching him at Morrissey's. "Could there be someone else?"

"Perhaps. But they could not be both a man and an adorable little old lady. And I've seen—or heard—of each at various times. Nothing makes sense."

"Troubling." I reached for his hand, and he pulled me in.

"Troubling indeed." He rested his head on top of mine. "You can at least take comfort in knowing your enemy in the blackmail matter."

"Perhaps. I'm still uncertain of any way out of this."

"I'm uncertain of something as well."

"What's that?"

"How is it that a lawyer has a sister who runs a sporting house? Was that the reason the dreadful Assistant Commissioner called her an abomination?"

"Close, but not quite." It was, I knew, time to tell him the whole truth. And to hope he would take it with his usual common sense and kindness.

Though this was quite a thing, even for him.

"Then what?" he asked. "Rhetorical hyperbole? Even a fallen woman does not usually fall so far."

"Well, she's not exactly a fallen woman."

"The matron of a sporting house certainly qualifies as fallen, Shane."

"Actually," I took a breath, considered temporizing one more time, and then decided to just throw out what I knew. He is, after all, an unusually enlightened sort for a British aristocrat. "She's not exactly a woman."

He sat up and looked down at me. "What do you mean?"

"Well, as Dr. Silver explained it to Marie and me, some people are born with a soul that does not match their body."

"So she-"

"Was born Paul's brother and is now living as his sister."

A puzzled stare for a breath. Then: "How does it work, exactly?"

"Well, apparently, the person feels they are a woman in a man's body. You can see how uncomfortable that might be."

"Indeed." As he continued, I could tell he was thinking it through. "Quite a difficult way to live. One would probably wake up every morning feeling like their true self, only to realize they're trapped in the wrong body. Very sad."

"Yes. Not an abomination at all. More like a cross to bear, if I may borrow a phrase from Father Michael."

"So what do such people do?" He reached for my hand.

"Well, they either try to ignore their feelings, or they find a way forward somehow. Remember that story a few months ago of the Civil War veteran in Yonkers?"

"Oh, yes. Decorated infantry sergeant—with a secret. That's right. She left a family in Pennsylvania and simply posed as a man for the next forty years."

"Precisely."

"And that's how it went for Paul's...sibling?" The pause told me he was trying to speak of the matter as precisely and correctly as possible.

"Apparently christened Allen, but always understood it was wrong. Allen became Alice and was, of course, cast out by the family."

"No doubt." He gave me a puzzled expression. "How-"

"Well, apparently, one day Allen just left Boston and started a new life in Five Points as Alice. Apparently, there was a very small inheritance, so Alice likely used it as a stake to set up her new life."

"And no one knew?"

"Not a hint. As far as the family was concerned, Allen went West to find his fortune. That's what I was told at Paul and Marie's wedding."

"And there it rested."

"It did. Until Alice came backstage to wish Marie well last fall, and Paul decided to mend fences as far as they could safely be mended."

"Which is not, even in our enlightened new century, very far."

"Not a bit. They exchange letters, and she occasionally sends a pretty house gift or a treat for the children. Apparently, Paul slipped down for tea every once in a while."

"Which is not necessarily a problem. Many men visit a sporting house on occasion."

"I suspect it's frowned on by 'Muscular Christianity.'"

"No doubt. But in general, most folks don't worry about it too much unless it becomes a public matter."

"Say, in a splashy police raid."

Gil nodded. "Precisely."

"One would need a motivation for that. As I understand it, Miss LaJoy is current on her protection money. You know those houses pay off the coppers."

"I did not, but I suspected as much." He gave me a sudden, sharp look. "You've seen Miss LaJoy?"

"Tommy and I—well, Eddie—visited her a few days ago. One would never know."

"No?"

"No. She's a beautiful woman, and I can only imagine life as a man was uncomfortable at best."

"And you gave her very close study."

"I did."

"With all of your theatrical knowledge."

"Yes."

In the moonlight, Gil's face turned sharp and contemplative. I could almost hear his wheels turning. "No one in Five Points seemed to be aware of her secret?"

"Not a bit," I confirmed. "Everyone spoke of her as a good lady and an ethical businesswoman. A few suggested she was unusual, but that seemed to be a reference to her class and culture, not to anything else. Not a hint."

"And if there were a hint, you would have heard it."

"Something like that? Absolutely."

"So now we have to ask ourselves the most important question: how did the Assistant Commissioner know?"

"How-"

Gil held my gaze. "There are only a few possibilities, and none of them reflect especially well on him."

"And some might provide a way to turn the tables on our blackmailer."

"Exactly, *mo chridhe*." He kissed the top of my head. "I hate to be in the position of telling my wife to head off to Five Points, but I think you and your protectors need to talk to Miss LaJoy again."

"We do. We might even be able to come up with a plan."

"One can only hope."

I snuggled in closer to him. "Well, thank you for easing my mind, *mes epinards*."

"Of course." He leaned in for a kiss. "Since we're both awake, and neither of us has an early engagement..."

Chapter Thirty-Two: For Queen and Country

The next day began with another lightning bolt.

And not a good one.

When I slipped downstairs, perhaps five minutes after Gil, in our usual vain effort to avoid Tommy's knowing smile, my husband was standing alone in the foyer, holding the phone.

He didn't look up when I reached the base of the stairs.

"What's wrong?" I asked.

"Aldrick did not wake this morning."

The quiet shock of his tone told me his friend was not merely lying abed after a late night.

"Oh, no."

"That was his man, calling to cancel our morning visit—because he died in the night." Gil shook his head. "Just—died."

I put a hand on his shoulder. "I'm so sorry."

"So am I. He was a good man. And a good friend."

"Was he in ill health?"

"No more than any other man dicing with the half-century mark." His jaw tightened, and I knew he was tamping down the entirely natural pain of loss. "Apparently, he had tea with Lavinia Ten Broeck and Cecily Bridgewater yesterday, some sort of courtesy thing, decided to take a tray in his room in the Residence instead of going to dinner…and just never awoke."

"Terrible." I rubbed Gil's arm, and he tensed a bit.

200

Even with his wife, he was fighting the show of emotion.

Men really should weep and throw things the way women are allowed to do at such moments. Grief is ugly and messy, and pretending it isn't, only harms the friends left behind, not to mention insulting our lost ones.

In this case, though, I was far less worried with the conventions of grief, and far more about the untimely death. Sir Aldrick had seemed to be in the pink of health when I met him a mere week or so ago.

And Gil was right, he was a bit young to just die in his sleep on a random night.

If only for this reason: if such a thing could happen to Gil's friend, it could happen to Gil—and I could not bear to entertain the possibility.

But I did have to entertain an equally grave possibility.

Gil had told me he felt as if someone was one step ahead of him.

He is, undeniably, a supremely rational lawyer, without a touch of the influence of Aunt Ellen's natural Irish connection to things unseen. Of course, he is also half Highland Scots, a Celt in his own right. But neither his mother nor he, seemed susceptible to the vibrations and vapors Aunt Ellen sensed.

So, if Gil said he felt someone was ahead of him, he meant he had literal, concrete reason for the feeling. Meaning there might well be some kind of malign plot at work here.

Honestly, I would have preferred some supernatural evil. I could just ask Aunt Ellen to reason with the spirits, and all would be well again.

Unfortunately, I suspected we were dealing with a malignant human. Or humans.

And Aunt Ellen could not reason with them. Though, I might seriously consider sending her in with a shillelagh if it came to that. Considering the possible suspects, Aunt Ellen might well enjoy getting a little of her own back. Our own.

"You look unusually troubled, *mo chridhe.*" Gil said, gently taking my hand.

"This is exceedingly troubling."

"I promise, I am not going to die in the night of some unexpected illness." I narrowed my eyes. "I'm not worried about that—or I wasn't until just this instant."

"No?"

"No." I shook my head. "I do not think it was simply your friend's time."

"What do you think?"

I took a breath. How to start this discussion? Better to just do this.

"Is it possible that someone else does not want you to find the answer?" I asked.

"What do you mean?"

"Well, if you were to report back that you could find no definitive evidence of anything, that certainly supplies an answer—and an answer some people might find very useful."

"But it might not be true."

His tone was clear and almost childish.

To my beloved Barrister, truth matters above all. Whether or not it was what some of his friends wanted to hear. If someone hoped for an answer that was no answer, or if they hoped Gil would lead them to a way to destroy evidence, there might be all kinds of bad things going on in the background.

Up to and including death.

I took a breath, held his gaze. "If all evidence to the contrary is removed, one way or another, the truth might not matter."

"The truth always matters."

"To you."

He stared back at me for a moment. Breathing, absorbing it. Trying to discount it—and unable to do so. "You think someone from the Court might be-"

"It's not unthinkable. A border lord, after all, can't be unaware that there are factions."

"But murder…"

"I'm sorry, my love, but a group of people who could calmly stand by and let thousands of my ancestors die in the road is not a group that would scruple to remove a few more people who know too much."

"There's no way to say this without sounding prejudiced, so forgive me." He took a breath, a guilty twist to his mouth.

"All right." I suspected I knew what was coming.

"You're speaking of Irish lives. The Court—and unfortunately many of my countrymen—did not consider them important."

"You mean, they didn't consider the Irish human." I'd seen enough of the attitude, and not just from Britons, to be able to say it coolly, if not happily.

"Probably true. And you know I-"

"I know. And I know what your great-uncle did for his tenants." Gil's late relative was one of the few landlords who had actually tried to mitigate the potato famine, suspending rents and even bringing in food. I took a breath, continued: "I suppose this wasn't the best example, but I'm trying to make the point that the Court will do what it has to do and ignore what it has to ignore."

"Do you suspect a setup, as Mr. Coughlan might say?"

"How can it be a coincidence that your friend at the Consulate collapsed last night—just a day after Colonel Vandergrift's stroke? Not to mention the missing report in White Plains, and your feeling that other people are a step ahead of you?"

"When you lay it out that way, it's certainly suggestive." Gil's jaw tightened as he continued. "But my friends and I have all taken an oath to Queen and Country and surely-"

"It's not the oath, my love, it's how you interpret it. You believe doing your duty requires you to find the truth and bring it back to your friend. Others may believe duty requires them to make sure it's never known."

"At this moment, it appears there's nothing to know. Hints, shadows, and conjectures, but nothing certain."

"They may not want to take that chance."

Gil shook his head. "I can't deny the possibility."

"And they might come for you."

"That, *mo chridhe*, is highly unlikely."

"If someone killed Sir Aldrick…"

"Sweetheart, Sir Aldrick was a functionary, and a knight. The bare lowest rung of the aristocracy. I am a Duke. I cannot even be tried in an ordinary court of law."

"If this is a faction of the Court..."

A dry little smile. "I have held this back because it was so sensitive. But it's important to ease your mind. My errand does not come from a mere courtier, but from someone immediately involved."

As he took a breath and held my gaze, I suddenly understood.

"The friend of your friend."

"Yes."

"Well," I said with only a little edge in my voice, "the friend of your friend might want to make some effort toward protecting you."

"I could also make an effort toward protecting myself." He studied my face for a moment. "It is a pretty morning—do you think you might enjoy a velocipede ride today?"

Chapter Thirty-Three: Wheels Within Wheels

Tommy, who'd returned quite late from his Broadway night with Cabot, was more than happy to put off our trip to Five Points until after my spin around the park. Hetty, as it happened, was practically lifting the phone to call me, because we were at the point where bright warm mornings were running low.

Easy enough, then, for Gil to put together a packet while I changed into sports clothes and send me on my way with it, a kiss, and a reminder to stay with my protectors when we visited Miss LaJoy. I suspected my day would be far more pleasant than Gil's.

Hetty was pinning on her hat in her foyer when the housemaid let me in. Dr. Faustus, her ancient, cranky marmalade tabby, looked down on me from the landing, sniffed, and padded away. His usual.

"So glad we got a decent day," she said, turning to me.

"Yes—a very pleasant surprise," I agreed. "Especially after a dull dinner at Marie's with the Assistant Police Commissioner."

"Ugh," she said. "How is she?"

"Dinner was wonderful, but she wasn't." I met her gaze. "Better not to say too much."

"I suppose." Her eyes flicked over me and landed on my hands. "Marie's not the only one in a mess, is she?"

"No. There's more than enough mess to go around."

"Any of it news-worthy?" she asked.

"Not yet. Hopefully never."

"You'll owe me one...or a few."

"Absolutely."

"You're good for it." She smiled. "Loris loved that interview."

"Good. Before we head out, lock this in your desk." I handed her the packet with Jamie's snap of the letter, Gil's notes, and one of the copies of *Trent's Illustrated Gazette.*

"What is it?"

"The greatest story I hope you'll never have to write."

Her brows knit, and her gaze sharpened on me. "What do you mean?"

"This is a bit of insurance. The Barrister is involved in a very grave matter, and, if anything untoward should happen, we want a record of the truth."

"Untoward? Are you in danger?"

"The risk is small but not non-existent. Some of his very British friends may not play by Marquess of Queensberry rules."

"Really."

"Really." I sighed. "But he doesn't quite believe it."

"They don't." She looked at the envelope for a moment. "Rowan couldn't conceive of one of his lawyer friends suborning perjury until he saw it happen right in front of him in court. It's one of the few bad things about deeply ethical men."

"You're right. They simply can't see that kind of evil because they're not capable of it."

"I guess the good part is they aren't."

"Perhaps."

She took a breath, held my gaze very seriously. "When you say something untoward, Ells, do you mean you could be at risk, too?"

"Possibly. But I doubt they'd expect him to involve his tenement skivvy wife."

"Nobody's called you that, have they?"

"Not in his presence, for sure. But I'm constantly aware that without the protection of his name and title, I'd just be more Irish vermin."

"Rather harsh, don't you think?"

"You're Scots, Hets. It's different for the Irish. Not to mention Jews. There are some people who just don't consider us human. And that my husband has betrayed his class by marrying me."

"Even now?"

"No one's said it in my earshot, but I'm sure some wonder why he troubled to marry me, when surely he could have gotten what he wanted with a smile and a few shiny trinkets."

Hetty's eyes widened. "Nasty creatures, these Brits."

"Some of them." I tapped the packet. "Which is why we need a measure of protection. If anything happens to him, this tenement skivvy will make them pay dearly. And what you've got there will make some very important people very unhappy."

"How unhappy?"

"Unhappy enough that I'd rather not put you at risk by knowing unless you absolutely have to."

Despite her obvious concern for me and Gil, the prospect of a good story made her eyes gleam. "Well, if it comes to it, we'll make every kind of trouble."

"Indeed, we shall. These people have no idea what we bold American women—that *is* a quote—are capable of when threatened."

"The problem, though, is what the aristocrats may be capable of."

"How true." I looked at the foyer clock. "Well, we still have time for a good ride."

"That we do." She dropped the packet in her drawer and locked it. As we walked out, she gave me a sharp look. "Perhaps you can tell me your impressions of the Assistant Police Commissioner, at least."

"Certainly. Why?"

"I hear he's preparing to launch some sort of public morals campaign."

"Really."

"Apparently quite bothered by the soiled doves of Five Points." She pronounced the term with the same disdainful awe as I did.

"You mean the girls who'd rather make a living with their bodies than piecework?" I asked pointedly.

"Exactly those girls." Hetty scowled as she climbed onto her cycle. Though a proper maiden lady, she, like I, saw no reason to judge. "Interestingly, I'm told he wasn't bothered by the ladies of the night until quite recently."

"Really."

"Apparently was known to have a connection with one of the house owners—I don't know which one."

"That's unusual, isn't it?"

"I'm not an authority, of course, but I think any kind of connection is discouraged. And for a member of the Police Commission to be friends with a sporting house owner?"

"Sticky."

"Very." She smiled. "What was he like?"

"A stick," I said with perfect truth. Hopefully, Hetty would never need to know he was also a blackmailing wretch.

"Not a surprise from that column in the *Republican Star* last night."

"Oh?" It must have hit the streets just as we were having dinner, and blackmail.

"The usual screed about how red-light districts harm the fiber of our country and our good Christian men."

"Well, that makes sense." Even if our Assistant Commissioner had been in the midst of something very un-Christian when the piece was published. Irony is a magnificent thing. I kept the thought to myself, keeping the conversation on safer ground. "He spent a great deal of time last night droning on about Muscular Christianity."

"Not another one."

"Another one?" I nearly missed a turn.

"It's all the rage among a certain type of man. We've got a few of them at the paper. One of them asked me why I am taking a man's job."

"Bet that went over well."

"He has no idea how close he came to meeting his Maker then and there." We shared a grin.

"It's all right." She followed the path around a curve. "They'll really love my next story."

"Oh?"

"I'm interviewing the country's first woman ordained minister." A grin. "Turns out Mrs. Blackwell—that's what she answers to these days—still lives over in Elizabeth, New Jersey. She's a suffragist, and I thought it would be interesting to talk about women and religion."

"And what God thinks about all of this New Woman stuff?"

"Maybe. Honestly, I just want to see what she's like."

"I can't wait to hear."

We chewed over Hetty's plans, which also included an exposé on factory safety—and more happily, an evening out with Rowan for a Bar Association benefit in December. While I was careful not to pry, I knew—and she knew I knew—the fact of appearing on Rowan's arm for such an important night was an announcement.

Privately, I suspected Rowan was trying to soften her up for a much bigger question by asking her to the event. Maybe even planning to propose in the coming weeks, so she could attend as his fiancée. The possibility concerned me just a bit, not because I thought Rowan wanted an Angel in the House, but because I wasn't sure he'd done enough to make it clear to her.

On the other hand, he'd happily backed her stunt trip to Chicago last spring, hanging about telegraph offices waiting for word and even ferrying copy to the *Beacon*. So he was clearly all-in. Now, if Hetty would bend just a tiny bit on her opposition to marriage…

Perhaps seeing the way Gil's and my marriage was turning out to be a great joy without destroying my career would give her some encouragement.

I did not, however, say this. If Hetty wanted my thoughts on combining work and marriage, she would ask for them. Still, while I remain firmly opposed to meddling, I'm not opposed to giving a friend a nudge toward happiness.

On that morning, though, there was no time for nudging. As soon as we turned out of the park, Hetty and I both hopped off our cycles, exchanged a quick hug, and dashed off in our separate directions, promising a good, long coffee chat soon.

As I stepped out, she handed me her copy of the *Republican Star*, folded to the Assistant Commissioner's screed.

We must protect our fine young men from the cesspits of iniquity...

It looked like there were close to a thousand words more in the same overheated vein. I didn't have time for that nonsense.

Right now, it was time for the duchess and the diva to slip offstage for a bit...and for Eddie Hurley to head down to Five Points.

I didn't know it might just be his last trip.

Chapter Thirty-Four: Trouble at the Sporting House

I n the foyer, Tommy was leafing through the mail and tapping his foot. "About time."

"You're the one who wanted to get a slow start this morning."

"That was an hour and a half ago." He scowled. "We need to get there and back quickly. We don't need to be in Five Points any longer than absolutely necessary."

"I agree. Give me five minutes." I dashed for the stairs.

"Just five. I still can't believe the Barrister is allowing you to go."

"He doesn't *allow* me to do anything," I reminded him sharply.

"Fair enough."

The trip down was uneventful, and the streets relatively quiet.

The same could not be said for Miss LaJoy's home.

My exceedingly limited experience suggested that early afternoon would normally be a quiet time at such a place, with the women resting up from the previous night—and prettying and preparing themselves for the next one. Rather like me during a tour, I supposed.

Not the most comfortable thought.

This was not, however, the time for contemplation.

Tommy lifted his hand to knock, and the door came open, with the young maid practically flying at us.

"Thank God you're here. I've sent to Mr. Coughlan because I don't know who else to call, but we need-"

A crash from the back of the house was followed by a cry:

"Get out of my house!"

"I'll leave when I'm good and ready!"

"You will not do this in my house!"

Tommy and I started running in the direction of the voices.

Miss LaJoy's serene drawing room was in an uproar. The lady herself was standing in the middle, holding her arms out, separating two red-faced, furious men. Her height—the only indication of her earlier life—was probably very helpful at this exact moment because she was able to glare directly at the antagonists.

One was a young man, with the sort of rounded face that was probably gentle and sweet under other circumstances. Just then, though, his large, light eyes were squinty, and his face contorted in rage as he stared down his enemy.

The enemy in question? Assistant Police Commissioner Duncan Maitland, as blazingly angry as the young man.

Well, didn't that add to the intrigue.

Tommy flicked his eyes to me. How were we to warn Miss LaJoy with him here?

In the event, the warning was moot.

"You don't get to insult my girl!" the young man shouted.

"Get over it, boy. Go to church and try to be a decent man."

"Stop this." Alice LaJoy's voice was cool and calm—much like her jurist brother's. "Matthew, why don't you just go upstairs and see Clover?"

"She's a woman, not a cesspit!" the young man snapped at the Assistant Commissioner. "I want you to take back what you wrote."

Now, I understood. That nasty little screed about the evils of the red-light district in today's *Republican Star* had not sat especially well with some of the regular visitors.

"Indeed not!" Maitland huffed. "Places like this are-"

"And what are you doing in a place like this?" Matthew, for that was his name, snapped back.

"Working to convert the fallen, of course." The functionary's tone was almost believable.

Or would have been, if I hadn't seen the expression on Alice LaJoy's face. Good Lord, how could someone so intelligent and ethical care for such a hypocrite? Leaving completely aside the issue of his absolute lack of masculine appeal, though one hardly could.

The heart truly is a mysterious thing.

Thank God I loved a worthy man.

No time to reflect.

"The hell you are. You're a damned hypocrite."

"I am entirely right with my God," Duncan Maitland said. "I suggest you get right with yours."

"I'll do you better. I'll send you to him."

The boy whipped out a gun.

So did Maitland.

Tommy put his arm in front of me.

I let him.

Alice LaJoy took a step back, but there was no fear in her stance or voice. "Stop this."

"I'll stop when he apologizes," Matthew said.

"I've nothing to apologize for!"

"Duncan," Alice began.

He ignored her. "Don't ask for trouble, boy."

Matthew leveled his gun.

So did Maitland, though from the shakiness of his grip, I could tell he wasn't used to handling weapons—and his hand was sweaty.

"You men can still stop this," Alice LaJoy said. "Call it a draw and back off."

Two guns wavered.

For an instant, there was a real possibility it could end without bloodshed.

And then Maitland's clumsiness decided for us.

He may have simply been trying to work his fat finger toward the trigger. Intent, at this moment, didn't matter.

His gun went off.

Matthew flinched and fired his own weapon.

I always forget how loud gunshots are. Even the blanks we use on stage can be deafening if you're close...never mind the sound of two real firings indoors.

It stunned everyone for a moment, freezing us all in place.

Then the realization and reaction.

Matthew fell back, clutching his leg with a whimper like a hurt child. Which, honestly, he was—probably no older than Jamie.

"Oh my God! I'm hit!" Maitland shouted, grabbing his arm. "Help me!"

Then, and only then, did anyone notice our presence.

"Hurley!" Alice LaJoy called, probably because it was easier than figuring out which one of us she wanted.

I grabbed a napkin from the tea tray and moved toward Matthew. "You're going to be all right, sweetie," I said, in the same tone I'd used with my young cousins when they had a skinned knee.

"Drop it, Maitland," Tommy snapped at the Assistant Commissioner. "You've done enough damage for one day."

"I'm-" he huffed, "I'm the one who was hit."

Tommy grabbed the gun away. "You shot a boy in the leg, you fool!"

The napkin I was holding on Matthew's leg was already almost soaked through. I raised my eyes to Alice. "He needs a doctor, now!"

The Assistant Commissioner's attention turned to me for just an instant.

The maid was in the doorway, frantically looking between me and Alice.

The lady of the house nodded. "Go get Dr. Ralston."

"What about me?" howled Maitland, flopping in a chair as the girl ran away.

Alice looked down at Maitland, obviously repulsed by what she'd just seen. But her voice was still gentle. "You've been grazed in the arm."

"It must be worse than that," he said.

"It's not," she said, picking up another napkin and dabbing at his arm, her eyes turning to Tommy and me. "What on earth are you two doing here?"

"We know who's blackmailing Paul," I said. Maitland was about to wish the kid had better aim.

At the sound of my voice, Duncan Maitland's gaze suddenly sharpened on me. "You're-"

"The absolute least of your worries, Assistant Commissioner," I said.

"You don't mean-" Alice began, breaking off in a shocked breath as the realization dawned. "You, Duncan?"

"You don't really think I could love an abomination?" he asked.

She pressed the napkin harder against his arm, and he cried out.

"You're the abomination!" she snapped. "Using my family against me? What *are* you?"

"A man on the way up." He managed a confident tone that turned my stomach. I could only imagine what it did to Alice. "Never hurts to own a judge."

"You don't own anyone, Mr. Assistant Commissioner." Her face hardened, and she squeezed his arm. "I own *you* now."

"Alice..."

"You," she said in a tone of ice-cold command, "will address me as Miss LaJoy. And never again once I get you out of this house."

Maitland opened his mouth to speak, clearly unused to being so over-matched.

"What the hell is going on here?"

The voice was unmistakable, and unmistakably angry.

Connor filled the doorway, gun in hand.

There was nothing unsteady or awkward about his grip. If he fired, it would be because he meant to—and it wouldn't be a graze.

"You two were supposed to warn me when you came down here."

"We didn't have time," I said. "We just learned the truth last night."

"I called Morrissey's." Tommy met his furious glare with one of his own. "They told me you were asleep."

Shrug. Scowl. "Out a little late."

"Never mind," I said. "We've brought our message, and the doctor's on the way for this fellow.

"Am I-" the boy in question asked.

The fact that the bleeding was starting to slow, and that he had the presence of mind to ask the question were good signs.

I met his frightened gaze. "You'll live to regret this."

"And so will you," Tommy said to Maitland. "Assistant Police Commissioner shooting a boy at a sporting house?"

Maitland's face took on a gray cast.

"As I said, Mr. Assistant Commissioner," Alice cut in, voice cool but eyes showing the hurt. "You're mine."

"And mine." Connor smiled, coldly. "I should thank you two for bringing me this little gift."

"I won't say it's our pleasure," Tommy said.

A grim little nod. "Get Eddie out of here."

"The doctor will be here soon," I told Matthew as Alice moved in and put her hands where mine had been on the napkin.

"Thank you," she whispered to me.

"Wish we could do more," I whispered back.

Connor followed Tommy and me to the door, and walked us down to the stoop where people were starting to gather. Even in Five Points, two gunshots draw attention.

"Thank you, Connor," I said.

He grabbed my arm. Tightly, the fingers digging through the cloth of my jacket, deliberately making sure I felt it. Looked me right in the eye. And not the way he usually did. Cold, scary, and determined. When he spoke, it probably came out a good bit louder than he intended.

"Eddie Hurley is dead."

Hard to argue that.

Chapter Thirty-Five: The Duke, in the Studio

"Miss! Thank God you're home!"

Even for the rather dramatic Sophia, it was an electrifying welcome.

Not unappreciated, though, since it had taken far longer than I'd expected to get back. The first cab wouldn't take us because we looked so disreputable, between the blood on my cuffs and the grip of Maitland's pistol clearly visible in Tommy's belt. The cab we finally did get took the long way and got lost in the little streets around Washington Square, and we'd ultimately just paid him off and walked the rest of the way.

Tommy and I exchanged puzzled glances and turned to Sophia.

"Mr. Dare called—said he heard two men were shot at Alice LaJoy's, and we've been terribly worried."

"Preston was probably in the newsroom when the call came in, Heller." Tommy shook his head. "Going to be interesting to see how the Assistant Commissioner keeps this down."

"The Duke's up in the studio, Miss." Sophia's little face tightened with concern. "He's pretty mad—or scared—I'm not sure which."

Either way, not good for me.

I started running up the stairs.

Took a moment at the top, to catch my breath, then opened the door.

"Shane!" Gil crossed to me and pulled me into his arms. For a moment, he held me like he couldn't hold me close enough, a desperate and relieved embrace completely at odds with the British stiff upper lip.

"I'm all right, sweetheart," I said. "We were never in danger."

Gil released me and looked down at me for a long moment, relief and joy in his aspect. And then, something else.

Anger.

"What on earth happened?" he snapped.

I heard Tommy's running footsteps stop, caught a glimpse of him in the doorway, and shook my head slightly at him. This was mine.

He nodded but stayed where he was.

"You know we went to warn Alice about the Assistant Commissioner," I said.

"I'm aware." Gil's voice was sharp. Cutting.

Some nerve. My husband had encouraged me to warn her, for heaven's sake.

I explained in as cool a tone as I could manage. "And when we got there, the Assistant Commissioner was there—and so was a defender of one of the—young ladies. He wasn't pleased with that column in the *Republican Star* yesterday."

"Defending his girl's honor," Tommy added, clearly trying to help.

"You walked into the middle of a fight over a—" Gil threw his hands up.

"We were incognito," Tommy reminded him, walking into the studio. "And in any case, no one will breathe a word of this. The Assistant Commissioner is now at the mercy of Miss LaJoy—and us."

"How encouraging." Gil glared at us both.

I snapped back in defense: "We stopped him and saved Paul, and who knows who else-"

"You put yourself in peril." His voice was tight, barely above a whisper.

"I did not. Tommy and Connor were there. And you told me to warn her."

"Do you know what Dare heard?" Gil asked.

Tommy and I exchanged glances.

Preston must have asked his sources-

"Eddie Hurley is dead."

Gil snapped out each word as a blow. As he must have heard them.

Connor *had* said it. And during our unexpectedly long and difficult trip home, the words must have come back to Preston. And then to Gil.

"Nobody died," I said. "I'm sorry-"

I broke off at the absolute inadequacy of the apology, as Gil's eyes blazed into mine.

His anger filled the room, charging the air like the last moment before a thunderstorm. Just before the lightning splits the heavens.

Frozen, I waited.

"I'll not bury you!"

The explosion was truly terrifying. His voice was loud and raw, and rough with the Northern accent, his eyes wild.

Now what? I shrank back, honestly afraid of what might happen now.

Tommy tensed, clearly ready to defend me if needed.

Surely not.

I could not imagine Gil laying hands on me.

But I couldn't have imagined what came next, either.

A reaction even more terrifying than his blazing fury.

Grief.

He crumpled in on himself and began to cry, sitting down on the piano bench, sobbing like a lost child.

I motioned to Tommy to leave, and quickly crossed to Gil.

I put a tentative hand on his arm, and Gil pulled me in, clinging to me for dear life, still sobbing. I hadn't heard a man cry like that since Tommy after his father's funeral.

"Dear God, Shane. I-"

I did the only thing I could. I knelt by him, held him, whispered the same reassurances he gave me when I had a nightmare or an upset: "You're safe. I'm here."

After what seemed like hours, but was probably only a few minutes, his breath began to slow, and the sobbing stopped.

"I'm sorry, *mo chridhe*," he whispered in a slow, thick tone, when he was able to speak again.

"Nothing to be sorry for." I rubbed his back as I would an upset child's.

219

After a few more breaths, he pulled back and held my gaze, those usually cool pale blue eyes now red-rimmed and still damp. But no less intense.

"It is no longer only your life, Shane."

"I don't…"

"I've buried one woman I love." He took a ragged breath. "I cannot—I *will* not—do it again."

"I'm sorry. I didn't mean to scare you."

"I know." For several breaths, he just looked at me. When he spoke, his voice was gentle and gravelly. "What I heard was two men shot at Miss LaJoy's house. And someone at the scene said Eddie Hurley is dead."

"Connor said it," I explained. "He meant I'd better never go out like that again."

"He's right."

"He is." I put my hands on his face, looked him straight in the eye as I did when making a promise. "I'm safe. I honestly try not to take foolish risks."

"I know."

And then, as our gaze held, the valence of the moment changed. His eyes took on a familiar hot glow, and he pulled me to him.

"Is the door locked, Shane?"

"Here?"

"Any reason not?"

"None whatever."

I locked the door.

Some time later, he was watching me re-button my shirt when he reached out and gently touched my ribcage, lightly running a finger over the scar there, now faded to a thin red line.

A permanent reminder of my most serious brush with death, when I fought a madman bent on stabbing Gil.

"It is no longer your life alone," he said again. "Promise me. You will not be reckless."

Since I hadn't been reckless in the first place, it was an easy vow to make. "I will never be reckless."

He pulled me closer. "I cannot lose you."

I leaned in. "I'm sorry I scared you."

"I'm sorry I lost my temper."

"But the making-up was quite pleasant, *mes epinards*," I said, leaning in for a kiss. He had not yet buttoned his shirt, and I rested my hands on his chest.

"We may have to argue more often. Preferably about smaller matters." His hand moved from the scar to a much more pleasant place. "And make up frequently…"

It should surprise no one that we were very nearly late for dinner.

Chapter Thirty-Six: Calm Before the Storm—or Show

Dinner, and the night after, were surprisingly restful, considering all that was in play. Of course, it was just a lull in the action.

Our table was quite full for a simple and convivial dinner: Preston and Greta came over, and Cabot joined Tommy after a busy day of books. Jamie regaled us with tales of his explorations of the city, and Preston tried out lines from his upcoming column.

We determinedly kept conversation light and pleasant and did not bring up the unpleasantness of the day. After all the *sturm und drang* it was a joy and relief to escape for a bit, even if everyone at the table knew escape was exactly what it was.

Next day, with a performance and Lavinia Ten Broeck's reception ahead, I tried for as quiet a day as possible, sleeping late, and stretching out on the chaise in the parlor in my favorite violet tea-gown.

Of course, considering recent events and all else that was in play, my serenity and solitude did not last. I was giving it my best shot, trying to divert myself with a fascinating novel about Queen Elizabeth and Mary, Queen of Scots, when Sophia scooted into the room.

"Madame Marie and her sister, miss."

Sister?

I marked my book and stood to welcome my visitors.

Marie walked in, arm in arm with Alice LaJoy, unmistakable to me because of her height, but nicely incognito thanks to a broad-brimmed midnight-blue hat with a lovely point d'esprit veil.

"Sophia, please call for tea for the ladies."

"Of course, miss."

I motioned to the settee and took my usual chair, leaving the book and afghan on the lounge.

Alice LaJoy marked them, and the tea-gown, and gave me an apologetic glance. "You're performing tonight."

"I am, but that's hours from now…and I was hoping to know how things turned out."

"Which is exactly why we came over," Marie said. "All's well that ends, as they say."

"Did I hear Madame Marie is visiting?" Gil walked into the parlor, with Tommy behind him. "And…"

"My sister," Marie said firmly, nodding to Alice.

"Ah. A pleasure."

"Probably not," Alice replied with a dry smile. "Considering yesterday's events, I wouldn't be especially pleased to see me, either."

"None of it was your fault," I reminded her.

"Not entirely true. I opened my home to a viper. I should have seen him for what he was, but instead I allowed myself to think that someone like him could be a friend to someone like me."

"It's not wrong to want a friend," Tommy said.

"I'm sorry to be indelicate," I began, "but I do not understand how you struck up a friendship in the first place…or what he was doing there yesterday."

"We actually met at church."

Everyone stared.

"I go to the early-morning service at Grace Church. Incognito, of course. But we shared a hymnal one Sunday. And talked. A few months later, he followed me home."

Tommy let out a low whistle, but everyone else thought about it, listening with wide eyes.

"It could have been quite awful," Alice agreed. "But I brazened it out.

Invited him in for tea. I should have known when he walked in that he was actually thinking about blackmail."

"He was a friend from church," Marie said. "You wanted to believe."

"I did. How bad could someone I prayed with be?" She shook her head, then spoke with a dry, bitter edge to her voice. "Good people, I am the *Protestant* whore."

"Nell Gwynn," Gil said, recognizing the famous quote from Charles II's mistress—a poor girl made good as an actress, unlike the aristocratic Catholic who was the Merry Monarch's other bedmate.

"She was a good person who ended up in questionable circumstances, too," Tommy said.

"She did what she could with what she had," I added. "Not sin, but survival."

"Oh, I think she loved Charles," Marie said. "And it's pretty clear he loved her. Love can happen even in impossible places."

"It may," Alice said. "But it didn't this time. Just something like friendship. And then I made an even worse mistake," she said. "I sought out my brother."

"That was not a mistake." Marie shook her head. "He is your brother."

"But if he hadn't come to the house to see me, Maitland would not have seen him."

"Oh," I said. "That's how he figured it out."

"Yes." She nodded. "He asked me how a woman from such a good family could end up doing what I do. I gave him what I thought was an appropriately vague answer—I was afraid of losing his friendship, if you can imagine—and left it."

"But he looked up Paul." Gil, who had just spent a significant amount of time checking records, went right to the final piece. "Discovered there was no birth record for a sister and put it all together."

Alice nodded. "And decided to use it. Wretch."

"But why was he there?" Tommy asked.

"Marie called me this morning to warn me."

"That's what we were trying to do," I said.

"I didn't want to believe it. I sent to him, telling him I had something important to tell him...and that's when Matthew walked in and saw him."

224

"The fight," Tommy said.

"Right." Alice sighed. "At least we all came through."

"Came through with the upper hand, I expect." A sharp note in Gil's voice suggested he was not entirely pleased with the price of the victory.

"True." Alice's face hardened into a grim smile. "I do not think any of us will have to worry about the Assistant Commissioner again."

"And the boy?" I asked.

"He'll live. Probably be back at the house next week as if nothing happened." Alice's face softened. "At some point, Clover will break his heart, but not today."

And that would have to do for a happy ending, I supposed.

Marie patted Alice's arm. "We should probably go."

"One more thing before we do." Alice turned to me with a concerned expression.

"What?"

"I may be safe now, but I'm not at all sure you are."

"What do you mean?" I asked.

"Someone is following you." She looked around the room. "May I speak freely?"

"Absolutely." Gil nodded. "We are in the family here."

"All right." A faint smile. "I like that. In the family."

We nodded. Welcoming her as we could.

"I think it's the old Englishman who's been lurking about Morrissey's for the last month or so. I've seen him coming out of there a few times, and I'm told he's been around the neighborhood."

Of course, none of us asked who her sources were.

"So, an old Englishman's been wandering about the neighborhood?" Tommy asked.

"Yes. He's done a decent job of trying to appear casual, but Da Morrissey says he was following your man here."

An old Englishman lurking around after Gil—and us? It fit all too well with my suspicions. I nodded to encourage her.

"And yesterday, when I looked out the window to see if the doctor was

225

coming—he was walking away. Probably following the Hurley boys again."

Tommy scowled. So did I.

"Thank you for letting me know," I said. "We'll keep a good eye on ourselves—and the Duke."

The peer in question nodded. His contemplative expression suggested he might finally be ready to believe my doubts about his aristocratic friends.

Alice nodded. "Please do. I'd hate to think of anything happening to you after all you've done to help me."

She held out her hands, and I clasped them, as I'd do any woman friend's. "You've been dear and kind. Perhaps we'll run into each other occasionally in the park."

"I'd like that," I assured her. "I know we have to be careful of the lines, but you're quite a lady, Miss LaJoy."

She smiled. "As are you. Watch over her, Champ. And yourself."

"I will." Tommy bowed to her. "And you stay safe."

"Well, now that I have an Assistant Police Commissioner in my pocket, I imagine we'll be just fine."

As she pulled her wrap close, her serene face cracked open in a naughty child's impish grin.

We couldn't help joining in.

"I hope the rest of your day is as successful."

So did we.

After she and Marie left, carefully taking separate cabs, I did indeed get a couple of hours to read and doze on the chaise. It was almost time for me to go upstairs to prepare for the night and check with Rosa to be sure she packed everything I needed for the reception, when I heard a messenger at the door.

A few moments later, Gil walked into the parlor, an envelope in hand, a stunned expression on his face.

"What's this?" I asked, putting down my book and sitting up, silently vowing to myself that I would throw everyone out of the house and take a day on the chaise sometime soon.

"Colonel Vandergrift sent it." He shook his head, holding out the packet.

"After all this, I hardly believe it, but here it is."

He watched me as I did the same. The Colonel's note was simple, just a brief apology for taking the letter out of the packet he'd sent us, out of a misguided desire to protect his late sister and her friend. The letter was not much longer, but far more important.

And real, because it was just like the one Jamie had authenticated.

"Good Lord," I breathed.

"Precisely. This answers everything."

"It does. So now-"

"Come along, you two!" Tommy yelled, as if this were any other day. "You've got a show to do, Heller."

I handed the packet back to Gil. "This will have to wait a bit."

My husband sighed, holding my gaze.

I squeezed his arm. "Can't disappoint the paying customers."

Chapter Thirty-Seven: In the Ten Broeck Library

That night, I turned in a surprisingly good performance for all the excitement that had come before. It was, I suppose, actually rather relaxing to be at the center of fictional danger and drama instead of the real kind.

After the show, the only sign of the last few days we'd had was Gil's standing a bit closer to my chair than usual, and Tommy keeping a surreptitious eye on Gil. Which Gil knew, but carefully did not acknowledge.

Finally, the three of us, plus Cabot, took a cab over to Lavinia's home. Her situation seemed similar to Great-Aunt Cecily's; the male heir of the clan, her nephew, had built a new home further uptown, leaving her to occupy the old family seat.

It looked like we were the last to arrive; Cabot had told me Great-Aunt Cecily was attending, and while I couldn't see her as we walked in, I could tell the drawing room was full.

Lavinia, now in an elegant evening gown, of jet-spangled black crepe with a large and probably priceless early paisley cashmere shawl, held court in the foyer and urged the gentlemen to partake of the punch and refreshments.

Not me, though.

"I wonder if you'd like to see my library," she asked. "Cecily tells me you love to read biographies, and I have a few that might interest you."

"That would be lovely," I replied.

Gil and Tommy gave me a careful glance, clearly willing to come along, but I shook my head. I was surely in no danger from a sweet older lady.

Not a bit.

"See, dear, I have all of the first editions of Mrs. Strickland's books on the Queens and Princesses of England," she said as she led me into the dim room, darker still because of the mahogany shelves lining the walls and the heavy, deep-red leather furniture. The oil lamps scattered through the room gave it a warm and engaging glow. Welcoming, not menacing.

"How impressive," I said. "I've read later editions of the Queens of England series, but the books on the Princesses are very hard to find."

"Well, perhaps you would like to borrow one. Of course, you'll have to return it at tea." She gave me a warm little smile.

"That would be wonderful."

"Would you like a glass of sherry?" she asked, moving to the drinks cart and picking up a glass. It looked like she'd poured two already.

Prepared to host me—in the midst of everything else?

Perhaps just the Knickerbocker matron in her element, arranging every scene to her satisfaction.

Still, I was a little surprised—libraries are a masculine purview and usually do not have sherry on offer—but certainly I needed refreshment after the show, so I accepted with thanks. "It's been a rather long day."

"I don't doubt it." A maternal smile as she handed me the glass of sherry.

"And over here is my First Folio."

I followed her to the display case and looked down at Shakespeare, today opened to Lady Macbeth's first soliloquy. It should have been a warning.

"Come, why don't we sit over here and chat for a moment?"

I took the settee opposite her, enjoying the swirl of my amethyst cut velvet skirt as I smoothed it.

"That's quite a ring. Lavender fancy diamond?"

"Yes. A wedding present from His Grace."

"Ah, those British aristocrats. That was Bertha's mistake, too."

Interesting that she brought up her late daughter so readily. She'd never done that before. "How so?"

"Bertha thought she actually had a chance at a happy life with the prince.

Silly girl."

I took a sip of the sherry, which wasn't as good as what we keep at Washington Square, as I noticed that Lavinia Ten Broeck was watching me with a strange intensity. Had I not still been tired from the performance and all the recent drama with Alice LaJoy, I would have caught it sooner.

Still, I didn't feel any sense of danger or menace. Besides, after reading the letter Colonel Vandergrift had sent, I suspected I knew a good bit more about her daughter's affair than she did. I offered as kind a response as I could: "Surely all girls are a bit silly when they fall in love. And at least you have the consolation that she knew love before she died."

"People set far too much store on love." Lavinia Ten Broeck's mouth twisted. "You know I can't let your husband tell anyone what he's learned."

Despite the blazing fire in the grate, my thick gown, and the afterglow from the show, a note in her voice gave me a sudden chill. Perhaps if I found out what she knew I'd know better how to handle this. "What's he learned?"

"Don't play innocent with me!" she snapped.

Uh-oh. I caught my breath and waited.

"He thinks he's so clever, but my stupid nephew Nicholas told me he was asking about the Academy of Music Ball, so I knew what he must be after. Easy enough to arrange invitations to that ridiculous reception of yours...and a tea at the Consulate with that arrogant friend of his."

I lowered the glass, stunned by the realization she'd been tracking Gil all along. Everyone underestimates old ladies. Even people who should know better, like me.

"That's fine. You've drunk enough, I'm sure."

The chill deepened. "For what?"

Her watery blue eyes sharpened into cold evil. "Don't worry, you'll be unconscious when I slash your throat. Probably be gone by the time he gets here to take the blame."

So much for a safe visit to the library with a cute little old lady.

Whatever she'd given me, it hadn't yet taken effect. I had a chance. Perhaps a good one if I played the scene well. I blinked as if trying to clear my head. "How does that protect poor Bertha?"

"Don't say her name!" she snapped. "A Jewish mongrel like you can't begin to understand what a stain such a thing is for the Quality."

"She told you there was a secret marriage," I said slowly, a logical, and hopefully lucky guess. "A comforting story to ease a mother's conscience."

"It wasn't just a story!"

Bertha's own letter gave the lie to that. In her tear-stained farewell to Colonel Vandergrift's sister Philly, she said she was being sent away because of her adventure with the Prince, and the "trouble" afterward.

I took a long breath. I still *felt* entirely sharp, but I kept my voice slow and began to slur a bit. "You had to believe it."

"I have no record, but it's true. She was a good girl."

I let my eyes drift closed for a moment, then brought them open again. Where was Gil? How was she planning to bring him in? I'd have no trouble taking her in a fair fight, but I didn't know how long I had until whatever was in that glass started working.

Between my eyelashes, I saw Lavinia reaching behind a cushion on the settee. Excellent. The sooner she came at me, the better. "I'm sure she was a good girl. But even a good girl can't resist a prince."

"You couldn't resist a Duke."

"Different thing." I let my voice trail off on the last word, then kept my tone deliberately light and slurred for the next sentence. "I waited for my marriage bed…"

"You rotten slut!" Lavinia pounced at the words, as I thought she might. She was angrier, but I was younger and faster, and before she knew what happened, I was standing over her. I grabbed the knife hand and held her wrist tight. The last time I'd been in close combat involving a knife I'd lost track of it, with disastrous results, and I wasn't going to let that happen again.

"Stop."

Gil stood in the darkened doorway. I wasn't sure if he was talking to me, or Lavinia, but it didn't much matter. He had a pistol, which neatly ended the knife fight.

When did he start carrying one?

Lavinia startled, but I kept my grip on her wrist—and she dropped the knife.

My knees suddenly wobbled, and I sat down hard on the settee. For a moment, I wasn't sure if it was the narrow escape or the drink.

"It doesn't matter, sonny." Lavinia Ten Broeck said, cackling evilly as she looked at me. "Your tenement skivvy wife's already done for. Greedy whore drank enough."

"Then you are too." He held the gun on her.

"What? You'd harm a sweet old lady?"

"I'll do whatever I have to do to protect her." His eyes were as cold as the steel of the barrel. "What did you give her?"

Lavinia just smiled. A sphinx.

Gil took aim. *"What did you give her?"*

I had no doubt he'd kill for me.

The old lady laughed. "Just a little something to make her docile enough to kill-"

"She did not."

Everyone turned at the brisk tone coming from the darkened back of the room. Great Aunt Cecily Bridgewater raised a glass as she walked toward us. "Lavinia, you don't really think I'd let you harm these darling children to protect a girl forty years dead?"

"Hush, Cecily. I don't have much time left, and I won't let them ruin her name."

"No, you hush. Bertha made a mistake. And she lied about it right up to her deathbed to spare you."

"She-"

"I'm sure God's long since forgiven her, Lavinia." Great-Aunt Cecily held her longtime friend's gaze. "I'm not so sure He'll forgive you."

"What do you mean?" Lavinia drew herself up, trying for offended shock.

"I know what you did." Her friend's voice was slow and sad. "You slipped something in that poor man's tea at the Consulate, didn't you? Thank goodness I saw you putting the laudanum in the sherry this time."

Without another word, Lavinia Ten Broeck grabbed the glass from Great-

Aunt Cecily and took the sherry in a shot. She sat down on the settee opposite me, eyes sharp, waiting.

"Well, then," Great-Aunt Cecily said. "I think we may need to call a doctor. And the police."

"I am not entirely certain whom to call," Gil said, putting the pistol in his belt and taking a long, hard look at Lavinia.

"Don't call anyone," the old woman said. "I've wanted to be with my daughter for the last forty years."

I opened my mouth to remonstrate, but nothing came out. How could I argue with her?

No one else seemed to know what to say, either.

"Bertha? Her name?" Lavinia Ten Broeck finally asked Gil, in the same die-away tone I'd pretended minutes before.

"There's no record of anything," he replied, his tone almost gentle. "And despite all of the gossip, I haven't been able to get definitive confirmation of the identity of the young lady who slipped in to see the Prince."

Lavinia smiled faintly. "Thank you."

"It's for her, not you," he said, his eyes icy. I knew he would offer no quarter to a woman who had killed his friend and tried to harm me. "A girl shouldn't be remembered for her worst mistake."

For a stanza or more, we let that settle. Then Lavinia Ten Broeck's eyes drooped closed.

"Go home, children," Great-Aunt Cecily said. "I'll take care of Lavinia."

She held our gaze, with just a tiny glint of steel in the depths of her still-lovely deep blue eyes. And sadness. Great-Aunt Cecily was about to lose one of her last old friends.

Considering her losses, though, Lavinia was probably better off with the laudanum than the police. Even though no jury would send a woman her age to the electric chair, there was no penitentiary that could safely hold her. I might even argue she'd paid her price over the last forty years…though Gil likely would not be interested in hearing it.

He put a hand on my back and guided me out of the library.

In the foyer, Tommy and Cabot were waiting.

"What happened?" Tommy asked.

"A misunderstanding," I said, looking to Gil.

"Mrs. Ten Broeck thought we had something to do with an old family grudge," he added, nodding to the door. "And she seems to have taken ill. Your great-aunt may wish to send for a doctor."

"I will see," Cabot said, turning for the library.

Tommy looked at us both, assessing. "You'd think there had been quite enough drama."

"But no." Gil shook his head. "I believe I'd like to take my wife home."

"Good idea. We'll see you later."

Gil walked with me to the door. As I climbed into the cab, I turned back to see Great-Aunt Cecily looking out from the library window, a wistful expression on her face.

I understood completely. How could something that began with such excitement and joy end so badly?

We were distracted by the events of the night. It is the only explanation, though not an excuse, for the fact that we climbed into the waiting hansom, without a thought. Only after it began moving did we realize we were not alone.

The man sitting opposite us was familiar. Immaculate in black tie. Gray-haired and bearded, plump, with a round face that should have seemed friendly, except for the absolutely cold eyes.

Like Connor's.

It was the man I'd seen from the window the day we went to tea at the Consulate, what seemed like a lifetime ago. In Morrissey's. At the dedication. In Five Points, Alice La Joy had seen him following Gil. And tonight, he had been in the crowd at the reception.

Here was the person who'd been a step ahead of Gil the whole time. And probably a much more serious threat to him, and us, than Lavinia could ever have been.

Now he was sitting across from us in a cab. And we were sitting across from him. Probably looking unhappy. Exactly like Aunt Ellen's vision.

Just once, I wish that woman would see something cheerful.

If we got out of this, I might send her a list of happy things she could look for.

"You." Gil's tone suggested he was not surprised.

The man smiled. Chillingly. "A pleasure to see you, Leith."

"The pleasure is yours alone, I'm afraid."

"I would not judge so hastily." He leaned back into the cushions of his seat. "I expect we may be able to come to an amiable resolution here. Especially considering your lovely wife is involved."

"My wife is not involved. Her presence is—"

"Let us not insult one another, Leith. You treat your wife as an equal, despite her clear inferiority in both nature and upbringing, and I must assume she knows everything you do."

The insult was probably a deliberate provocation. I shot Gil a glance to remind him not to take the bait.

"She is not in this," Gil said. "It is not her sphere."

Careful use of the very term he'd thrown to protect, not demean, me at the reception.

"Really?"

"You know this is a matter for men and discretion," Gil said. "Do you really believe I'd expose her to it?"

"I have no reason to believe you," said our carriage-mate. "And I do not."

"That is your choice. But you are making a dire mistake if you think threatening her will get you anything you want." He held the man's gaze for a moment, then spoke the next words slowly and carefully. "You've been trying for a while, haven't you? It was you who left that charming calling-card in her bouquet."

The glass. Of course, who would know a vile British schoolboy trick but a vile adult who was once a British schoolboy? I clenched my hand, feeling the twinge from the healing injury.

My attacker, for that was what he was, just acknowledged the accusation with a small flick of a bushy brow.

"As much as I would enjoy making you pay for that," Gil said, his tone suggesting unspeakable tortures, "we shall have to content ourselves with the resolution of the matter."

"Oh, shall we?"

"The investigation is at an end." Gil returned the deadly gaze with a deadlier one. "There is evidence of an entanglement. No record of anything with bearing on larger matters."

"On this, at any rate, we agree. I assume the evidence of the entanglement has been destroyed."

"Actually, it is currently in an envelope in the hands of a friend. Should anything untoward happen to me or Her Grace, the friend will deliver it to a reporter. Who will be only too glad to find herself above the fold."

"Well played." He nodded.

Not to mention gentlemanly of Gil to add an extra layer of protection for Hetty with that mythical friend.

"Even the British Empire cannot always kill its way out of things," I said.

He looked at me as if I were a cat that had quoted Shakespeare. And then turned back to Gil. "We are, then, at a standoff."

"Not at all." Gil gave him a chilling smile. "We are, quite simply, done. You may report to whoever sent you that the matter is closed, which is the same report I will make to my friend."

"Precisely." The man bowed to me slightly, but deliberately. "I do not believe I congratulated you on your marriage, Your Grace."

"One doesn't congratulate a bride." Gil glared. "You didn't think I'd miss the insult."

A scowl. "This matter should never have been entrusted to a man who so obviously betrayed his class and upbringing."

"I do not know who sent you, but my errand came from the highest circles."

"Not *the* highest." Dry little smile. "She is not dead yet."

"No indeed. And she is not in the habit of killing her way out of things, to use my wife's trenchant phrase."

"She does not need to be." The man studied Gil and me for a long moment. I thought of the consulate worker who'd fallen down the stairs…and of Gil's friend Aldrick, who did not wake up.

"Also," Gil continued, his voice even sharper, "she is not given to class or religious prejudice and has great respect for artists."

"She did not marry one."

A muscle flicked in Gil's jaw. Everyone in the carriage understood the vulgar insult implied in the statement. It was not the first time someone had suggested my husband had no need to take the trouble of marrying me, and it would not be the last.

But it was one of the more chilling.

I was still back at the comment that Her Majesty did not need to kill her way out of things. I had no doubt Lavinia was responsible for some of the death and mayhem that had surrounded us in recent weeks. She, I believed, had accidentally poisoned Grover Duquesne at the music collection dedication in an effort to make sure Colonel Vandergrift did not reveal what he knew. And taken another run at the Colonel when she failed.

Great-Aunt Cecily's reference to the Consulate suggested she believed Lavinia had also killed Aldrick...but there was also the employee who died in a mysterious fall. Not to mention the sudden illness of the White Plains coroner and the disappearance of the records. Lavinia could not possibly be responsible for everything.

Which pointed very strongly to present company.

I looked to Gil, who returned my gaze for a moment, then focused on our seatmate.

"Answer me this, only, then." Gil's tone was ice cold, deathly serious. "Did you have anything to do with Aldrick's demise?"

The man's face softened suddenly, shockingly, and for an instant, he looked like he might cry. "No. He had tea with the dear little old lady who held tonight's reception just before he collapsed."

"That's why you were here," I said.

"I suppose I owe you a small debt of gratitude, Your Grace," the man said, his mouth twisting as he pronounced the title. Like it tasted bad. Probably did, addressing it to me. "You'd have done better to kill her, though."

"There was laudanum," I said. "You can hope."

"I no longer indulge in hope." He took a long breath and one more look at both of us. "I am told this modern world of ours is an improvement. I cannot say I find it so."

"That's your right," Gil said. "Wrong-headed though it may be."

The man nodded to Gil, then knocked on the partition. "I will find my own way home. A pleasant night to you both."

Barely waiting for the cab to stop, he stepped down briskly, moving surprisingly quickly for a man his age.

As we moved away, we watched him disappear into the darkness.

"I'm sorry I did not believe you, Shane," Gil said finally.

"You couldn't see it. You were too close."

"And I wanted to believe that we're..." He broke off, searching for a word.

"Better," I said bluntly. "You wanted to believe all of that stuff about nobility and ethics and rules—because you follow them."

"I do. And I suppose I did believe we were better." He held my gaze. "Not better than you, understand. Just—better than the ordinary run of the world."

"Ah."

"You knew this all along."

"I'm Irish—and Jewish. I know what the Crown is capable of." I patted his hand. "And what happens when people stop seeing others as human?"

He laced fingers with mine, gave me a searching glance. "You don't think I—"

"Never. From the moment we met, I knew you considered me as good as anyone else."

"Even though I called you theatre people?"

I smiled. "Well, that was why I made you duel me. I wouldn't have tried to teach you a lesson if I didn't think you could learn one."

"The first of many useful lessons." He leaned in and kissed me. "Perhaps another when we get home..."

"By all means." I snuggled into his embrace. "Home, together."

As Gil handed me down from the cab, I saw movement across the street and tensed.

The shadow stepped into the glow from the gas lights.

Connor.

Before he even acknowledged me, he looked to Gil, who shook his head.

So Gil had made another plan besides Hetty.

I wasn't sorry he had—or that he called it off.

Connor nodded. Turned to me and tipped his fedora, with the smile he reserved for me.

As usual, Gil either did not see, or did not acknowledge it. No matter.

Gil and I turned for the house. The parlor light was on, and I recognized a familiar tall, slim silhouette in the window. Jamie. Waiting up for us. I really do love that boy.

On the stoop, I looked up at Gil.

"You…"

"I do what I must to make sure my family is safe. And take help where I need it."

"I understand."

"And approve?"

"It's not for me to approve. But I don't argue with a safe resolution." I took his hands and met his gaze squarely. "It *is* a safe resolution?"

"*Mo chridhe*, we could not be safer if we were in the Crown Jewels vault."

Another cab pulled up.

Both Gil and I tensed for a moment. And then let out a long breath in relief as Tommy and Cabot climbed out.

"I believe you two have a bit of explaining to do."

Even in the weird glow of the gaslights, I could see the sharp concern in Tommy's face.

"We do, at that." Gil motioned to the door. "As good a time as any for a family council."

Chapter Thirty-Eight: In the Family

We began by pouring whisky.

No family discussion of matters this dark and dangerous could take place without at least a drop of the creature.

If nothing else, hopefully it would warm the chill from Lavinia's desperate run at me—and the cold evil of the Queen's man.

The drinks cart is my purview, of course, and I poured generous, but not sloppy, portions of our very best, long-aged whisky. The really good stuff we keep for special occasions.

Once the gentlemen were served, I reached for one more glass and hesitated, wondering if perhaps I should stick to sherry.

"Have a drop, *mo chridhe*," Gil said, "medicinal, for your nerves after the events of this evening."

"Medicinal," I agreed, and poured a half portion for myself.

Tommy chuckled as I sniffed it, then gingerly took a taste.

I'd probably had whisky once or twice before, always associated with a very serious matter, usually a death or other disaster. But never had I tasted anything this good. It was like liquid smoke and fire in the best possible way...like kissing the god of fire, perhaps.

"Come, then," Gil said. "Let us sit. We're all going to need to be careful of ourselves and each other for a time, I'm afraid."

"Is this tied to those old letters you had me authenticate, Pater?"

"Yes, son. In due time." He took a sip of his own whisky as everyone sat and arranged themselves, then sat in the wing chair he favors opposite Tommy. Amusingly, Cabot and I were on the settee—both seated like decorative spouses. Appropriate and ironic at once.

Jamie, of course, sprawled over most of the other settee.

Gil took another taste of his whisky, savored it, then nodded. "Right, then. I hardly need tell you this matter stays in the family."

Cabot moved to stand. "Perhaps I should leave."

"You're family," I said.

Cabot glanced to Tommy.

My word, or Gil's, was not the first that mattered here.

Their gaze held for a long moment before Tommy spoke, in a tone suited to a vow: "You are, as far as I'm concerned."

They smiled together.

"Well," Gil said, with a wee grin of his own, "now we have settled that, to the matter at hand. You'll know I've been looking into a matter for a friend."

"A friend?" Jamie asked.

"In this case, perhaps," Gil replied with a slight shrug, "it could be a rather presumptuous description. But there's no doubt he will count me as a friend going forward."

"He's in your debt," I said.

"Our debt," Gil corrected. "All of ours, at this point, considering the effort involved."

"Meaning?" Cabot asked.

"Meaning we've all been involved in finding as much of a resolution as possible to this matter, and we've all been at some level of risk."

Tommy looked up from his whisky.

"Not particularly serious risk, Toms," I said quickly. *At least not 'til just now,* I thought.

Gil shook his head. "Serious enough, I'm afraid. No point in trying to shade the truth now."

"It's all right, Barrister," Tommy said. "Any time Heller tells me there's no danger, I assume there's at least some level of peril or she would not be mentioning it."

"Wise indeed."

My men exchanged the dry little smile I usually found maddeningly patronizing.

After the events of the evening, it was almost comforting. I took a sip of my whisky.

"Well, Pater, what's this all about? Ancient letters?" Jamie asked. "Old newspapers? What happened forty years ago?"

"The Academy of Music Ball." Cabot looked from Jamie to Gil to me. "Which means…"

"The Prince of Wales," Tommy said.

"You are correct." Gil bent down toward his whisky but didn't drink. "During His Highness's visit, he had a—connection—with a lady."

"Not Great-Aunt Cecily's friend, surely." Cabot blinked. "Lavinia Ten Broeck would have been close to forty then."

"Her daughter, right?" Tommy asked. "And she ended up in White Plains, didn't she? That's why you went to look at the records."

"Yes. Bertha Ten Broeck, daughter of Lavinia, went to stay with her brother and sister-in-law in White Plains after the—entanglement. And there she died. Of a hemorrhage, so described."

Jamie winced. "Hemorrhage? What kind of-"

"We don't know. Everyone who might have attended her or known is dead." Gil shook his head. "The sister-in-law registered a baby girl just a few weeks later. The passage of time makes it very difficult to be sure about anything other than the bald dates recorded."

"Is there any indication that the daughter…" Cabot began.

"There's nothing to suggest the parents of the girl—now woman—are anyone other than the ones recorded. And there's no way to prove anything now." Gil sighed, and then took a sip.

"More," I added, "there's no hint of a marriage, neither a legal wedding nor any kind of informal vow. Even though Bertha apparently told her mother she'd made a secret marriage to soothe her conscience."

"Are you suggesting there was a child?" Jamie asked.

"We honestly don't know," Gil said. "Bertha may, in fact, have simply died of a hemorrhage. She may have had a baby who died. Or the daughter raised by her brother and sister-in-law may be hers."

"And the Prince's." Cabot's eyes widened.

"And forty years later, there is no way to prove anything." Gil shook his head. "No evidence of her connection with the Prince other than that one letter she sent the Colonel's sister."

"Another letter," Jamie said.

"Yes. The Colonel held this one back. She referred quite clearly to an involvement."

"But less clearly to the man," I said. "She called him simply 'my prince.'"

Cabot shook his head. "As any young woman might call her swain."

"As any number of hopeful ladies did call you," Tommy teased his friend.

Cabot laughed, and blushed. "It's true. A fellow who's known as a catch will draw a certain amount of florid description."

"I've heard of it." Gil swallowed a smile along with a bit of whisky.

"And anyone wanting to argue against Bertha's involvement with the Prince would seize on that," Jamie said. "The letter's virtually useless."

"It is," I agreed.

"Certainly, there is no evidence of a marriage that would make this a public matter," said Gil.

"And," I added, "no reason to upend the life of a woman unless we're absolutely certain she's not who she has always believed she is."

"So it ends here?" Tommy asked.

"Lavinia Ten Broeck took a large dose of laudanum this evening," Gil said. "She may or may not live to answer for her crimes."

"What crimes?" Jamie looked confused.

"At the very least, the death of Sir Aldrick," I said. "We know she had tea with him just before he went to bed and did not wake up."

Gil's jaw tightened, and he contemplated for a moment. Then: "Also, she poisoned Mr. Duquesne at the music collection dedication. She was attempting to kill Colonel Vandergrift over his sister's letters and what he might know. Ultimately, she did manage to get to his home and poison him."

"Thankfully, he's recovering," Tommy said.

"As is Mr. Duquesne," Cabot said. "So she may only be responsible for one death."

"As far as I know," Gil said. "The fatal fall at the Consulate may be—and a death back in Britain related to this matter almost certainly is—the responsibility of another."

"Another unknown to this house," I added. It seemed like the best and simplest explanation. We could trust our dear ones not to reveal anything, but we did not want to give them even more dangerous knowledge.

"Is that other person still a threat?" asked Tommy.

"No," said Gil. "We've settled matters."

"Are you sure?" Jamie asked.

"If I were not, he would not be sleeping safely in his bed tonight." Gil's tone left no room for discussion, holding my cousin's gaze.

Tommy's eyebrow flicked as he absorbed the true meaning of the comment.

"So this matter is settled," Cabot said.

"It appears to be so," Gil agreed.

"But there are unanswered questions!" Jamie remonstrated. "Don't you want to know? Doesn't the lady in White Plains deserve to know?"

"If we knew anything certain to tell her, she absolutely would," I said.

"What would you have me tell her?" Gil asked. "That there's some possibility—which we cannot prove and cannot legally pursue in any way—that she-"

"That she might be the daughter of the Prince of Wales!" Jamie cried.

"And she might not, too," I added. "We have nothing but speculation. No records, no testimony, no letters."

"Just a poisonous green ribbon," Jamie said.

"That's truly all." Gil nodded, took a sip of his drink.

"So it may be best to let the past bury its dead." Cabot shook his head. "Some secrets don't need to be carried forward."

"Everything is still there," Gil said. "The letters and papers will go in our safe, as will all of my research. And if later, someone wants or needs to know, it will be there."

"You won't send it to the family?" Jamie asked.

"Maybe one day." Gil's tone suggested that day would be after we were all long dead.

Fine by me.

"So this adventure is over," Tommy said. "And we've all come through."

"It is," I said, lifting my glass, "and we have."

Jamie raised his. "Then, to the next adventure."

"A safer one," Cabot said.

"And happier," Gil added.

We could all drink to that.

And we did.

Epilogue: A Crowning Moment

London, August 1902

A unt Ellen did not especially approve of my singing at the Coronation, but Madame Lentini was in raptures at the thought that her protégée had reached such a pinnacle. The Met even proved willing to adjust my performance schedule when the King took ill at the last moment and the service was postponed. And so it was that a woman born to an Irish father and Jewish mother in a Lower East Side tenement found herself in the Choir of Westminster Abbey on that August day, in a cream brocade gown with the Tallach pearls and Leith coronet.

My mother and father had to be looking down from Heaven in absolute amazement.

While I was not unaware of the honor, neither did it escape my notice that having me sing the first hymn after the "Vivat" processional chorus spared the more hidebound Peeresses from walking in with me. It also allowed the Lord Chamberlain to assign me a congenial and comfortable seat with Gil's sister Madeleine, temporarily back from Australia while the Foreign Office reshuffled under the new regime.

The service was exactly like we'd read in history books, full of glitter and pomp and spectacle. A show grander than any I'd ever played. And yet, still there was a moment, just a flash, as the Archbishop blessed our new monarchs, when I saw the King and Queen's faces and realized they were taking it as the holy dedication intended.

Perhaps they weren't so bad after all.

After the ceremony and the procession back to the palace, there was a lull in the action, as some participants rested, some posed for pictures, and others wandered about, taking advantage of a once-in-a-lifetime opportunity to speak with exalted figures they would never meet again.

Madeleine and her husband, a Scots peer from an ancient seat near Edinburgh, stayed with me, happily regaling me with stories of Australia. We were laughing about the fact that everyone thinks koala bears are sweet little creatures when they're actually nasty, surly beasts, when a page came up to me.

"Your Grace, the King requests you join him and the Duke."

Madeleine's deep blue eyes gleamed. "You two shall have to report back."

"No doubt."

I followed the page down a corridor into a room that was probably some kind of parlor but looked more like a museum gallery to me. One wall was dominated by an eighteenth-century painting of one of George III's daughters and her dogs. On the far wall, a sizeable Winterhalter portrait of Queen Victoria and her children gazed down at me.

The King, now a tired, aging man instead of the cherub on the wall, was sitting in a large chair beneath the painting, with several counselors standing around him, and Gil a bit further away.

"Well, my lady Leith," the King said, using an appropriate if only slightly informal form of address, and taking an appreciative look at me in my robes. "As beautiful as your voice."

Gil tolerated the look for a moment because it came from his Sovereign, but then narrowed his eyes slightly.

"Erm, yes." His Majesty coughed, nodded to Gil. "We have asked you both here to award you the Victorian Order, given only for meritorious service to the Royal Family."

"Thank you, Your Majesty."

Gil and I bowed—and very nearly spoke—in unison.

"It's my pleasure. The two of you cleared up quite a difficult matter for me."

"It was our pleasure," Gil said.

I nodded. "An honor I never dreamed of, Your Majesty."

"I am told it is impossible to kill one's way out of things." His Majesty's aspect became very cold. I suspected our friend from the carriage was not doing nearly as well under his new monarch.

"It's been said." Gil met the King's gaze with equal steel.

Very definitely a thing among men. British men.

The King turned to regard me. This time, there was no lust, but something wistful and respectful. "Her Late Majesty, my mother, would not have understood you, Miss Shane, but she would have heartily approved of you."

No higher praise.

A few minutes later, with our new honors duly added to our ceremonial attire, the page guided us out of the room. In the hall, with more subsidiary royals gazing down at us from the walls, Gil turned to me.

"You look like you've seen the angels themselves."

"I've never sung at a coronation, never mind been praised by a king. It's quite a moment for a poor orphan from the Lower East Side."

A grim little smile from Gil. "We put four Saint Aubyn lives on the line for him. It's the least he can do."

"Not holding grudges, surely." We did not, after all, know until months later just how perilous that autumn night had been.

"Never forget, sweetheart, I am a border lord. I'm not dazzled by the English Crown."

"Well, dazzled or not, we'd best start saying our farewells." I nodded to the huge cabinet clock that dominated a wall ahead of us. "It's getting quite late."

And now, the happy and proud grin I'd come to treasure in recent months.

"Yes, the young ladies shall never forgive us if we miss nursery tea."

I returned the grin. Our twin daughters are a rather demanding pair. "We won't forgive ourselves."

Acknowledgments

As always, thanks first to my editor Verena Rose, and agent Eric Myers for making it possible to continue Ella's adventures.

Much appreciation to my Sibs in Sisters in Crime, National, New York/TriState and Connecticut chapters, and to my writing buddies in the Short Mystery Fiction Society, Cozy Mystery Village, and other groups. It may be possible to survive a publishing career without writer friends, but not to thrive.

And of course, to my families of blood, work, and affection. You make everything possible.

With love and gratitude,

Kathleen Marple Kalb

About the Author

Kathleen Marple Kalb describes herself as an Author/Anchor/Mom...not in that order. An award-winning weekend anchor at New York's 1010 WINS Radio, she writes short stories and novels including the Ella Shane and Old Stuff series, both from Level Best Books. Her stories, under her own name, and as Nikki Knight, have been in *Alfred Hitchcock's Mystery Magazine, Black Cat Weekly, Mystery Magazine*, and others, and short-listed for Derringer and Black Orchid Novella Awards. Active in writer's groups, she's served as Vice President of the Short Mystery Fiction Society and Co-VP of the New York/Tri-State Sisters in Crime Chapter. She, her husband, and son live in a Connecticut house owned by their cat.

AUTHOR WEBSITE:
  https://kathleenmarplekalb.com/

SOCIAL MEDIA HANDLES:
  Facebook: https://www.facebook.com/Kathleen-Marple-Kalb-10 82949845220373/
  Twitter: https://twitter.com/KalbMarple
  Instagram: https://www.instagram.com/kathleenmarplekalb/

Threads: @kathleenmarplekalb
Bluesky: @mysterymarple.bsky.social

Also by Kathleen Marple Kalb

Ella Shane Mysteries:
A Fatal Finale (2020)
A Fatal First Night (2021)
A Fatal Overture (2022)
A Fatal Reception (2024)
A Fatal Honeymoon (free novella – 2024)

Old Stuff Mysteries:
The Stuff of Murder (2023)
The Stuff of Mayhem (2025)

Vermont Radio Mysteries – As Nikki Knight
Live, Local and Dead (2022)
Live, Local, and LONG Dead (2024)

Grace the Hit Mom Mysteries – As Nikki Knight
Wrong Poison (2023)
Hound of the Bonnevilles (2025)

Short Stories in Magazines, Anthologies, and online, including:
"Public Affairs Homicide," in *Devil's Snare*: Best New England Crime Stories, 2024

"Mow Way Out," an Old Stuff Mystery, *Black Cat Weekly*, September 2024

"Things Look Different Up Here," in New York/TriState Sisters in Crime Anthology, *New York State of Crime*, September 2024

"Sorry Not Sorry," an Old Stuff mystery, M2D4, *Mysteries to Die for Podcast and Anthology*, Summer 2024 season

"A Fatal Saint Patrick's Day" (Ella Shane Mystery) in *Luck of the Irish Anthology*, March 2024

"No Angels Here," *Black Cat Weekly*, December 2023

"The New York Goodbye," *Black Cat Weekly*, September 2023

"The Telltale Request," *Mystery Magazine*, September 2023

"Second Chances are…Murder," *Malice, Matrimony, and Murder Anthology*, November 2023

"Pie a La Poison," in *The Perp Wore Pumpkin*, Misti Media, November 2023

"The Custodian of the Body," (Old Stuff Mystery), *Black Cat Weekly*, May 2023

"This Never Happened to Wolfman Jack," *M2D4 Podcast* August 2023, season anthology, November 2023

"Don't Mess with the Boss Cat," *CatsCast Podcast* by Escape Artists, June 2023

"The Annual Mud Season Homicide," *Alfred Hitchcock's Mystery Magazine*, May/June 2023

"Owl Be Damned," *Mysteryrat's Maze Podcast*, January 2023

"Blame it on the Blizzard," *Deadly Nightshade: Best New England Crime Stories 2022*

"The Thanksgiving Ragamuffin," (Ella Shane Mystery) in New York/TriState Sisters in Crime Anthology, *Justice for All*. November 2021. Derringer Award Nomination

"Boss Cat Rules," in Donna Andrews Presents *Malice Domestic: Mystery Most Humorous*, Wildside Press, April 2025.

"Diana and the Princess," in *Sleuths Just Wanna Have Fun*, Down & Out Books, April 2025.

"The Last Diamond," *Mysteries to Die for Podcast*, February 2025